Altar and Throne

A Novel by

Ed Zaruk

For Susanne & Bill

[signature]

authorHOUSE®

AuthorHouse™
1663 Liberty Drive, Suite 200
Bloomington, IN 47403
www.authorhouse.com
Phone: 1-800-839-8640

First published by AuthorHouse 9/11/2008

ISBN: 978-1-4389-0453-5 (e)
ISBN: 978-1-4389-0451-1 (sc)
ISBN: 978-1-4389-0452-8 (hc)

Library of Congress Control Number: 2008907886

Printed in the United States of America
Bloomington, Indiana

This book is printed on acid-free paper.

Cover design by Carl Hileman

This is a work of fiction.
Only the heartache is true.

Author's Notes

The events in this novel are based in actual fact. However, I have taken the liberty to place some details outside of their real time frame for the sake of the story.

The characters are fictitious composites of real people from all over Canada, some more so than others. I do not want to leave the impression that all experiences at the residential schools were negative. The willingness of good people to work long hours in exasperating circumstances under a bureaucracy determined to minimize costs, can only be attributed to dedication.

Throughout this novel I have chosen to use both the words Native and Indian. The term Indian was in common use during much of this story's time frame and is a more realistic portrayal of the dialogue of the people involved. In narrative, I have endeavoured to use Native to dignify these people, many of whom are my personal friends.

Those who experience the loss of their loved ones in this book have their own view of death, and deal with this tragedy in diverse ways that allow them to overcome their grief. I have endeavoured to portray all these ideas as they affect their emotions, yet have not held back from letting some question the basic precepts of their beliefs.

I chose to place the story in the beautiful Lake of the Woods country surrounding Kenora, Ontario for several reasons. First, I wanted to use a real town, and Kenora, as well as the surrounding area of Northwestern Ontario, was home to one of the largest float plane fleets in Canada. Native people in this area have suffered terrible injustices, and my familiarity with the place allowed me to give their story a sense of reality. It is my hope that *Altar and Throne* may be a bridge-builder between our two communities as well as an engaging read.

Ed Zaruk

One

Jack Redsky, a member of the Fish clan and full-blooded Ojibway, looked up to see the float plane disappear over the trees. Sharing the realm of the eagle, it reminded him that the coming of the white man to the Lake of the Woods had changed life for his father and grandfather, some for good, some for bad, but mostly it just complicated things.

As a heritage from these two men, Jack had been entrusted with the legends and values that had served his nation from times unknown. Even as the white man's society eroded his culture, Jack learned carefully the lessons taught him about how to deal with change.

"Be like a tall tree," his grandfather had said. "Bend when the wind blows. A tree that does not bend will fall. Bend, but keep your roots in our sacred Indian soil."

The winds of change blew gently on Jack when Ted Corrigan came into his life more than two decades ago. Jack's father had fished around the point from the Corrigan's camp on the Lake of the Woods, often tying up at the long dock made of old telegraph poles, to chat with Ted's father, Charlie.

As was his custom, Charlie would invite Jack's father to the lodge where they relaxed, rolled cigarettes from a can of tobacco, and smoked in the shade of a veranda. That summer day, Jack who'd just turned eleven, sat in the boat watching a white kid about his age fish off the end of the dock. Unlike anything Jack had ever seen, his fishing pole reflected a sparkle of sunlight whenever he would swing it. All Jack had used was a willow stick with some string and a hook. It fascinated him the way yards of string seemed to follow a shiny lure in a long arc before falling into the lake. Hopping out when called, Jack ran barefoot down the dock to stand beside a boy shorter than him, unable to keep his eyes off the new rod-and-reel he was using.

"Hi, what's your name?"

Jack continued staring at the fishing pole, wondering what the words, in a language he had never heard before, meant.

"I'm Ted," the boy said, extending the rod and reel.

Jack found himself gripping the steel fishing rod with both hands, the boy beside him indicating he should swing it over the water.

Jack swung it like his father's axe when cutting down a tree. Un-spooling in a big tangle, the line jerked tight dropping the lure into the water within jumping distance of his feet. Jack felt his ears get hot as the kid beside him laughed. He handed it back, hanging his head, but watching sideways as the white kid sat down on the weathered wooden planking and began working the line off the spool. Rewinding it, Ted stood up and handed the rod back to his new friend. Then accompanied by the strange words, he showed Jack how to hold the rod, moving his thumb on and off the reel while making a practice swing beyond the dock. Jack tried it again, this time dropping the lure some thirty feet out in the lake.

"Hey! That's good."

White teeth gleamed against Jack's smooth, brown skin. Ted nudged him with his elbow transmitting a universal message to try it again. Ten minutes later, Jack had the hang of it, plunking the lure into the lake almost as far as his new friend could do. Enjoying the thrill, Jack almost let go of the rod when the line snapped tight and the tip bent over. The hollering and yelling beside him along with a slap on the back, encouraged Jack to start reeling in the line, all the while fighting the jerking rod in his hands. Moments later, a Walleye danced on the surface, a brass lure hanging from its mouth.

They spent the summer together, speaking in a language neither understood yet communicating as only friends can. In the heat of the day they swam in the cool water of the Lake of the Woods, afternoons were spent exploring the surrounding forest, and evenings sitting on the dock. With fishing lines hanging in the water, they watched as the sun painted the sky orange, scarlet red, then faded to deep purple as the day drew to a close. Jack learned what it was like to sleep on a feather mattress. Ted loved the nights he spent sitting on furs in the tepee, listening to Jack's father, tell stories in the Ojibway language, which, although understanding only a few words, he knew from the skillful motion of hands were about hunting.

Just as fate had brought them together, it continued to overlap their lives as each grew to manhood in their separate worlds. They both married and had children. Jenny gave Jack three sons who all slept together. Ted and his wife, Diana, settled into a newly constructed house with running water and a bedroom for each of their two girls.

Good memories, Jack thought, raising the rifle Ted had given him for a wedding present, feeling the cold steel draw warmth from his fingers while he squinted through the sights. Every autumn, when the leaves turned golden, Ted stood beside him on the hunt. This year they were determined to take the big buck that had been growing fat on Jenny's garden.

Antlers filled the gun sights. Jack lowered the rifle a tiny fraction, settled the stock against his shoulder, and eased the trigger back.

TWO

Abe Williston loved Northwestern Ontario from the air. Vast panoramas of trees and rivers stretching to the horizon under an ever-changing sky, swamps with bone-white tree snags reflecting the afternoon sun, the Lake of the Woods with its thousands of islands. Now, descending with mechanical problems, it all disappeared as he made a forced landing on the lake. Tying his float plane to a tree in the middle of nowhere, he tested the knot. If he had to break down anywhere, this was probably not a bad place to be.

The day had started off a pilot's delight. Gorgeous fall sunrise painted in orange against long wisps of cloud high in the sky: the cool smell of algae drifting up from the lake, early morning ripples lapping the shore, smooth air to fly in. By mid-afternoon, Abe had made three trips in his old biplane built a few years after the Great War, and already obsolete, moving two prospectors and their gear to a place known only as an X marked on his flight map.

When his dad had died of pneumonia, the farm in Saskatchewan had become too much for his mom to look after. Abe had no interest in growing wheat, so they sold it a few months before the stock market crash that brought on the depression. Unlike his father, who considered it a waste of time and money, his mom had always encouraged him to become a pilot. Now she insisted he use the money to follow his dream of owning an airplane.

Abe could have taken it all and bought a newer aircraft, but his mom would have had to go to work. He refused to let that happen, accepting only enough to arrange for financing of his present plane from its previous owner. Long hours and lots of mechanical work had seen him pay the loan off over the last two years, but the old biplane was showing its age.

Little things kept causing big problems. Today it was a broken fuel line forcing Abe to land in a bay near the Long Grass Indian Reservation. What now separated him from help was a half mile of trees and brush. Satisfied his knot would hold, he checked to make sure all the switches were off, then stepped from the float. A shot rang off in the distance as he tucked his sleeping bag under one arm and walked into the forest.

THREE

When the single shot echoed out of the forest, Jenny Redsky stopped picking beans from her garden behind a wood-frame house built three years ago by the government of Canada. The house had two small bedrooms and a kitchen with an adjoining area used as a living room. The toilet was forty feet outside the back door.

In the quiet that followed, she smiled to herself and went back to picking, gently working the beans from corn stalks around which they had become intertwined.

She always looked forward to Ted Corrigan taking a week off from his job with the Canadian Pacific Railway and spending a few days with her husband, Jack. If they got a deer, Ted would probably leave in the morning for his father's camp.

Jenny brushed away a fly from the side of her head thinking how good life was as a gentle breeze rustled the leaves, some displaying autumn colours about their edges. A little hand tugged at her wool skirt. She looked down into black eyes tinged with gray.

"Here, Mommy."

Jenny took two bean pods from her youngest son, Michael. "Thank you." Placing them in her woven basket, she pointed to another pole. "You want to get me three from that one this time?"

Michael broke into a grin and scampered off. Jenny knew her son liked to use numbers. She was thinking he understood them very well for a boy of four when a commotion behind broke her thoughts. Jenny watched Michael's two brothers chase barefoot around the back of the garden. Where had the years gone? she wondered, as Pete, her oldest, dashed by holding a big bull frog by its two hind legs. Close on his heels, Johnnie kept hollering, "Give it to me. I found it first."

"No way." Pete looked back at his younger brother. "I saw it first," the words lost as his foot caught a fallen log, sending him sprawling. Johnnie leapt on top of him before he quit rolling. Free of Pete's grasp, the frog sprang into the air as the two boys started grappling for each other in a good-natured wrestling match.

Jenny had learned to ignore her sons' constant play fighting and took her beans inside as Michael ran over to join the fray. She was cutting and snapping them in a galvanized wash pan that served as her sink when, through the little four-pane window, she saw Jack and Ted, each holding an antler, dragging a deer carcass out of the trees. Wiping her hands, she hurried outside.

Jack met her with a smile as wind ruffled the tips of black hair resting on his shoulders. "Here's your big buck, Jenny." Letting go of the antler in his hands, he allowed the deer's head to fall sideways.

Ted, shorter than either Jenny or Jack, let go his, and the animal's head rolled on the ground. "Jack nailed him right in the neck."

"He'll go a hundred and twenty pounds." Jack moved beside his wife, rubbing the small of her back.

"So he should, all he's eaten from my garden." Jenny touched her man's arm, feeling the hard muscle. It always gave her a tingle. She'd come back to that thought later tonight. "We'll give your folks a hind quarter."

"And make new winter moccasins for us all," Jack said, leaning his rifle against a tree. Taking out his hunting knife, he carved out a loin strip and handed it to his wife, "Supper."

Pete, Johnnie, and Michael ran up. Michael kicked the deer's head.

"Hey!" Jack grabbed his youngest son by the shoulder. "The Great Spirit gave us this one. He runs no more so that we may eat. Do not abuse the Great One's generosity."

FOUR

Plagued by a few late season mosquitoes that continued feasting
on his exposed skin, Abe trudged through a stand of Jack Pine,
wondering if he was lost. He should have dug out the pocket compass
from the emergency pack instead of trusting his sense of direction. From
the air, the reservation had appeared just over a rise of land running back
from the lake. Down here, it was a wall of trees and swamp.

Abe slapped another mosquito on his neck. He skirted a small
lake, looking for the sun, now low in the afternoon sky and hidden by
trees. Topping a rise, Abe came upon an outcropping of rock covered
in blueberry bushes, their branches empty. A clear view of the land
before him revealed the Lake of the Woods curving into a bay. Abe
had wanted to nurse his plane over the ridge, then land and paddle up
to the reservation's old dock, but he'd run out of air space.

Half a dozen frame houses clustering together formed the nucleus of
the reserve. A dirt track ran to the shore where log cabins were scattered
along the bay. Tepees dotted the open spaces between. Occupying the
highest ground in the middle, stood the church.

He wasn't sure how much help the Indians could give him, but knew
them to be resourceful people on what little they had. A few steps down
the ridge and the reserve was swallowed up by the trees, but he knew where
he was headed and soon broke into a clearing behind the reservation.

Ted Corrigan was the first to spot Abe walking out of the bush.
"Well, look who we have here."

Abe recognized Jack Redsky from previous flights to the reserve. The woman he didn't know. Three boys ran over and danced around him as he addressed the white man. "Ted! Am I ever glad to see you."

Ted rubbed a hand through his crew-cut hair. "What did you do? Fall out of the sky?"

"Well, sort of. Broke a fuel line. Landed on the other side of the rise. Think you could tow my plane over here?"

Shaking his head, Ted said, "Let you down again, huh? About time you got rid of that old wreck."

"Well, it's all I've got." Abe could feel blood rising in his cheeks. "I'm not running a damn railroad."

"I was only kidding." Ted balled his fist and nudged Abe on the arm. "Give us a hand stringing up this deer. Jack can skin it while we get your plane."

Still holding the strip loin in her hands, Jenny asked the pilot, "You staying the night?"

"Well, I don't mean to..."

"Of course he is," Ted said.

Jack took Abe's sleeping bag and tucked it under one of his wife's arms. "Always room for one more."

"Venison strips, fresh beans, and corn on the cob," Jenny said, walking to the house. "Hope you're hungry."

***

Long Grass Reservation's doorway to the world was a decrepit wharf made of two floating logs tied to shore with a rusty cable. Small poles laid crossways, in equally poor condition, made up the decking. Rolling a barrel of gas along them caused the whole structure to wave up and down, and it wasn't uncommon for Abe to break through where the poles were either loose or missing. He finished tying up the floats of his plane while Ted waited, holding one wing. "I sure do appreciate this, Ted."

"Ah." Ted waved the comment away. "Seriously, Abe, you should look at getting a bigger plane."

"Been thinking about it. Hear there's an outfit in Montreal making a float plane especially for the bush."

"Noorduyn Aviation."

"Yeah, that's the one." Abe stood up.

"You done?"

"Yep, lead the way." Abe followed Ted off the dock as night swallowed up the sunset.

Jenny fried venison until, one by one, the men pushed their plates away, protesting they were full and for her not to cook any more. Abe dug in and helped as, by the light of two candles, the deer was cut into strips and readied for drying.

Ted pulled out his pocket watch and flipped the lid open. "Twelve-thirty."

Ten minutes later, Jack blew out the candles, said goodnight, and followed his wife into their bedroom. Abe took off his trousers and shirt, then crawled into his sleeping bag on the living room floor. Jenny had laid out some furs for him to sleep on. Ted got the couch, mainly because he was short enough to fit on it. Abe would have hung over by a foot.

Tired as he was, Abe couldn't fall asleep, Ted's snoring made it all the more difficult, as he lay thinking. Jack was a lucky man to have a wonderful wife. Then there was Ted's close friendship with Jack, something unique and rare, even among whites. Jenny, with her three kids and loving husband. Closing his eyes, Abe's thoughts drifted to his plane. He really needed to get something better, the thought vanishing as his world of reality faded to dreams.

FIVE

Williston Air Services had chartered to the Rabbit Lake Residential School in its first year of operation. Tied in with the local church, Abe had found himself flying Father LaFrenier to outlying reservations every other Sunday.

Hauling fish in a two-seat biplane, then taking a priest for a ride next was no easy task. The first time it happened, Abe heard nothing but complaints about the smell. He'd mentioned it to Ted one day and next morning the CPR Express delivery van dropped off a case of pine-smelling cleaner that was used on the passenger trains. Father LaFrenier's complaints abruptly ceased.

The old biplane let Abe down twice more that year, last time in the dead of winter when he was forced to land miles from help and would have froze to death if not for an Indian trapper by the name of Ignace Two Bears who happened along. It was ten days before he and his mechanic got the plane back to Kenora.

Eleven weeks later his new Norseman bush plane rolled off the assembly line in Montreal. Abe had ordered it on floats, and with the melting of the lake ice, he rode the train east to pick it up.

Now that Williston Air Services was operating a Norseman on floats, it needed a lot more revenue. Abe aggressively went after government work, much of it involving the Department of Mines and Resources, which also had responsibility for Indian Affairs. One spin off from this was an increase in work for the residential schools.

At the beginning of September, Father LaFrenier, from the Rabbit Lake Residential School booked Abe's new plane for three flights. The first was to the Long Grass Indian Reservation carved out of land west of the Lake of the Woods in Northwestern Ontario that bureaucrats in Ottawa considered useless. The reserve comprised four hundred and forty-two acres of land, three islands, some of the most appealing shoreline on the lake, a small Jack Pine forest, and swamp, lots of swamp. Hunters by tradition, and fishermen by necessity in the summer, Indian men scraped out a living from the lake. Abe often flew their catch to Kenora. Occasionally when a big sturgeon was in the load, he'd see smiles on the faces of his Native friends because the buyers always paid top dollar for them. Today the Government of Canada wanted the children from this reservation taken to the Rabbit Lake Residential School. Father LaFrenier was here to see it done.

Abe didn't like the idea, but had come to realize that if he refused, Department of Mines work would dry up. He simply couldn't afford to operate without that money, so he followed the priest onto the reservation.

First call was the Chief's house. A woman with gnarled hands opened the door allowing the aroma of cooking meat to drift out. Deep lines on her dark-brown face told of wisdom gained from past generations. "Singing Dove, my child. It is time for the children to leave for our school."

Bowing her head respectfully, the old woman chided the priest as she had done every year since he had started coming for the children. "Our Great Chief Saskatcheway was promised a school on our land."

"The Great Fathers in Ottawa say I must take them away. They want me to teach them how to live in the white man's world."

"They need to learn the ways of our fathers."

"It is more important they learn the ways of the Father in Heaven."

"This is so. You may take them."

The formalities over Father LaFrenier set about gathering the children, most of whom were not ready to depart.

Abe watched the group of kids grow in number while following the priest through the reservation. When the Norseman had arrived, he'd been thankful for the increase in business until that September day when Father LaFrenier crammed nineteen kids into an airplane designed to carry only ten people. Abe knew he was overweight and in gross violation of federal regulations. Mentioning it to the priest brought a response in no uncertain terms; there was only money for one flight. Leaving weeping mothers and angry fathers standing on the dock, Abe taxied into the bay and, with engine noise filling the cabin, he wound on extra flap and worked the overloaded plane out of the water for the flight to Kenora.

The following two days brought flights from three other reservations, every one overloaded. Each ended in a parade of silent kids trudging from his plane to an old hay truck with open sides that carried them away to the residential school.

A flight to a mining exploration site with drums of fuel filled out the last day and Abe went home early, if you could call eight o'clock early.

SIX

Abe noticed that entire families were missing from the reservations after their children had been taken to the residential schools. Fishing was off so much he was combining the loads from Long Grass with those of Shoal Lake, barely giving him a decent overload. Under the weight of eighteen tubs of fish and near empty fuel tanks, the plane sat deep in the water as it plowed through choppy waves trying to take off. Pulling and pushing the elevator controls, Abe rocked it back and forth until the floats rode up on the step. When he felt the plane leave the lake, he eased back the controls and, loaded with considerable more fish than the government said she could carry, his Norseman staggered into the sky. On the seat to his right sat a cardboard box. Abe was hauling it for free.

He'd finished loading seven Long Grass tubs against the Shoal Lake fish when Susan and Ignace Two Bears had walked onto the dock with it. "Hi there, Abe," the tall Native man said, shifting the weight of the heavy box in his hands.

"Ignace. Hello, Susan." Stepping off the cargo ladder onto the float, Abe pointed to the box. "Outgoing freight?"

"Actually," Susan said, "it's a box of dried fish and meat. We're wondering if you could drop it off where Jack and the other families are camped."

Abe knew the camp. He'd often flown over its three tepees since they were set up two days after Father LaFrenier had taken Pete and Johnnie away. Along with two other families, Jack and Jenny had found a spot by a small beach on Coney Island. There was a larger camp on reservation land along Devil's Gap set up by those with children in St. Mary's School south of town.

Abe walked along the float and opened the front passenger door. "Stick it up on the seat."

Letting go of the door handle, he stepped onto the dock allowing room for Ignace to climb into the cabin. Moving beside Susan, Abe asked, "How long do you think they'll stay there?"

"I don't know. This is so unlike Jack. He's such a pillar of strength around here, but without his sons he seems to be adrift."

"Well, it's not only Jack and Jenny. I'd guess there are at least a couple dozen families camped on the lake around Kenora."

"It bothers me," Susan said as Ignace stepped back on the dock, "they can only visit their kids for a couple of hours on Sunday. What are they doing during the rest of the week?"

Abe knew, and pondered how best to reply. Ignace took his wife's hand in his, their white and tan fingers entwining. Susan sensed Abe's reluctance. "They're drinking," she said.

"Yes."

Her shoulders sagged. She squeezed her husband's hand. "Will it never end?"

Abe looked at Ignace. No wonder Susan fell in love with him. Shiny-black hair long at the shoulders outlined handsome Native features chiselled into his face. The man shook his head. "Our people suffer much when their children are away. It is why our forefathers asked for schools on the reservations when they signed the treaty."

Treaty Three. Abe didn't know much about its details, only that each time the government interpreted some clause, the Indians got the short end. Of them all, he figured the church-run schools were doing the most damage.

"The sooner winter comes, the better," Susan said.

"I do not think so." Ignace's voice was soft against the waves gently breaking on the shore. "Their loneliness will follow them here, and during the long winter nights there will be a lot of trouble."

There was nothing Abe could do to help, except deliver the parcel. He looked in the cargo door to see the ice melting on Shoal Lake's fish. "I'd better get going." He hopped onto the float and closed the two-piece cargo door.

"Don't take it personally, Abe," Susan said.

"Why not? I'm white. I charter to the Federal Government and the churches." He turned the door handle with more force than necessary. "That makes me part of the problem."

Ignace let go of his wife's hand and moved toward Abe, now standing with one foot on the front step. "*Needjee*," he said in Ojibway, placing his hand on the pilot's shoulder. "My friend, it is not the colour of your skin we see. Your heart is big, and you share it with us. With that we have no problem."

"Thanks. Coming from you, that means a lot, Ignace." Abe had climbed into the cockpit and had waited for Ignace to untie the plane before Susan and her husband used the wing strut to push it backward and turn the plane toward the bay.

Now that he was airborne, the big Pratt and Whitney engine working hard to keep the load of fish aloft, Abe settled back for the forty minute flight to Kenora. Dropping into the bay, he ran the Norseman in on the step. Slowing about a couple hundred yards out, he hoped no government inspectors were watching his approach to the pier with the back of his floats almost under water. Once the fish was unloaded, he put a few gallons of fuel in each wing tank and started out again for another load of fish out of White Dog, only this time instead of taking off, he taxied to the Indian encampment on Coney Island. About a hundred yards offshore, he shut off the ignition then opened his door as the engine died and the propeller wound to a halt.

Jack Redsky waved from the shore as Abe climbed down onto the float and beckoned him. Jack's boat was lost in the sunlight reflecting off a gentle ripple on the lake's surface. With virtually no wind to push the plane, it sat in one spot as Jack approached. Catching a line thrown him, Abe tied the end to the front strut.

His Indian friend joined him on the float. "Good to see you, Abe."

"And you, too. How's it going, Jack?" Abe asked.

"I should be fishing."

"It would help my revenue. I'm only making one trip between Long Grass and Shoal Lake."

"It is that bad?"

"You should know."

Jack lowered his head. "Yeah."

Abe pointed south. "Go back home, Jack."

"When the ice comes."

"That's a couple months away."

"Yes, but we can stay and see our sons until the ice comes. After we leave, it will be a long winter without them."

"How's Jenny taking it?"

"Very hard. She misses the boys, and her garden back home."

"I'll ask Susan to help out there."

Jack's face brightened. "Jenny is with child again."

Abe slapped him on the shoulder. "That's great. Congratulations. You going to order a girl this time?"

Jack smiled and thumped his chest. "A man should have many sons, but I will ask for a daughter, for Jenny."

One of Canadian Airways' planes, heavily loaded, began taking off along the channel. Barking exhaust from the short summer stack made speech impossible so Abe wrestled the package out of the cockpit. "Here," he yelled as the plane roared by.

Jack took it.

"Susan and Ignace sent it for you and your people. They're worried about you folks."

"There is no need for that."

"They hear reports of drinking."

"Not here. Tell them I will not allow it." Engine noise from the plane, now climbing and banking north, diminished, allowing the men to talk without hollering. "Some white men tried to sell liquor here a few days ago. I ran them off."

"Not with a gun, I hope."

"Nah, just stood up tall and threatened to scalp them." He laughed.

Abe smiled.

"Still, I found William Two Crows drunk with his woman last night."

"Take your people home, my friend."

"When the Ice Moon comes."

Abe bent down and held the boat as Jack stepped into it with his heavy parcel. After setting it down he moved to the back and wound the starter cord around the outboard's flywheel. "Next year my sons will not go to the church school."

"They need an education." Abe untied the rope and threw it in Jack's boat.

"Do they? We will never be allowed to fit into the white man's world, so why let our kids lose their language and way of life?" Jack pulled the rope and the engine coughed to life in a puff of pungent blue smoke.

Abe remained on the float, watching him leave. Why? Because my friend, Abe thought, if the Ukrainians can fit into our society and still keep their culture and language, then you can, too.

Abe flew steady for the rest of the week. During all that time Jack's boat never moved off the beach. Sunday morning Abe noticed that it and two of the three canoes were gone when he took off for a flight to Red Lake with a government survey crew. Banking north, Abe saw the town's police boat with two men in it heading straight for the Indian camp.

SEVEN

Ted Corrigan idled his big mahogany speedboat through the First Avenue bridge, then pulled the throttle all the way open. Water boiled out the stern until the twenty-eight foot long-deck launch built up speed and a white rooster tail rose in its wake. As spray blew ten feet out each side, the exhaust pipes, now out of water on the rear of the boat, rumbled in Ted's ears. He loved these occasions alone in the *Foxey*, running flat out. He knew why his father had so faithfully looked after this boat. He'd have to start taking better care of it. The canvas covering on the engine hatches looked like old flannel, and varnish peeling loose from the mahogany was beginning to haunt him. He vowed he'd have the boat redone next spring.

This year the engine had been tuned up and Ted figured the 'old girl' would top twenty-seven miles an hour in calm water. He lifted his head above the windshield to let the air blow on his face and rustle his short crew cut.

Cutting a swath through the choppy water of Safety Bay, he tore past Coney Island. To his right, another cruising boat was out. Ted recognized it as the town's police boat. If ever there was a boat to match his, it would be that one. He'd seen it up close many times, a triple cockpit boat. Loaded with six or eight policemen, it plowed through the water, but on the odd occasion when he'd seen it go with only one person, the bow came right out of the water. It was supposed to be faster than the *Foxey*. He'd never been up against it, so there was no way to know, although he figured his boat had the edge, especially since it had been tuned up.

Ted studied the Hacker-Craft's sleek lines as she crossed his bow heading into the bay on Coney Island. Sergeant Farnell was at the wheel. Ted wondered what he was doing out so early Sunday morning. The answer wasn't long in coming.

Farnell ran the big boat onto the sandy beach, then he and another man jumped out. Neither were in uniform. Ted couldn't hear them, but three or four dogs danced around the men, snapping at their heels. On his way up from the beach, Farnell took out his revolver and shot two of them.

"Bloody bastard!" Ted reefed back the throttle, settling the *Foxey's* stern deep in the water as he cranked her around in a tight turn. Standing up, he idled toward shore, watching as an old Indian woman appeared out of the center tepee. Farnell walked up and shoved her to the ground, then started kicking out the wooden poles of her tepee.

Just like Farnell, Ted thought, closing in on the shore. Not satisfied beating drunks in town, he has to come out here on his day off and pick on old ladies.

Above the idling engine, Ted could hear a dog bark as it lunged at Farnell. The woman got up and started yelling. Ted could hear her calling Farnell names in Ojibway. He didn't know that much of the language, but the words she was shouting at Farnell he'd heard when with Ojibway men; they didn't reflect favourably on his mother.

Ted watched Farnell kick another support out as the woman grabbed his jacket. Swinging around, he tried to shake her off, but she danced behind him, holding his coat with one hand and beating on him with the other. She let go when the second man curled his arms around her, lifted her up, and hauled her off his boss. Ted could have seen some humour in it if he didn't detest Farnell so much.

By now the *Foxey* had drifted within an arm's length of the police boat and neither the sergeant nor his companion had noticed.

Not sure what to do, Ted continued watching. Farnell was more than he could handle, let alone take on the two of them. Disengaging the propeller, Ted floated beside the Hacker-Craft. Reaching out to keep the two boats from bumping, he felt the rope used to tie off the back end. Pulling it over, he gathered about eighteen feet of line. Turning in his seat, he was knotting it to a rear cleat on his boat when someone shouted.

Farnell and his partner were racing for the beach. Ted reversed the propeller, hitting the throttle. The *Foxey* backed around, snugging up the line and swinging the Hacker-Craft sideways. Ted swung the bow around while shifting to forward, dragging the captured boat off the sand. He opened the throttle more as the two men cut down the distance. Things moved so slow. If Farnell got on board his boat... Ted took out his jack knife, knowing the sharp blade would cut the towline in one slice.

Instead of following straight out, the Hacker-Craft slewed sideways as Farnell waded into the lake. He was up to his waist, slowing in the water as his boat, a mere three feet away, moved out of reach.

"Corrigan, you bastard! I'll get you for this." The rest of what he said was lost in the *Foxey's* rumbling exhaust. Farnell turned back and waded toward his companion, now launching the canoe. As it went by, Farnell tried to climb in, upsetting the canoe and spilling his partner into the lake.

Finding it hard to believe these were the best men on Kenora's police force, Ted roared with laughter at the vaudeville act until his eyes brimmed with tears. After towing their boat a couple hundred yards off shore, he cut it loose. Once again opening the throttle, he sped off toward the Keewatin Channel, satisfied he'd done his good deed for the day.

Three weeks later when the wind became chilled and ice began forming in the shallows, Ted pulled the *Foxey* out of the water. Next morning, it snowed.

EIGHT

Flying in twenty-five below weather inside the Norseman was a whole lot more comfortable than the open cockpit of his old biplane. Even though the heater would only blow warm air at the best of times, Abe enjoyed his first winter of operations with the new plane.

Cindy came to work for him the next spring. Straight out of business school, she asked if Abe would hire her for the summer so she could gain experience as a receptionist. Bouncy little girl with a ponytail, she looked so discouraged when Abe hesitated. He hired her even though he couldn't afford it. First time the hospital phoned to say they were sending a nurse over for a mercy flight to the Long Grass Reserve, Cindy got all in a flap. Abe calmed her down saying it would be just like any other flight. He didn't add, until we get there and find someone with a leg sliced open or their fingers all mashed up. Kathleen O'Brian, the Public Health nurse arrived as Abe was fuelling the second wing-tank.

Cindy couldn't hold back and asked right off what the emergency was.

"Singing Dove sent word that one of the women is going into labour."

"Kids are born out there all the time, Kate. What's the emergency here?" Abe asked.

"The baby's in a breech position. Doc Payton wants her brought in. He thinks he might have to do a C-section."

"Okay," Abe said, picking up Kathleen's medical bag and opening the passenger door. "Let's get going. I want to be back before dark."

The emergency case was Jack Redsky's wife, Jenny. Too many people got involved with moving her to the dock and more showed up to help load her into the airplane. Flying into a headwind billowing out of thunderclouds gathering in the northern sky ate up the evening. Darkness shrouded Safety Bay when Abe flew over Coney Island. Spotty raindrops on the windscreen weren't helping his visibility. The lights of Kenora's main street and its businesses illuminated the right-hand side of the bay, but the shoreline blended into black where it met the water on his left. Hospital lights reflected in the water well away from where he had to land. Abe flew into the darkness, feeling for the lake's surface.

Jack, who'd held his wife's hand up until now, moved into the passenger seat beside Abe. His coal-black eyes searched the darkness below. "Good thing the lake has waves. You will see the water."

Peering out his rain-spotted window over the big cowling covering the engine, Abe knew different. Abandoning the approach, he circled the hospital, again flying over the edge of Coney Island, and lining up for a second attempt, letting down lower, searching for water he could not see.

Jack pressed his face against the side window. Abe opened his. As engine noise roared in, Jack looked over to see Abe leaning toward the window, listening while he closed the throttle until the plane was barely flying. The steady bark of the big radial was re-assuring as he skimmed the unseen surface. Abe continued down very slowly, waiting until the exhaust noise bounced back at him from the lake underneath. This was it. Jamming the throttle shut, he pulled back on the controls.

"Too high!" Jack shouted as the Norseman literally fell six feet, hammering the toes of both floats into the water.

Kate's shriek was buried amidst crashing and shuddering in the cabin. "Abe! For God's sake."

"Sorry, Kate. I'm sorry." In front of Abe's eyes the cross braces on the windshield vibrated into a blur. Water spiralled out from the propeller, spraying into the hot engine and covering the front windows.

Jenny moaned, grasping Kate's arm. She wiped Jenny's sweating forehead. "It's okay. Everything's fine."

Jenny's eyes squeezed shut as another contraction started.

"We're going to be all right," Kate said, then hollering over her shoulder, "aren't we, Abe?"

"Yeah." Abe waited for his heart to slow down. "We're okay."

Cylinders crackled and popped as he taxied the last hundred yards to the dock. A waiting ambulance took all Abe's passengers to the hospital. After checking his plane for damage with a flashlight, he opened his office door, went in, and made coffee. The pot began shaking in his hands as he tried filling it under the tap. Unable to control his shaking, he set the pot in the sink and turned around, grabbing the counter behind him, leaning against his hands until they stopped twitching. He vowed never to land in the dark again, ever. A stack of maintenance reports and bills needed his attention. Three cups of coffee and an hour later the door opened.

Jack Redsky stood in the opening. "I had no place to go."

Abe waved at him. "Well, come on in, Jack." Pointing to the pot, he said, "Coffee's not that old, probably rot your guts out, but you're welcome to it."

Jack nodded, walked over and poured a cup, then slumped down into an old sofa chair that never seemed to get thrown out of the waiting area. "Hard landing."

"Yes, well, I don't always get it right. How's your wife?"

"The doctor said he would do his best. I do not know what to think. He is going to cut Jenny open to save the baby."

Abe didn't know much about Caesarean births. "Perfectly safe," he said to reassure Jack. If Doc Payton was doing it, well, they didn't come much better, he thought to reassure himself.

"I walked back to town. Saw your lights on, you do not mind if I stay?"

"Of course not. Make yourself comfortable. I've got to finish this paperwork."

Jack drank half his coffee before rolling his head to one side and falling asleep, his snoring filling the small office. Abe called it a day and put his feet on Cindy's desk. She found them both sleeping at five o'clock the next morning.

Jack woke first as she made fresh coffee. "Hi. I'm Cindy. That's my boss with his boots up over there. Were you on the mercy flight last night?"

"Yes. My wife is in the hospital."

"How is she?"

"I do not know."

The aroma of perked coffee began filling the room as Cindy walked over to her desk. "Well, let's find out." She swept Abe's feet off the desk. Ignoring his groaning, she dialed through to the switchboard. When the operator answered, she greeted her. "Marg? Good morning. Put me through to the hospital, please. No it's not an emergency."

Cindy's older sister Olive, was the night receptionist on duty and filled her in with all the details. "Thanks, Sis. What are you and Al doing Sunday..?

"I mean after church...

"How about we catch the Argyle to Coney Island for the day. It's supposed to be warm...

"Well get back to me when you know...

"Good...

"Bye." She hung up. "Mr. Jack, you are the father of a darling little daughter."

"My Jenny? What about her?"

"She's fine, bit sore from the stitches, but the Doc says she'll heal like new."

"I am going to see her." Not waiting for the coffee to finish, Jack bolted for the door.

Abe stretched, griped about growing older and walked over to the sink. Cindy poured two cups of coffee as he splashed water on his face. "When you going to get married, Cindy?"

"Not while I'm working for you. All the eligible men are asleep by the time I get off work."

Abe threw the towel at her.

Jack returned a couple hours later when Abe was pumping water out of the floats, a gurgling sound inside the last compartment telling him it was empty. He stood up as Jack stepped onto the float. "How's your wife, Jack?"

"Very tired. I left her sleeping."

"And your daughter?"

Jack's eyes beamed with pride. "Beautiful."

Abe slapped him on the back while shaking his hand.

Jack broke into a big smile. "She is so cute. Lots of black hair, round face, nice brown skin. Ten fingers and toes."

Abe laughed. "How about breakfast?"

Jack looked down.

Abe knew why. "I buy every new father that rides in my plane breakfast. Come on."

On their way up to the café, Abe found out they had named the little girl Elizabeth.

NINE

Abe glanced at his passenger while taxiing into the bay at Long Grass. The man's black robes blended with the depressing atmosphere filling the cabin. Neither had spoken on the flight out. Killing the engine, Abe allowed the floats to bump against the dock. Usually there were a couple of men from the reservation waiting to help, but today the dock was empty.

"Where is everyone?" Father LaFrenier said, opening the door. "This year they knew when I was coming."

Abe turned to the hawk-nosed man. "Perhaps Singing Dove knows."

The priest shot him a cutting look, then climbed out, tangling his flowing gown in the ladder rungs as he stepped down onto the float. Abe tied the plane to the dock, then followed the priest ashore where he gathered twenty-one kids for the coming school year. As usual, Abe was expected to fly them to Kenora in one trip.

Jack Redsky's oldest, Pete, squatted between the two front seats.

"What are those pedals for, Mr. Williston?"

"They turn the airplane, Pete." Abe pushed on the right pedal with his foot and the Norseman skidded sideways in the air.

"Just like my Dad does with his outboard motor."

"Yes, but in a plane you have to drop the wing at the same time. Like this." Abe turned the controls with his hand and the plane banked in a sweeping right turn.

"If you want to go the other way, you press the other pedal and drop that wing?" Pete asked, pointing across Abe's chest.

"That's right." Abe patted the boy on the shoulder. "Keep that up and you could be a pilot."

Pete lowered his head. "They don't let Indians fly airplanes." He looked up at Abe. "But we are good fishermen."

"Pete," Abe said, speaking loud against the noisy radial engine drumming off the cabin walls, "you can be anything you want in this world. No law says you can't learn to fly." At least Abe didn't think there was.

"I want to help my Dad fish."

"Good, you catch'em and I'll fly'em out. How's that?"

"Great."

Abe tied up the Norseman at the Second Street seaplane base in Kenora before allowing anyone to get out. The priest came first, waited for the plane to empty, then marched the children off the dock to the old farm truck with open hay racks on the back that this year stank of cattle. Much of the life had gone out of their eyes as they filed past Abe, some with small suitcases, most with a bundle of clothes wrapped in a blanket. Watching the truck drive away, Abe slammed the door on his plane.

Sitting in his office, he needed to file reports and catch up on paperwork but found he couldn't concentrate as the sun settled in the sky. He'd just as soon quit working for the churches, but the Federal Government paid his bills, and he needed the revenue. Abe felt he'd sold his soul that afternoon. Well, not his, but those of twenty-one Native children.

TEN

Throwing the red buoy marking the end of his net back into the water, Jack Redsky began his journey home. The lake had yielded only two small Walleye and a four-pound Pike which lay gutted in the bottom of his boat. When Jack tied up at the dock, with its patchwork of logs and hand-sawn boards, two stars shone in the sky and fading sunlight crowded the northwestern horizon. Stuffing his meagre catch in a sack, he started up the path to his house.

A strange feeling came over Jack while reaching for the doorknob. Usually the sounds of his two older sons could be heard through the thin door as they wrestled or teased their mom. Tonight, only silence greeted him. Opening the door, he stepped into the light of a coal-oil lamp to see Jenny sitting at the kitchen table, breastfeeding their daughter, Elizabeth. The vacant stare in her eyes startled Jack into dropping the sack of fish and rushing to her. He could tell she'd been crying. Dried blood covered her buckskin dress. "Jenny! What's wrong?"

Jenny lifted his hand to her cheek as tears flowed once again.

Jack knelt beside her.

"Oh, Jack, it was horrible. Michael, he..."

Jack now understood why the house was so quiet. "The boys?"

"Gone."

"Michael! What about Michael?" His smiling eyes flashed in Jack's mind. Little touches of gray in them.

Jenny let go of her husband's hand and pointed to Michael, sleeping on the couch. Jack got up and walked over to him. Michael was different. Always wanting to know about people and why they did

29

things. If ever Jack could manage it, his youngest son would be the one to get a real education. His heart raced when he noticed blood all over his son's shirt. Even worse was the bandage covering his right ear, it too, brownish with dried blood. Reaching out, he touched his favourite son, who stirred slightly before settling back into a deep sleep.

"What happened?" he asked, returning to Jenny. "And where are the boys?"

"They're gone."

"Gone where?" Jack raised his voice, something he never did to her, unless he was drunk.

"He just took them, and Mary's three boys, the Castel kids, and a bunch more."

"Who, Jenny? Who took them?"

"They went in Abe's plane."

Jack slammed his fist onto the table. Jenny jumped at the sound, then closed her eyes as the baby let go of her breast and began to whimper. Lifting little Bethy over her shoulder, Jenny patted her back.

Jack ignored his daughter's fussing. "Father LaFrenier." Jack spat the name out covered in poison. That priest with his religion was a constant thorn in the side. It seemed that his god, who did nothing but hang on a cross, was always short of money. The tribe had raised enough to build a church when what they really needed was a school, and the church had to stand on the highest ground. The men had put together the money to build it in one summer, giving up many good fishing days. It was either that or have the Indian Agent hold back government money from them.

So they built the church, and Father LaFrenier hung his god on the wall. Once a month he arrived in Abe's Norseman to check on him and ask for more money. Everything he did had to be paid for, often with money that came directly from the Indian Agent. His god demanded that everyone get married again in his church, the traditional ceremony wouldn't do. When some refused, they had problems with government money that should have gone to their families. Father LaFrenier and money seemed to go hand in hand. The less money he took away, the more trouble they had with the Indian department. Now, for the second time, the priest had taken his two sons just when they could start helping him in the boat.

"Don't blame Abe."

"What happened to him?" Jack pointed to Michael. "Why all the blood?"

"When Father LaFrenier came for the boys, he... Pete did not want to go, and tried to pull away. The priest took out a long ruler and threatened him."

Jack felt blood rush to his ears. "He struck them?'

"No, not the boys. Michael."

"Michael?"

"He kicked the priest in the back of the leg while he was pushing the boys out the door."

"LaFrenier struck Michael?"

Jenny nodded and sniffed while wiping tears from her face. "Yes. The ruler had a steel edge that sliced open a big cut behind his ear."

From all the blood, Jack figured it must have been deep.

"Michael screamed as the priest reached for his arm. That's when Abe stepped between the two of them."

"Abe?"

"He shoved the priest up against the house, yelling in his face. Said if he ever laid a hand on Michael again he would kill him."

"Abe said that?"

She nodded. "The man went white. I mean really white, he was so scared. Abe told him to never strike Michael again, ever, then let go, and went back to his plane."

"Pete and Johnnie?"

"I don't know. At the residential school, I guess. I was trying to stop Michael's bleeding. Singing Dove came over and put a poultice on it. She said it would leave a scar."

Jack was shaking. "No damned priest is going to strike my kid and take my sons." He walked over to the closet and took out his hunting rifle.

"No, Jack!" Jenny put the baby down and ran over to her husband. "No, Jack. Please." She grabbed his arm. "Don't go."

Brushing her aside, he checked the clip. "That man is not going to keep my sons." He started for the door.

"Jack!" Jenny grabbed his arm again, but he shook her off as she stumbled to the floor. "Jack, no. No!" Tears flooded down her face as the door slammed.

ELEVEN

Crossing Eighth Avenue South, Abe walked past the big Corrigan house and turned into the yard of a more modest dwelling where he boarded with a little Ukrainian woman he knew only as Mrs. Litynski. There was a Mister Litynski, Yuri actually, but he worked with a track maintenance crew stationed out of Ignace, a hundred and fifty miles to the east. Abe had only seen him three times.

The smells of fresh cooking pervaded Mrs. Litynski's house. If it wasn't for her, he'd be skinny. As it was, long hours of wrestling freight and fish had given him enough muscle to fill out his short-sleeve shirts. He usually found something on his plate that seemed like it had been made minutes before he came in. Supper, no matter what time of day or night, always started with a bowl of borscht. Tonight was no exception and Abe filled up on cabbage rolls before stepping out the back door to enjoy the warm, late-summer evening.

Laurenson Creek was a wide canal that ran back inland from the Lake of the Woods. Three bridges crossed it, connecting the south of town to city proper. Walking toward the water, Abe cut through Mrs. Litynski's garden, now maturing as the season wore on. Scarlet-runner beans grew beyond the tops of ten-foot poles. He wondered how his landlady picked the top ones.

Swatting away the occasional mosquito, Abe stood by the water and took a deep breath of the evening air, trying to wash away the day's events. He shouldn't have manhandled the priest, even though it was easy. The man was all tough and bluster until he came up against someone more powerful. Abe wondered how the priest stood up against God.

"Hey, Abe."

Looking next door, he saw Ted standing on his boathouse dock, waving him across. A tall thin man, wearing a white shirt with black trousers and suspenders, was stepping into the cockpit of a long-decked, mahogany speedboat. Abe recognized him as J D Riley, Ted's brother-in-law, who was a passenger conductor on the railroad. People had a habit of calling him by either his initials, J D, or his last name Riley. It had taken some time for Abe to figure out they were both the same person.

"We're going over to Lodge's. Want to come along?"

"Sure."

"Well, get over here."

Abe admired the sleek boat as he walked onto the boathouse dock. It was a J W Stone boat, designed to be fast. Abe knew the story; Ted's father had bought it from the police after they'd taken it from smugglers caught running whiskey across to the States. The big engine, housed under long chrome-trimmed covers up front, was idling on gasoline, its exhaust burbling out two stern pipes, now under water. Abe stepped in as Ted reversed away from the dock. Taking a cup from J D, he was careful not to spill its contents as Ted shifted into forward and opened the throttle a little. J D Riley only bought the finest of whiskey.

Ten minutes and three bridges later, Ted switched the engine over to kerosene and opened the throttle as they broke out into the bay surrounding Kenora's waterfront. Raising its nose, the *Foxey* built up speed, sending water spraying out each side and leaving behind a long white wake that trailed huge waves. Abe knew. Many times they'd rocked his Norseman while taxiing across the bay.

The town of Norman slid by on their right, then just before Keewatin, Ted turned left and followed the channel to Lodge's camp. Built on the west side of an island he owned, Harry's cottage, as he referred to it, was a two-story house with an attached boathouse and screened-in veranda, fitting for Kenora's Justice of the Peace. Harry stood on the dock waiting for them to come alongside. The *Foxey* was twenty-eight feet long, and once it was tied up, plenty of room remained to park another boat behind. Harry's big cruiser, Abe knew, left a lot less room inside the boathouse.

J D, holding the bottle in his right hand, stepped out and walked up to his host. "Harry, you old reprobate."

"I'm surprised you aren't shoveling coal into an old steam locomotive," Harry said, taking the rope and tying up the boat.

"Not my type of work."

"Well, you must be doing something right," he said, patting Riley's flat stomach. "Ah, I see you brought the pilot. Good," he chuckled, "maybe we won't have to listen to Ted's old war stories." Directing his guests up a flight of stairs, Harry followed them into the screened-off room above the boats. J D's bottle was gone in twenty minutes, but no one worried. Harry had a well-stocked bar and they opened their first twenty-sixer of Crown Royal.

Abe's head was getting light when they found out about his trip to the Long Grass Reservation earlier that day.

"It's about time we started teaching those Indians," Harry said.

"Teach them what?" Abe raised his voice. "Do they fly airplanes?" He turned pointing at Ted. "Would the CPR let them run steam engines?" he asked, stumbling through the words. His tongue wasn't working like it should.

"English," Harry said, interrupting Ted, who was about to answer. "Teach them how to speak correctly."

"Dammit, Harry, they speak perfect Ojibway," Ted said.

Harry stood up. "All they talk about in that language is hunting and fishing, and their legends and stories."

Ted swirled the ice in his drink. "That's their heritage."

"All in the past. Not worth saving." Harry refilled his glass, offering the bottle around. "They need to learn the white man's ways if they're going to make it in this world."

"How about their religion?" Abe asked.

"There's nothing wrong with teaching them religion."

"Balls, Harry." Ted accepted the bottle, filling his glass. "We're supposed to be different with all our creeds and churches?"

"They have so many spirits and ideas, I don't think they can keep them straight," Harry said.

"Jack Redsky keeps them straight." Ted pointed south with the neck of the bottle. "He's a pretty happy man."

Harry tapped his forefinger on the table. "We teach them Christianity because that's what's right." His finger emphasized the point.

"That's what's white," Abe countered, not sure why he was arguing with Kenora's Justice of the Peace.

"Look, Abe," Harry said, "I'm not against Indians, they're part of our country. I just think we need to do a better job of teaching them the things we know."

"You think the residential schools will do that?"

"Yeah, I do. The sooner they adopt our ways, the better."

Abe drained his glass. He was getting nowhere, and couldn't even figure himself out now. Certainly he wasn't going to worship the spirits. Still he didn't feel it was right to take Indian children away from their heritage and families to turn them into brown-coloured white kids.

Red sunlight filtered through the screens as darkness fell on the warm evening. Ted was onto his Great War stories as J D dozed in his chair. Finally, after midnight, they all staggered downstairs and struggled to untie the *Foxey*. Ted put her in forward, driving the bow on some rocks before managing to reverse the propeller and back out into the channel. Opening the throttle wide, he sped off into the night following the green and red navigation lights casting a glow across the bow. When the first bridge appeared out of the darkness, he never slowed a bit. Abe closed his eyes as they roared into the opening.

"Shit," Ted hollered as the beautiful boat scraped the concrete, shaving mahogany off its side. Running wide open through the creek, the *Foxey* trailed two-foot waves, washing into boathouses and slamming small boats against their docks. Ted, who'd get irate and threaten blue murder when anyone else did it, couldn't have cared less.

Abe didn't remember running the *Foxey* inside the Corrigan boathouse, or falling through the door of Mrs. Litynski's house, but he did notice the clock when he went to bed. It read twelve fifty-five. Four hours later, his landlady woke him up.

TWELVE

Reeds swayed in the gentle night breeze as Jack Redsky walked onto the dock. Small waves rubbed his open wooden boat against two old tires he used for bumpers. Setting his rifle in the bow, he checked the spare gas can. Satisfied there was enough fuel for the trip, he turned to start the outboard, his pride and joy, the biggest on the reservation, an Evinrude Fastwin, fourteen horsepower. Opening a valve on the aluminium fuel tank surrounding the flywheel, he turned the needle valve three-quarters open, pressed the carburetor float down until a few drops of gas dripped into the boat, then let go. He flipped the choke shut.

While winding the starter cord around its groove on the flywheel, he thought of Father LaFrenier in his black robes. They reminded him of a crow. Yanking the cord in anger, he ripped the end off. Making a new knot, he tried again. On his third pull, the engine coughed to life and the boat sped off through the water. Straddling the rear seat in a sitting position, Jack advanced the spark lever and fiddled with the needle valve. Once the motor settled into a steady drone, he swung out of the bay and started the long trip to Kenora.

A combination of wind blowing in his ears and water rushing past the boat lulled Jack to thinking. He looked beyond the darkness into the stars. Where was Kitche Manitou when he needed him? Never had he killed a mother deer with her fawn. He tried not to overfish his part of the lake, even throwing back the odd big female he felt would survive. All his life he'd taken care of the Great Spirit's precious earth, but where was He now?

The white man's religion with its idols and crosses had nothing to do with the land. Father LaFrenier only talked about a dying man on a cross. And money, always money. How could a man who preached love leave some families too poor to buy winter clothing? Now he'd taken away his two sons again.

Silver moonlight reflected a broken line across the lake as Jack rounded the point to open water. What would his sons learn in the white man's school? English? His religion? How to fit into his society? Pete and Johnnie needed to learn how to fish and hunt if they were going to look after a woman and raise a family. What little money the Indian Department gave out disappeared before the poor got it.

Letting his hand dangle in the water rushing past, Jack thought of the lake. Until the coming of the airplane it had held back the white man's intrusion on their life. It gave them fish in abundance, and water for Jenny's garden. Life on the reserve was simple and happy. He was determined to get his boys back. What good was a family without sons?

The full moon moved behind scattered clouds in the eastern sky to be replaced by Jenny's face appearing in a vision. Tears of grief flowed down her cheeks. Shivers tingled in Jack's spine as death overlaid the image. Shoving the lever on the outboard, he turned the boat around and started back to the reservation. Still Jenny wept. He looked over his shoulder, toward Kenora and his sons. The vision vanished.

Shutting off the engine, Jack allowed the boat to drift on the still water. Above were all the stars, his friends, yet tonight they gave him no comfort. The Great Spirit had abandoned him. His sons were gone, his wife alone in her grief. Inside, his heart hurt, crushed by a weight the white man had placed on it. Jack broke down and wept. Tears washed salty down the weathered skin on his face.

Looking skyward, Jack extended his arms to beseech the Great Spirit. As he called out in prayer, his words echoed across the waters. The weight became lighter on his heart. He sat, waiting for the answer he knew would come. Waves lapped against the side of his boat. He dared not think in case he missed the answer.

A loon called in the distance. Jack remained motionless. The haunting cry came again. Two calls, he thought, two sons. Starting the outboard, he turned for Kenora, unaware the loon was calling out a third time.

Jenny, Michael, and the baby would be alone tonight. Tomorrow he'd have the boys back home and his family would be together again.

THIRTEEN

Mrs. Litynski always saved the fresh cream she skimmed from the bottle of milk that arrived at her doorstep every morning. Serving it with cooked oatmeal was the only breakfast she made. Abe could think of no better way to start the day. This morning it tasted more like mucus. He could feel it getting matted on the hair that coated his tongue. After each spoonful, he took a sip of coffee to wash it off.

Standing at her kitchen counter, the little Ukrainian woman mentioned nothing about the night before. She must have known, with all the commotion Abe made stumbling in. She talked on about her garden and made Abe's lunch. "I pick beans today. I can them all, but for you, I save best ones. We eat tonight with broccoli."

Abe tuned out her words, which wasn't hard to do with the constant pounding inside his head. He hoped the morning air would cure it as he stepped outside. After walking to the seaplane base at the foot of Second Avenue, he still needed to tread softly and avoid any sudden turns. Opening his office door, he stepped inside.

Cindy liked her boss's easy manner. She adored his curly brown hair and hazel eyes that made him look so handsome. She liked how his nose came to a soft point. If he didn't shave every day, it showed. She wondered what it would be like to kiss him, but not today. "You look like a dead fish dragged ten miles over broken glass." There wasn't a drop of sympathy in her voice.

"I was out with Ted Corrigan and J D Riley last night."

Cindy lifted the tin coffee pot from a little hot plate that sat on top of the filing cabinet. "Will you never learn?" She rolled her blue eyes before picking up a ceramic mug. "Let me guess. You went over to Arnold's," she said, while filling the cup and handing it to Abe.

"Harry Lodge's." He took a sip, burning his tongue.

"Same thing." After seating herself behind the counter, Cindy started listing off the day's flights. They had a business to run and, if Abe wanted to do his share with a driving headache, that was his problem.

She knew Abe was only picking it up here and there, like telegraph dots and dashes. Prospectors up north. Load of fish to come down. She'd have to repeat it all again later when he asked about destinations.

Abe was staring at a calendar on the wall. "What's the weather forecast?"

Cindy pushed back her short blonde hair. "What you see is what you get." In the window behind her, the sky had lost its morning pink and was turning to cobalt blue. "Highs will be in the mid-seventies, so don't overload on the fish run."

"I never do."

She cast an incredulous look as Abe shuffled out the door.

The smell of fresh water drifted in on the breeze as Abe walked across the weathered planking. His Norseman, CF-MAZ, wasn't the only plane on this side of the dock. Doc Woods had one of his Canadian Airways planes parked behind, and a private Stinson owned by an eastern mining company took up the last spot.

Running a hand along the smooth wing strut, Abe allowed its coolness to penetrate his skin. Stepping up, he reached overhead and cracked open the gas tank drain. No water. Good, he thought, then gingerly stepped down and walked to the front of the float, the smell of engine oil drifted from under the cowling. Standing beside the propeller, he noticed a line tied to the spreader bar. Squatting down, he recognized Jack Redsky's fishing boat with the big Evinrude engine. Abe sat against the cargo ladder, his head pounding between both temples. He wasn't going anywhere for awhile. He knew of pilots who flew half drunk, but even with a splitting headache, he wasn't going to risk piling up his plane just to match their stupidity.

Rippling waves rocked the plane gently as Abe watched Jack Redsky's boat bump against the float. And where was Jack now? What was he doing in town? When no answers came, Abe sighed, trying not to watch sunlight sparkling off the morning water. Headache or not, he had flying to do. Untying Jack's boat, he paddled over to J W Stone's boat yard and asked Walt to look after it until Jack returned. While walking back to the office it struck him that Jack must have left Long Grass last evening to get here before dawn.

FOURTEEN

Jack's eyes had felt heavy with sleep as he shut off the outboard and steered his drifting boat alongside Abe's Norseman. With all the spaces taken at the public pier, he had no choice. Jack knew that Abe would move his boat to a safe place. He resolved to give him the next Muskie he caught for his troubles.

Rose light bathed the eastern horizon as Jack walked off the dock, the rifle Ted had given him in his right hand. All was quiet as he crossed Main Street by the Kenricia Hotel and made his way to the CPR freight sheds. The sky had turned cobalt blue when he passed the Co-op and followed the road to Brett's pit, some three miles east of town.

He was about to cross the railroad tracks when the moan of an approaching steam whistle sounded. Moments later a steam locomotive thundered by pulling Tuscan red passenger cars. Jack had never been on a train, never had a reason to go anywhere the iron tracks went. His life centered around the reservation. Even standing here he felt out of place. The dining car rumbled by, inside people eating at the tables. What type of life did those people have, if they had to eat while travelling so fast?

Robert Coldwell recognized the lone figure standing beside the eastbound passenger train as he pulled up in his old Ford pickup truck. "Hey, Jack, want a lift?" he hollered above the coach wheels clicking on the rails.

Jack opened the truck door without replying and got in, holding the rifle between his legs, butt to the floor.

Robert glanced at it. "Going hunting?"

"Nope."

"Okay. So, where are you off to, my friend?"

"The residential school."

"With a gun?"

Jack looked at him. "Yes."

Robert saw an intensity in Jack's black eyes that suggested he ask no more questions, and when the last passenger car went by, he put the pickup in gear.

A mile down the road, Jack spoke. "How many kids you got?"

"Three, all girls."

"You want a son?"

Robert thought on that a moment. Sure he'd like a son, someone to carry on the family name and inherit the farm. There was no doubt that his girls would marry and give him many grandchildren to bounce on his knee when he was old. He'd have to be satisfied with that as his wife had nearly died giving birth to their last daughter. Doc Payton had told him in no uncertain terms she couldn't do it again.

"I'll get three sons when the girls marry."

"It is not the same."

"True."

"The soul of a man lives on in his sons. A man teaches his sons how to be like him. There is not much time to do this. Soon they grow to men. It is not for the church to take them away."

Now Robert understood. Every time he went to town, he passed the residential school. He remembered going to school in a little one-room building, his friends always laughing and playing tag in the yard. It was different at the residential school. The kids seemed listless if they were out in the morning. Most afternoons he would see them working in the barns or fields. Part of their training, he'd heard. To him it was more like slave labour. He went to school to learn reading, writing, and arithmetic. His dad taught him all about farming.

Clearly, he saw what was bothering the Native man seated beside him. "Jack, you can't fight the system."

"I do not want to fight. I want my sons back."

The brick buildings of Rabbit Lake Residential School were just around the next bend. Robert pulled over and shut off the engine. Turning to face Jack, he said, "They won't let you. The government says they have to go to school and you don't have one on the reservation."

"We have the wife of Ignace Two Bears. She can teach them."

Robert knew Susan personally, a wonderful white woman who enjoyed teaching children; fell in love with Ignace and left her position at a college in Winnipeg to live with him on the reservation. She was one of the most contented women he'd ever met. "Yes, Susan teaches the little ones on the reserve but the government doesn't employ her. It pays the church to teach them." Convenient and cheap, Robert thought. Trouble was, the Indian Department got what it paid for, and he didn't think it was worth even that.

"Jack, look, how about you come out to the house for coffee. Maybe we can work something out so the boys can come to the farm on weekends. You and Jenny are welcome to visit when you can. We have an empty bunkhouse available."

Jack's jaw muscles tightened. "No." He looked straight ahead out the windshield. "Pete and Johnnie are going home with me."

"Perhaps you could leave your rifle with me. It wouldn't look good walking into a school full of children with a gun, would it?"

Jack never gave an answer. Robert waited through the silence.

Jack opened his door. "No. I will keep it."

"I can drive you the rest of the way."

"I will walk." Jack closed the door and placed one hand on the open window. "Thank you, my friend."

"Jack." The Indian looked at Robert as he continued. "Violence is not the answer. Think back to your forefathers. They always lost to the white man's government."

"I will not lose my two sons." Jack stood back, allowing the rifle to point downward.

Robert stared out the front window. He didn't want this man walking into the residential school with a gun, yet outside of forcibly taking it from him, knew there was little more he could do. He'd call the police as soon as he got home. Pushing the starter pedal with his right foot, he fired up the engine and drove away.

Jack watched the dust cloud until the pickup disappeared around the bend. Three ducks flapped their wings and splashed water as they took off from the slough beside the road. Circling around, they flew overhead toward the reservation. Last night, Jack recalled, the loon cried two times. Today three ducks flew home. If the Great Spirit had changed his mind he wasn't going to, and strode off toward the school.

FIFTEEN

Built at the turn of the century before the world went to war, Rabbit Lake Residential School was part of Canada's commitment to education in the treaties signed with the Natives of Northwestern Ontario. A convenient way to do this was by employing the churches who already had a foothold in the reservations. What evolved was the 'Altar and Throne' arrangement. The government supplied the funding, the churches everything else. Slowly, but surely, over the years, harmful mutations sanctioned by government bureaucracy changed the purpose of these institutions until they became a tool for stripping the Indian of his language and culture.

Jack didn't notice the brickwork done by British masons, or the stone steps of granite as he walked up to the school's front door, but he was aware of the prejudice to his Indian culture contained within its walls. The brass opener felt cold to his touch. Turning it, the big oak door opened easily. He walked into the white man's world.

No children were around. He'd seen a few working in the barn. Pete and Johnnie were not with them. Looking both ways along the hall, there was not a single person to be seen and it left him wondering where to go. It could not be as difficult as hunting deer, he thought and turned right, his rubber boots treading quietly on the linoleum floor. Jack studied the plaster walls. This was not the forest. He had no idea where to look for his sons. Bad medicine filled the air and he was seized with an urge to run from the building. Jenny would be waiting. Turning around, he started back toward the entrance when a door to his right opened and Father LaFrenier stepped out.

"What are you doing in here?" his voice loud and harsh. "We don't allow Indians on the premises without an appointment, and especially with guns."

Jack spoke in a soft voice. "I want my two sons."

The priest's eyes hardened, his lips curling in a cruel sneer. "You can't have them until next spring. They're wards of the government. We'll look after them. Now, run along." He made a dismissive gesture with the back of his hand.

Jack stood his ground.

"Run along. I have things to do." Father LaFrenier turned to walk away.

Jack reached out. The priest froze when he felt a hand settle on his shoulder. Wheeling around, he swatted Jack's hand. "Don't touch me, you filthy heathen."

The words stung Jack. Had he not gone to the church on the reservation? Had not the priest married him and Jenny before Michael was born? He hadn't given much to the church, yet it was more than most. Raising four kids wasn't easy on the little money fishing brought in. Jack wanted his family to be together, growing up happy in the world he knew, even if they were poor. "Where are my sons?"

"You don't seem to understand," Father LaFrenier started to say. Jack eased the rifle upward. Fear grew in the priest's eyes. He cleared his throat. "Yes, well, ah, maybe you could visit them."

A door opened behind Jack. He was puzzled when the priest relaxed.

"Officers! You're just in time."

Jack looked over to see two policemen entering the hallway. Both were drawing their revolvers. Jack turned back to the priest. "I want my boys."

Father LaFrenier ignored him. "Arrest this man!"

"Drop the gun, Indian," the first officer yelled. "Drop it now." He raised his pistol.

Jack continued looking at the priest. "My sons."

Footsteps started along the hallway.

"The sins of fathers are visited upon their children, the Good Book says."

"Where are they?" Jack's voice echoed off the walls.

Footsteps started running. As Jack turned, the priest ducked into a doorway and three shots rang out.

SIXTEEN

Standing beside a month's worth of supplies, the four prospectors, dressed in outdoor gear and new hiking books, waved as Abe took off. He'd made a note in his logbook of their location and penciled in a reminder on the day he was to pick them up. This time of year there were quite a few notes in his book of men and locations that only he knew. If he didn't show up they'd have to walk out, or starve.

Sunlight beat in the airplane windows, adding to the heat radiating off the firewall, slowly cooking his feet. Ten minutes out of Kenora, Cindy came on the radio informing him the next flight was cancelled. The police had requisitioned his plane for a trip to Long Grass Reservation.

Abe swung around behind the hospital and with Coney Island on his right, landed well out in Safety Bay. While taxiing in, he spotted a police panel truck sitting on the dock, its rear doors facing him. Swinging the left wing over the dock, he jumped out and grabbed the strut, dragging the plane to a halt. Two uniformed policemen, lounging in the shade of an open-roofed shelter, watched him tie off the left float. Not until after he'd secured the rear, did they move. Abe walked over to Cindy, who'd come out of the office. "What's up?"

"I don't know. They drove out here twenty minutes ago and booked your plane. I managed to juggle things back."

Abe looked over Cindy's shoulder. The big man, with hairy arms that strained the cuffs of his short-sleeve shirt, was Sergeant Farnell. Abe had once seen him kick an Indian so viciously he broke two ribs. It was common knowledge that most white men Farnell found drunk,

50

especially local businessmen, would get a ride home. Indians in the same condition always ended up in jail, and sometimes the hospital. Abe had no time for the man's bigotry.

"Williston," Farnell called out, "open up the freight door."

Abe ignored the order. The man wasn't going to tell him what to do around his own airplane. When Farnell walked up to him, he asked what the freight was.

"Meat." He rolled back laughing. When it died down, he opened the panel's rear door.

Cindy screamed, then held a hand over her mouth as she ran for the office. Inside Abe could see a body covered in blood. Stepping closer, he stopped and rounded on the policeman. "You bastard!"

"Don't go running off half cocked. He was about to shoot Father LaFrenier."

Too bad he didn't, Abe thought. "You kill Jack?"

"Me and Harold here; we put three rounds into him." Farnell smirked.

Abe wanted to punch the man's teeth down his throat.

"Open the door, Williston. I haven't got all day."

Abe did as directed and stood aside as they each grabbed a foot and dragged the body out of the panel truck, letting it bounce to the ground. Abe heard the head crack against the wooden planking. The two policemen lifted the body into the airplane, leaving it with one leg hanging out.

"Bill the reservation," Farnell said, strutting off and climbing in the front seat of their vehicle. Abe stood, every muscle spring tight, his fist clenching and opening as the panel truck rolled off the dock. One day, Farnell... He chopped the wish short.

Moving Jack's leg inside, Abe rolled him over on his back and covered him with the ground sheet from his emergency supplies. After fuelling up the wing tanks, he walked into the office to find Cindy sitting on the old couch, colour drained from her face.

She looked up. "That's horrible. Poor Jack."

Abe rubbed the back of her neck. "You going to be all right?"

She nodded. "Yes. I mean no! I've never seen a dead person before. All that blood." She buried her face in both hands. "Why did it have to be Jack?"

"Take the rest of the day off, Cindy. Lock up here." Abe stepped back outside. "We're closed for business."

Clear of the dock, Abe pulled the throttle lever back and the engine came to full power as the propeller eased into fine pitch. With only Jack's body on board, the Norseman should have been airborne in twenty seconds. Abe's eyes watered as he let it ride on the step, well beyond the hospital, past Norman. He figured the plane would lift off when it was ready, but it continued skimming the surface, as if Jack's spirit refused to allow it to take flight.

A hot tear ran down his cheek. "Time to go, Jack." He drew back the controls ever so slightly and CF-MAZ reluctantly rose into an azure blue sky.

The engine's steady drone closed in on him, drifting his thoughts into the past. With sorrow heavy on his heart, Abe remembered the first time he'd met Jack. It had been on his second trip to the reservation in his biplane. At that time he was just another Native man who had helped unload and load freight. Later when the old plane had let him down, he'd stayed the night, feasting with Jack and Ted on venison strips Jenny had cooked. That was the first of many occasions he had eaten with Jack. But now there would be no more meals with his happy, outgoing friend. Abe shifted in his seat, scanned the horizon through the spinning propeller, then looked at each instrument in front of him. His shoulders sagged. Glancing back, he saw the body covered by his ground sheet. Looking forward, tears streamed down his face as he flew Jack home in a cloudless blue sky.

SEVENTEEN

Ted Corrigan arrived home to an empty house. He knew his wife Diana, and their two daughters had left earlier. As senior yardmaster for the Canadian Pacific Railway, he was responsible for the operation of all rail traffic in the Kenora yard. Regular hours, something quite rare on the railroad, had allowed him to plan time with his family at their camp on the Lake of the Woods. He was looking forward to a pleasant evening fishing. Gathering up his fishing rod and tackle box, he stepped out and took a deep breath of air, much better than the smoke and cinders around the yard office. Loudly cursing the starlings in Diana's garden, Ted walked down a set of steps leading to the boathouse. Inside, tied to one of the walkways that ran down each wall, was the *Foxey*. As part of his father's estate, the boat had remained in the family. Polly, his sister actually owned half of it. When Ted suggested they sell it, she flatly refused. Fine for her, living up in northern Manitoba with her husband who ran tractor trains into the tundra across frozen lakes in the winter.

Raw mahogany showed along the side he'd scraped on the bridge. His father would roll over in his grave if he knew it was there. He should have repaired it but there never seemed to be the time. Oh, to hell with it, he thought, setting his tackle box under the seat. Nothing a little fishing wouldn't cure. Reaching for the key, he turned it in the ignition.

Ten minutes later, after passing through the offending bridge, he swung right toward town. At Don's Live Bait he'd buy a dozen minnows for the girls. Abe's Norseman roared to life, heading west toward Keewatin on the step. Ted watched it, expecting it to climb out quickly, wishing he was in the right-hand seat. He'd have been a pilot if the CPR didn't pay so well. When the plane ran into the distance without leaving the water, Ted continued watching. Something wasn't right. He swung the *Foxey* in a tight turn, creating a huge wave off the stern that ran toward the hospital grounds. Opening the throttle, he followed the Norseman, constantly losing ground as the plane skimmed along the surface of the lake, sending out two thin white wakes. Ted was relieved when Abe lifted off in a lazy climb down by Keewatin. He sure wasn't in a hurry to get into the air. Throttling back, Ted watched the plane bank and slowly head south before he turned around and headed back to town.

While cruising by the public pier, Cindy came running out of her office, waving both hands. Ted slowed to a stop, then reversed back to the pier. Shutting off the engine, he drifted into the spot vacated by Abe's Norseman.

"Did you hear about Jack Redsky?"

"Hear what?"

"He's dead."

"God, no!" Ted stood up in the boat. "How?"

"Sergeant Farnell shot him."

"What the hell did he do that for?"

"Jack was out at the residential school. They say he was going to kill Father LaFrenier."

"Too bad he didn't," Ted said, stepping onto the pier. "Where's Jack's body?"

"Abe just left with it."

Now it all made sense. The long take-off, the slow climb into the air, the lazy turn south. Abe didn't want to do this flight.

"Mr. Corrigan?" Cindy touched his right arm. Ted looked at the girl, her face moist with tears, sadness filling her blue eyes. "Jack's boat was tied to the Norseman's floats this morning. Abe moved it to J W Stone's. Do you think we should leave it there?"

"Hell, no. Once word gets out Jack's dead, the locals will strip it bare." Stepping back into the boat, Ted turned to Cindy. "You going to be all right?"

"Yes. I'm over the shock of it now. Abe told me to take the rest of the day off. I don't think he'll be back tonight."

"You're probably right. I'll look after the boat. You run along and don't worry about it."

Cindy forced a smile. "Thank you."

Ted fired up the *Foxey,* and as it idled across to the boatyard, Jack's death descended like a black cloud on him. An honest friend, how often he had called Ted that. *Needjee-* my friend. There would be no replacing him. Untying Jack's boat, he towed it home and put it in Diana's bay of the boathouse.

Walking into the empty house had the feeling of being lost in a dense forest. The girls and their mother were up the lake, and expecting him for the weekend. His heart wasn't in it. Standing in the living room, Ted looked around. Where was the value in all he owned when a good friend and large portion of his childhood memories could so quickly be snatched away? Reaching into the china cabinet, he took out a crystal glass tumbler, then picking up a bottle of scotch, filled it to the brim.

EIGHTEEN

Two Native men held the Norseman as Abe drifted against the reservation's dock. Sitting a moment, he stared out the windscreen, knowing that when he went ashore, the news he brought was going to bring grief to his friends. Opening his door, he stepped out as the plane was being tied up.

"Hi, Abe. Whatcha doing here?"

"I have business with Singing Dove."

The man looked at his companion, then down at the knot he suddenly had trouble tying.

Abe noticed. Unexpected flights didn't always bring bad news, but somehow these people could tell when he flew in with it.

"She is in her house." The man never looked up.

Having lived seventy-seven winters, Singing Dove was treated with respect by all, including the Government Agent. Young women would seek out her wisdom. The elders of the tribe were not too proud to listen to her words, even when not invited. Of all her qualities, Abe felt most comfortable with her kindness, which she tempered with inner strength. Seldom did he visit when children were not playing in her yard or helping inside.

Standing in the open doorway, Singing Dove's gray hair, braided into a long pigtail, still shone with the luster of youth. Crow's-feet, and other lines etched deeply into her skin, told of long summers spent under a hot sun, winters too cold to remember, and death. She had lost three children and her first husband to the Spanish Flu. Her eyes met Abe's. Black as the depth of night, they asked the question he had to answer.

Climbing the three steps to her door felt like scaling a mountain. Looking down on the frail woman, Abe said, "Jack Redsky is dead."

A crow cawed in the distance. Singing Dove walked back into her house. Abe followed, seating himself opposite her at an old wooden table. Still she did not speak.

Abe looked into eyes veiled in sadness, focussing in the distance. "His body is in the plane."

"He is at peace," she said, "to the west, in the land of clear waters."

Abe didn't know where Jack was, but liked the idea he was surrounded by lakes and trees. It just didn't make sense that he was sitting on a cloud in heaven. Jack was always close to the earth, so if God took him to heaven, away from all he loved, why was he in peace? Religion could be so confusing. When he was covering him with the ground sheet, the thought had crossed his mind that his friend was sleeping. Abe would leave him there, sleeping in the arms of Mother Earth.

Singing Dove spoke while looking out the window. "Pete and Johnnie suffer. Pete is strong, like his father. Johnnie will bear a heavy burden for which Pete will carry the guilt."

"They've only been away a day."

"Yes, but it is written on the wind. Dear Jenny. My heart is heavy for her. She has lost her mate and the souls of her two sons."

"The boys will return next spring," Abe said.

"Only one, and his spirit will be broken."

Abe sensed a foreboding in her prophecy.

"Jack's strength was his greatest gift to Jenny, but so few were the years he gave. I have known her since she was at her mother's breast. Only when Jack took her home did life come to her eyes. It will go out now."

Standing, Singing Dove started for the door. "Let us go."

NINETEEN

Leading the way, Singing Dove shuffled down the road, passed houses that were in need of paint and windows. To their right a voice called out. "Jack!"

Singing Dove stopped.

"Jack. No, please, no. Jack!" Holding up the hem of her blood-stained, buckskin dress with both hands, Jenny ran onto the dock, pushing men aside to reach the plane. Stepping onto the float, she grabbed the cargo-door latch and pulled. The door swung open, bounced off the fabric side of the plane, and banged against her shoulder. She pushed it away again and scrambled inside.

Kneeling on the birch floor, she tore away the groundsheet. "Oh, no!" She threw herself across Jack's body. "Jack!" Tears streamed down her cheeks as she cradled his cold face in her hands. "Why?" she sobbed. "Why, Jack?" She leaned forward and kissed his forehead. "Why did you have to go?"

Singing Dove approached. The crowd parted to let her through, closing behind as she reached the airplane. Hanging onto a wing strut, she placed a foot on the float and stepped down. The sound of Jenny's grief hurt deeply. Singing Dove discerned she needed time alone. Turning, she silently dismissed the crowd with a gesture. Uncertain at first, then with reluctance the group moved ashore. Abe, last off the dock, joined those waiting for the drama to unfold.

With a movement that reflected her many winters, Singing Dove stepped from the float, thinking of her young husband who was taken by the white man's disease. They said it came from the Great War in

Europe. Visions played out in hazy memory. Running Deer had been strong. He stood proud, a skilled hunter, there was always meat in her tepee. She remembered nursing him, puzzled that her medicines would not work. So many winters ago. She grieved, but there was no need for tears, Running Deer had died peacefully in her arms. Now, waiting for the woman inside Abe's airplane to mourn, she allowed more enjoyable memories to play through her mind.

A dog at the edge of the crowd barked. One swift kick to the ribs brought a yelp, and shut it up. Appearing from the north, *Kineu*, the eagle, drifted on the air currents overhead. When Jenny stepped out of Abe's plane, it accepted the ascending prayers then, carrying them aloft on powerful wings, circled, and flew west, toward the Land of Souls. All eyes watched it grow smaller, finally to disappear in a sapphire sky. As Jenny wept in Singing Dove's arms, the onlookers melted away, until only Abe stood waiting for the two women to move off the dock.

TWENTY

Alone for the evening with nothing to do, Ted rang up J D Riley. "Thought you were going up the lake for a couple of days," J D said, after picking up the phone.

"I'll go tomorrow. Got some bad news." Riley waited. He could hear Ted sigh. "Jack Redsky's dead."

"An accident?" J D knew it wasn't uncommon for fishermen to drown.

"No."

"Want some company?"

"Yeah."

"I'll be right down."

The Riley's lived along Laurenson Creek between the second and third bridges in a modest house with a small glassed-in front porch facing north. The Corrigan's had a screened veranda running the entire width of their house with a western exposure. J D walked in the gravel drive, his back bathed in the warm rays of an evening sun. Ted, seated in a wooden rocking chair, beckoned his brother-in-law inside.

Riley pulled the screen door shut. "So Indian Jack is dead."

Ted nodded.

"How'd it happen?"

"Farnell shot him."

J D turned his head and looked into the dying sun. "Hasn't changed much since school days, has he?"

"Gotten worse."

"Well, you'd know. I didn't have much to do with him as he was a few grades ahead. Always fighting, bullying anyone smaller."

"Avoided Andy Barrett, though."

"So he should have. Andy was the only guy who could match him. I certainly didn't." J D felt his crooked tooth and turned to face Ted. "In the line of duty, no doubt."

"At the residential school."

"What was Jack doing out there?"

"Don't know, but I'll bet even money it had to do with his boys. Want a drink?"

"Yeah."

Ted set his empty glass down and went inside, returning with a clean glass and a new bottle of rye. "Somebody should get Farnell in a back alley and put the boots to him."

"Never happen."

"You're right." Ted set the glass on a little side table his father had built using a pair of moose antlers for the legs.

Riley spoke as Ted opened the bottle. "Why does the town keep Farnell on the police force. Everyone knows how prejudiced he is."

"Most people around here wouldn't kick a drunken Indian," Ted said, making a sweeping gesture with the bottle in his right hand. "They leave it to Farnell to keep them out of places they're not wanted."

"Yeah, too many people quietly agree with his way of handling things."

"Not everyone. Since becoming the CPR policeman, Andy won't let him on railway property in uniform." After filling J D's glass, Ted sat down still holding the bottle in his right hand, thinking of how they had grown up detesting Farnell. Hobos and bums feared Andy. Most jumped from the slow-moving freight trains and walked through town. Oddly, Farnell never bothered these men. Ted filled his glass as J D picked up the one on the table and sipped the fiery liquid inside, then said, "Treats the Indians pretty decently."

"Farnell doesn't like it."

"Too bad." Riley rested his glass on the chair's arm. "The feeling is probably mutual, especially after that business with old Frankie."

"Old Frankie." Ted thought back to that autumn night, then began telling the story, embellishing it where he felt necessary. "How he survived the winters in town, I'll never know."

"Used alcohol for antifreeze," Riley said.

"Nah, Andy used to haul him down to the roundhouse and let him sleep in the boiler room. Watched out for him, like the night Number One was late."

J D sat and drank as Ted related the events of that day.

"She had a hot journal on the second baggage car, Riley. I remember that. Farnell had been waiting to put his mother onboard for a trip to Winnipeg. Frail little thing. Farnell hovered over her like a hawk when I walked in. Tore a strip off me demanding to know why I couldn't run a railroad on time. Said the waiting was hard for his mother. She became embarrassed as the other passengers looked at her.

"I told him running a railroad was a lot different than being a cop. You couldn't just kick things and have them move on. Some of the ladies snickered. God, he turned red. Marched right over and stuck his nose in my face. 'One day, Corrigan.' I remember the look in his beady eyes when he said that. Pompous bloody ass. Always pushing it.

"Well in walks Andy and sees us standing nose to nose. Comes over and asks if there's a problem. I didn't think so. He turns to Farnell and suggests he should be looking after his mother. 'We have Indians around here,' he said. The look on Farnell's face. Turned a dark shade of purple. That man's going to die from high blood pressure one of these days."

J D grunted an agreement while staring through the screen.

"I got Number One out five minutes late. Andy stood beside me as the passenger train pulled away. Farnell was at the far end of the platform. As the last car was going by, who wanders around the corner but Frankie, bumping into Farnell. Swearing at the little Indian, the big cop knocked him down. I tell you, Riley, Andy moved so fast he was beside Farnell before Frankie hit the cobblestones. 'This man bothering you, Frankie?' Andy says, helping him up. Made quite a show of dusting off the Indian's clothes.

"You should have been there, J D. With Frankie looking bewildered, Andy turned to Farnell and suggested he apologize. Farnell pushed Andy with one hand, telling him there was no way that was going to happen, even over his grave. Well, Andy grabbed Farnell's hand and twisted it while pushing his face against the brick wall. I walked over as Andy was telling him that striking a peace officer was against the law.

"Farnell threatened to arrest him." Ted laughed. Riley didn't bother, he'd heard it before. "Here's Farnell, arm bent behind his back, face pressed against the station wall saying he was going to arrest Andy. 'This is CPR property, Farnell.' I remember him putting some pressure on his arm. Farnell grunted as Andy explained how private citizens were subject to his authority while on company property. Farnell tells him he's a policeman. Andy spun him around. 'Don't see no uniform.'

"Farnell straightened his coat, then bent over to pick up his hat. He fired off a wicked look at Andy then spit on Frankie. 'You'll pay for this, Indian.'"

"Well he did, didn't he," Riley said. "Those words still haunt Andy."

"Strange how a man can fall through a plate glass window, cut his throat and bleed to death, and there be no blood around."

"So now Farnell's shot Jack." J D drained his glass and refilled it from the bottle.

"I'm sure going to miss Jack." Ted leaned back and closed his eyes. "Lot of good memories died with that man." After sitting in silence for a while, Ted spoke again. "Farnell should bloody well have to pay for that."

"I agree. A life's a life."

"Ah, we both know nothing will come of it."

"Why? Where's the justice in that?" J D leaned back in his chair. "We come in here, take all the best land and relegate these people to a life of poverty, then wonder why they don't fit in."

"Some of us make room," Ted said, a tear slipping from his eye as he thought of his friend.

"Not nearly enough do. The way I view it, we're all humans. Equal in the eyes of God. Isn't that what the Good Book says? A lot of folks treat their dog better." Riley put his half-finished drink down. "When's the funeral?"

"Don't know. Day after tomorrow probably. Takes three days to bury an Indian."

"Can't make it," J D said, standing up. "I'm scheduled out on Number Seven."

After the screen door snapped shut, Ted watched one of the few men he counted as a close friend walk out the driveway and up Second Street. Pouring what remained of J D's drink into his glass, he topped it up from the bottle. Taking a long swallow, he allowed the rye to burn down his throat. When he'd told Diana about Frankie, she found it hard to believe. Farnell went to church every Sunday with his mother.

Well sod it, Ted thought. Indian killers sit in the front row of the church, and people like me were blessed for killing Jerries during the war. When an Indian kills a white man, he's called a savage. What had Riley said? Equal in the sight of God. Ted drained his glass. Did God really care?

The moon had risen and a chill was creeping into the veranda when he finally stood up and felt his way inside, leaving the two glasses and half-empty bottle on the side table. Before falling asleep, he looked at the ceiling and softly said, "I think you do care, Lord."

TWENTY-ONE

Abe shifted on the uncomfortable couch he'd tried to sleep on all night. Susan and Ignace Two Bears had insisted he stay with them. From past experience, Abe knew the Norseman's chipped-up plywood floor was more comfortable but couldn't bring himself to sleep where his friend had lain. Although the body had been removed, nobody had cleaned the blood stains from the plywood.

Birds sang in the early dawn. Yesterday the air had been still, high humidity and a blazing sun sapping the life from those forming a quiet circle around the dock as they waited for some sign from Singing Dove. After the two women had left, Abe had helped move the body to Jenny's house for the wake.

He lay trying to visualize Jack's face, his smile, his eyes. The best he could manage was a vague outline. Slowly his features filled in: the broad nose, the dark hair, the heavy eyebrows, a smile forming on his lips. The noise of an outboard motor broke the peaceful dawn. Jack's memories vanished and the sound faded to the south.

Susan walked out of her bedroom and drew water for tea. "You awake, Abe?"

"Yeah."

"Good. Pour the water into the pot when it boils, would you? I'm going to get dressed."

Abe pulled on his trousers and buttoned up the same shirt he'd worn the day before. The water boiled and he had tea made by the time Susan returned. She poured herself a cup, refilled his, then sat opposite him at the table. Stirring her tea, she asked, "Why?"

The pilot looked up and said nothing.

"Why does the white man go on killing these people? Will it never end?"

Abe didn't know.

"It would have to be Jack. Of all the men on this reserve, he was the tower of strength. I hate to think what will happen to Jenny, now that he's gone."

"She has a family to care for. She'll manage."

"Will she? Her two sons are at the residential school. Her mother's old, her father's a drunk who's never lifted one finger to help his family. Marrying Jack was the only decent thing that ever happened to her."

"Now he's gone."

Susan brushed a hand through her long brown hair. "Lord, it's so unfair at times."

After breakfast, they walked over to Singing Dove's house, only to find it empty. They found her at the Redsky house holding Jack's baby daughter, Bethy, as Jenny, with two other Native women, three kids, and a man Abe didn't know, sat around Jack's body lying in a hand-made coffin.

Six-year old Michael was eating at the table. The women rose, each embracing Jenny and leaving before Singing Dove motioned Abe inside.

"They watch the body for three days," Susan whispered in his ear. "They'll bury him tomorrow."

Abe walked over to the coffin. Jack's eyes were closed, his skin a putty brown. Abe's heart felt heavy, a tear crept down his face. He felt he should pray. But why? To thank God for taking his good friend? To ask that Jack be taken home? He didn't even believe that himself. From dust you are and dust you will become. He'd leave it at that.

Walking over to the old woman, Abe knelt before Singing Dove. She reached out and wiped the tear running down his face. "Don't grieve long, my son. The Great Spirit gives us memories. One day you will enjoy them. Jack lives on in the souls of his sons. One will have the strength to be like him." She withdrew her hand.

Abe bowed his head, then stood. "I have to leave. There are people..."

"You don't have to explain, young man," Singing Dove said, placing a soft leathery hand on his cheek. "Jack would understand."

Abe nodded his head, then left the house.

Susan followed. "You'll be back tomorrow, won't you?"

"Yes, after I pick up three prospectors waiting for me north of Ball Lake."

"Good. I think the service is planned for two o'clock."

"I'll be here."

Susan touched his hand. "We'll all miss him."

"Yeah," Abe said, and walked down to his plane.

TWENTY-TWO

With sunlight streaming in the kitchen windows, Ted nursed his headache and made tea. Turning on the electric stove, he waited for the coils to glow red. Taking a little wire grill, he put it over the element and placed a slice of bread on it to toast. In a few moments curls of smoke told him it was done and he turned it over, then poured a cup of tea. He toasted a second slice. This was breakfast.

Idling the *Foxey*, Ted towed Jack's boat through the creek into open water, then, nudging the throttle until he was going about fifteen miles an hour, headed south with the flat-bottom boat riding in the speedboat's high wake. Overhead a brilliant orange sky reflected the sun's early morning light off the lake. Ted sailed through a sea of sparkling water thinking about adventures with his childhood friend. The time they had run barefoot through some cactus. Ted's mom was pulling prickles out of his feet for days. Jack had none. The day they climbed to the top of a spruce tree to look into a crow's nest.

Then there was the day Jack's lure snagged while they fished off the end of the dock. Jack pulled a little. "It is stuck on the bottom."

"Ah, give it a good reef. If we lose it, Dad has lots more fish hooks."

Jack bent the rod almost in two. "It will not come."

"No, no. Look! It's moving."

They watched the rod straighten. Jack reeled the line tight. Slowly it went slack again.

"You must have hooked a log or something," Ted said. "Keep pulling."

Jack worked the line in close, until it pointed straight down into the water. No amount of yanking and jerking would get it to rise. "It is not moving."

"Let's pull it on shore."

They ran along the dock, then stepped onto the beach and continued reeling it in. Jack handed Ted the rod. Standing with his bare feet in the water, he reeled in their catch, then scampered out of the lake when it broke the surface.

Not three feet from them an alligator snapping turtle the size of a wash pan stepped onto the beach, Jack's red and white Daredevil lure hanging from its jaw. Ted wound up the line until the tip of the rod was touching the turtle's beak-shaped mouth. Giving the rod a couple of sharp tugs, he tried to pull the hook free. All the turtle did was open his mouth, its eyes following Jack's hand as he reached down and gingerly took hold of the lure. Gently he began to twist the lure free.

"Jack!" His father's voice made him jump, jerking the lure still firmly hooked.

"Look out!" Ted yelled as the turtle's head turned, snapping its mouth shut. Jack felt the sharp upper lip scratch his finger as it bit the end off the rod, severing the line. The turtle's beady eyes continued watching them while it waved its head side to side. With the lure still hanging in its mouth, the green, algae-covered creature backed into the water, sinking beneath the surface.

Whenever the Redsky's showed up at the island, Charlie always invited Jack's dad ashore, and while they smoked, he and Jack had played cowboys and Indians for hours. Remembering those times, Ted smiled as he passed Sandy Beach, the sun turning yellow in the sky behind. Jack had always wanted to be the cowboy. *I made a damn good Indian,* Ted thought to himself, turning out of the main channel and skirting a red buoy.

The Great War in Europe had started the day after the turtle incident, he recalled, and another two years went by before he looked old enough to lie about his age, be accepted in the Army, and shipped overseas. Seventeen months in the mud of France, ended when a shell burst killed three of his fellow soldiers and tore up his right knee. He was sent home on the *Olympic*, sister ship to the *Titanic*. While many veterans preferred to forget, Ted's way of dealing with the horrors of war, was to turn every little event into a story.

The world wasn't the same after the war. Jack's dad had died while Ted served in Europe. He pieced together what had happened from other Natives he knew. His hunting party had killed a moose and was gutting it when a bear charged out of the woods. Taken by surprise, the other Indians froze. Knife in hand, Jack's father met the charging animal. While being mauled, he cut deep into the bear's chest, slicing up a lung and cutting its heart nearly in two. Before the others could pull them apart, Jack's father was dead. A bullet hole in the bear's front left shoulder, was later attributed to a group of white hunters, who had shot the animal and couldn't be bothered to track it.

Now Jack, the oldest of seven, set the nets around the point from Charlie Corrigan's camp. Whenever Ted was there, Jack stopped to visit. Charlie had always paid cash for the biggest Walleye in Jack's boat. Ted did the same. That they had different skin colour never entered into their friendship.

Flashes of sunlight danced off the waves as the *Foxey* sliced through the water, Jack's boat in tow. The morning air, losing its coolness to the heat of the day, rustled in Ted's ears. How often had he ridden through these islands and channels with his father? Long before he knew Jack. Now they were both gone. He sometimes wished he hadn't come back from the war.

The beautiful mahogany launch, with all its memories, was now his. Looking back, he saw Jack's home-made boat following obediently. Pulling up to the long dock his father had built, Ted tied up first the *Foxey*, then Jack's boat. Walking off the dock, he met his wife, Diana, on the porch. "Jack Redsky's dead."

"Oh, no!" Diana felt behind for a chair and sat down. "Poor Jenny."

Ted took a seat beside her, the silence between them broken by the sound of waves curling onto the beach. "The funeral's tomorrow."

"How'd he die?"

Ted told her.

"Farnell will get away with it, won't he?"

Ted nodded yes. But one day.., he thought.

"You know what hurts the most?"

Ted shook his head.

"Jack was one of the few men who accepted the white man as an equal. And who betrays that trust?" Diana looked at her husband who wasn't going to be drawn into her personal vendetta. "The church and the law. I hope Farnell and LaFrenier rot in hell." She got up and strode inside, leaving Ted alone with his thoughts.

Next morning, Ted, dressed in a pair of black pants and white shirt, helped Diana into the big boat. Wearing a black floral print dress, gray hat and black gloves, Diana waited while he tied Jack's boat to a cleat at the *Foxey's* stern. With the engine rumbling out of the exhaust pipes, they fell to their own thoughts as the miles slid by.

Little log cabins appeared along the shoreline as they approached Long Grass Reservation. Most were in a state of collapse, but a few showed signs of life. Not everyone wanted a new frame-built house from the government. A boat from the south pulled in ahead of them and headed for the dock across from Abe's silver Norseman. A tall figure in flowing black robes stepped out.

TWENTY-THREE

Abe cut short the day's schedule to fly into Long Grass for Jack's funeral. Arriving after one o'clock, he tied up at the dock and walked to Jack's house. Susan met him at the door. Inside, Singing Dove, who held baby Bethy in her arms, watched as Abe approached and ran a finger down the little girl's tiny nose.

The old woman turned her head as the sound of an outboard motor drifted in through the morning. "That will be Frank. He insisted on getting Father Pollard from North West Angle."

Following a quick knock, Frank opened the door, allowing the priest to enter first. Father Pollard entered in rush of flowing robes, acknowledged Singing Dove, then shuffled across the room to Jenny. With his straight brown hair, pink round face and broad nose, he looked like a pudgy abbot out of medieval times. Before greeting Jenny, he took her hands in his. "Bless you, my child." Letting go with his right hand, he offered it to the young woman to kiss. Looking down on her, he spoke again. "God needed another angel in heaven. He chose your husband. You must feel honoured." He made the sign of a cross.

The words revolted Abe. He reasoned that God must have millions of angels, so why did he need Jack, as well? If anyone needed him, it had to be Jenny, and his kids. In fact, Abe couldn't comprehend why he even had to go to heaven. Jack's life revolved around the earth. He definitely wasn't going to be happy playing a harp on some cloud, even if it was lined with ermine furs and not silver.

"God will look after you, my child. He has blessed you with much." Looking around the room the priest noticed that, although there weren't a lot of furnishings, what was there had been cared for and was about average, for a reserve house. "I feel God would want Jack to have a fine funeral. What I have in mind will cost only forty dollars."

"What!" Singing Dove, in spite of her years, jumped up startling the baby.

Jenny looked up, eyes wide. "But, I don't have forty dollars."

"I'll need that much to properly bury your husband."

Jenny broke down crying.

Susan stepped forward. "Father, isn't that rather steep? These people are poor. Rarely have they ever seen five dollars at one time." The priest gave her a disdained look. "Please, Father, have mercy on this woman. She has just lost her husband."

The priest stood erect, put the tips of his fingers together and looked to heaven. "Forty dollars. I cannot do it for less."

Jenny slipped to her knees, taking hold of the black robes in both hands. "Please, I beg of you, Father, bury Jack. I will pay you when I can."

"We cannot use the church without some form of payment."

"I have nothing."

"Ah, but you do. Your husband's boat and motor."

Abe stepped in front of the priest. "It's worth twice that. Besides, it isn't here. I left it tied up in Kenora."

"Oh, but it is here. I saw it being towed in as I arrived."

Abe, and Susan's husband, Ignace, stepped outside to see the *Foxey* moored behind Abe's plane with Jack's boat drifting alongside on a rope, the Evinrude motor tilted forward on its stern.

"Shit." Only Susan's husband, standing at Abe's side heard the curse as they strode off down to the dock.

Diana was stepping out of the boat when Abe approached. He reached to help her. Standing on the dock, she gave Abe a quick embrace. "Nice of you to come."

"Jack was.., ah..."

"A *needjee*," Diana said.

"Yes, a true friend."

Ted climbed out of the *Foxey*. Diana moved away from Abe. "Jenny?"

"She's taking it hard."

"Poor woman."

Ted stepped beside Abe as Diana walked off the dock.

"We've got a problem," Abe said, as the railroader, a head shorter than the pilot, watched his wife walk up the path. "The priest wants forty bucks from Jenny to bury Jack."

"She's got forty dollars?"

"Of course not. He wants to take Jack's boat and motor as payment."

"Whose here?"

"Father Pollard," Abe replied.

"He'd like that."

Abe didn't think Ted quite saw the seriousness of the problem. "Jack left a family behind. One of the boys will have to come back and look after his mother. Without that boat the family will be destitute."

Ted ran a hand through his brush-cut hair, then stepped around the pilot. "Well, let's just have a talk with that man." He stormed up the path, Abe hard pressed to follow. Opening the door without knocking, Ted, the shortest person in the room, ordered the women to leave.

Singing Dove gathered up the baby and shepherded Michael out the door. Susan guided Jenny out, holding her elbow. Diana followed.

Ted marched over to the priest, whose face had drained of its blood. "Been a long time, Sidney." Ted crowded the man as he tried to back away. Eventually, he had him backed against the wall beside Jack's coffin. "For a man who ran the biggest parish in Winnipeg, looking after two small churches and an Indian reservation is really quite a responsibility." The priest held up both hands. Ted didn't give him a chance to speak. "Sending your pregnant girls away by train." He shook his head. "We invented the telegraph."

"Please, not in front of these men."

"Why not, Sidney? They might have daughters that need protecting."

"They're Indian women." His eyes revealed he'd said too much.

Ted now held the high ground. "About this forty dollar funeral..."

"Did I say forty? I meant to say four. Jack was always good to the church."

"Still too much."

The priest's eyes darted around the room. "Two, then."

"Hypocrite." Ted reached in his wallet and took out a five dollar bill.

"I don't have change."

"Break the bill at Luther's store. Meanwhile, how about a receipt?"

The funeral started at two o'clock, with Father Sidney Pollard officiating, in Latin. Six men carried Jack's coffin to the graveyard and lowered it, facing west, into the freshly dug hole.

The priest said the standard ashes-to-ashes phrases, then left. While Jack's Native friends bid him goodbye in their traditional way, Abe's thoughts drifted away. "Ask anyone at Long Grass," the fish buyer had said. "They'll all tell you Jack Redsky is the best fisherman out there."

Abe didn't have to ask. When he had loaded tubs of fish in his airplane, he soon came to know Jack's were always the heaviest. When he'd kid Jack about fishing the lake out, his Native friend would blame the white man for eating too much fish. This good-natured banter didn't bother Abe, for he felt that of all the men on the reserve, only Jack viewed him, not as white, but as a friend.

Jenny treated him like a brother, often insisting he stay for supper. He remembered the first summer with his Norseman. It was a late afternoon flight and they'd unloaded drums of gas and were sliding two heavily iced tubs of fish in the plane when Jenny walked onto the dock. "Abe, when did you eat last?" she asked.

"Breakfast." Eleven hours ago, he thought.

"Well, stay and eat with us."

"I can't."

"Sure you can, my friend." Jack patted him on the back. "You said it was your last flight." Reaching into the plane, he picked out a big Walleye. "This is too much for us to eat." With the other hand, he had gestured Abe toward the house. Those had been good times.

Abe looked across the grave to see Singing Dove between Jenny and Diana, arms around both women. A tiny hand took hold of his fingers. Looking down, he reached out and picked up Michael.

"Why did Daddy have blood on his shirt?"

"He was..." Abe almost said shot. "He was hurt."

"Who hurt him?"

"The police."

After he said this, something deep inside the boy's eyes flashed into comprehension, the look that surfaced told Abe he'd said the wrong thing.

TWENTY-FOUR

Ted stood with his head bowed. He wanted to pray, but couldn't find any words to say to the God who took his childhood friend. Earlier, the ringing church bell had called the faithful to Jack's funeral. All the wooden benches had filled as relatives and friends gathered for the service. He and Abe had stood along the back wall of the little church.

Jack's body lay in an open casket up front as Father Pollard sent him to heaven. The Christian heaven, which Ted found distasteful because if it did exist, had to be full of Germans and British, who killed each other during the Great War. He doubted they'd make room for an Indian. The man hanging on a cross behind the pulpit certainly didn't embrace Jack's beliefs or way of life.

After taking Jenny as his wife according to tribal custom, the Christian God decided they were living in sin, whatever that meant, and demanded they be married in the church. Jack complied because Jenny believed the priest. It cost Jack a week's fishing. Reflecting on their time hunting together every autumn, Ted felt the weight of old memories fall upon his heart. He'd made sure the first deer went to his friend, Jack the hunter, at one with the forest. All life was sacred and Jack had explained the qualities of the Creator as he saw them in the natural world about them. Everything had its place in life. To take more than one needed was to displease Kitche Manitou. Jack would express sorrow for the deer they'd shoot, then thank the Great Spirit for his winter meat supply.

Ted tried to recall the words. 'I had need. No more will you run in freedom. Without you I grow weak. Give me your flesh for strength.' Ted found himself a little more selective when hunting, trying not to contribute to the white man's waste. But then he already had two four-point deer heads hanging on the wall, one his father's, the other his own.

Often he and Jack had watched the sun set in the west, rose petal red through clouds in an autumn sky, the promise of a better tomorrow, a tomorrow that would never come. Beyond the sunset, Jack would say, was a world of happiness and plenty, yet he often puzzled over the need to die in order to get there.

Well you're there now, my friend, Ted thought.

Jack had wanted to be buried overlooking the bay. Unfortunately, the graveyard, a plot of level ground surrounded by a weathered picket fence, lay behind the church whose front door opened onto the lake. Jack, the Native Indian, was now being buried among the Christians. Ted didn't for one minute believe his soul was there.

People drifted away from the grave. Ted walked toward the dock. A second set of footsteps followed. He allowed Abe to catch up as they continued down the path. Stepping onto the dock, they stood under the shade of the Norseman's right wing.

Sunlight danced off the rippling water as Abe spoke. "I'm worried about Jenny. Jack was her strength."

Ted stared off across the water as he lit a cigarette, flicking the match into the lake.

Abe scanned the bay. "Do you think the boys know their father is dead?"

"No."

"So, who's going to tell them?"

Ted continued gazing into the distance. Handling death left him with the feeling of falling into a well and never reaching bottom. When his own father had died, he never seemed to say or do the right thing. It was his sister Polly who smoothed over his grief. Besides, having two daughters, he wouldn't know how to approach the boys. "Jenny. She's their mother."

"I don't think so. You saw her today. She's barely hanging on. It's only Singing Dove who's keeping her sane."

"The boys saw you last when you flew them in. Why don't you tell them?"

"Me? Look, I'm not even married. How can you expect me to handle something like that?"

"Don't you care?"

"Sure, damn right I do. And you?"

"I'll lose my temper and punch Father LaFrenier. Nothing would please me more than to flatten that big French nose of his."

Abe laughed. "Good, you do that, it'll save me the bother."

"Tell you what, I'll talk to Diana. She'll go with you, young Johnnie will be on her mind."

Abe sighed. "Okay, I'll talk it over with Singing Dove and Jenny, then get back to you."

Diana and Susan came down to the dock as Ted climbed into the *Foxey*.

"You will look in on Jenny?" Diana asked. Susan nodded. "And let me know how things turn out."

"Of course I will." The two women embraced then Susan stood back.

Diana took Abe's hand as he helped her into the boat and undid the lines.

Ted turned the key and the engine roared to life, barking out exhaust underwater at the stern. "If you see Sidney, tell him to mail me my three bucks." He reversed the propeller and the big boat backed away from the dock.

Susan waved good-bye. Abe kneeled down and untied his airplane as the speedboat turned and thundered out of the bay.

TWENTY-FIVE

The dormitories at the Rabbit Lake Residential School each had ten beds, little money being spent on them. Many were old. All had been wetted in the last year; stains covered both sides of the mattresses. During the first days of the school year it was not uncommon to hear the sobs of loneliness as many, particularly the young ones, missed their mothers.

One small window, that did little to keep out the winter cold, allowed in very little nightlight. Once the two electric lights were turned off, darkness closed over ten sad boys. On the first night, one of the new boys had cried loud enough to be heard in the hallway.

Within moments, the door had swung open and a shadowy figure made its way to the wailing child. The first time this had happened he responded to the touch on his shoulder, calling out, "Mommy?"

"Shut up." The angry voice, heard by all, started the boy crying again. "I said, be quiet."

The child wailed on.

Pete, having been through this the year before, rolled on his stomach, pulling the pillow over his head and pushing it against both ears. The shrieks, although muffled, continued to get louder with each crack of the wooden ruler. Pete found his eyes watering, even though he knew that after two or three nights, none of the kids would cry out loud. They would weep with their face in the pillow. Pete missed his mom and dad.

When a small boy sobbed too loud, an older one sometimes slipped out of bed to calm him. But being caught out of bed after the lights were out, assured a beating. Still, the older boys did it.

Lying on his thin mattress, feeling the steel springs underneath, Pete stared into the darkness. He knew what death was. He'd been with his uncle after his female dog had given birth to eight pups. Holding one of the tiny furry animals under each arm, he followed his cousin, who held one pup with both her hands as she walked behind her father down to the lake.

Pete recalled the dread that surrounded his heart when his uncle took one of his pups and held it underwater. Bubbles came out of its mouth. It struggled, paddling all four little feet, and stopped moving. Although his cousin turned away, Pete watched each one die until five shaggy-haired bodies lay on the dock. It had been a long walk back. He could remember dragging his heart behind in the dirt as the limp, cold bodies hung under each arm.

Today, he had been told his dad died in an accident. Tears flooded both eyes. The top of his heart hurt. He stifled a sob.

When someone began crying, he blotted it out until, breaking through his own grief, he realized it was his younger brother. Slipping out of bed, he padded over to comfort him.

He touched his brother. "It is okay, Johnnie. I am here."

Wrapping an arm around Pete, Johnnie buried his face in his pillow trying to mute his loud sobbing. Pete fought back the urge to join him and knelt beside the bed.

"Johnnie, please. Shh. They will come soon." He patted his brother's shoulder. "It is okay."

Johnnie tensed, holding back, sniffing as he tried to control his crying by taking short, jerky breaths.

"That is better."

Johnnie bawled again. Pete broke down. Holding his brother tight, he too cried.

That was how Father LaFrenier found them when the lights came on. Seeing Pete out of bed, he rushed over, his black robes flowing around him and grabbed the boy by the arm, dragging him upright. "What are you doing out of bed?"

Pete, hauled out of his grief, looked at the man but said nothing.

"Answer me. I asked you a question." The priest shook Pete. "I expect an answer."

When he began speaking in his Native tongue, the priest slapped him. "Speak English."

"I... I... My brother needed me."

"Your brother needs a good licking for waking everybody up." Letting go, he reached down for Johnnie, who lay looking at him, tears streaming down his face.

In that moment, Pete took his first step toward manhood. Feeling the protection his dad had always given him, he knew he couldn't allow his brother to be beaten. Lashing out with his right hand, fingers closed, thumb sticking up, he struck Father LaFrenier. It was a glancing blow on the shoulder that continued on to strike the side of his face.

The priest went mad with rage. "You.., you.., heathen." Sinking his fingers into Pete's arm, he held it in a vise grip and dragged him out of the dormitory.

Calling another priest, he opened the door to his office and shoved Pete inside, who, tripping over his own feet, sprawled across the floor.

"Get up!" Father LaFrenier's voice filled the room. "Get up, damn you."

When Pete refused, Father LaFrenier hauled him up, laying him across the desk as another man entered the room.

"Hold him." Father LaFrenier shouted, opening a cupboard and taking out a riding crop.

Pete felt strong hands bend him over the desk. His night clothes were ripped off and the lash fell. Searing pain followed each stroke, and with it Pete's hatred of the white priest and his religion bore deeper into his soul.

TWENTY-SIX

Abe had secured a contract with the owners of Blindfold Lake Lodge to fly in their hunters booked for the fall season. He'd dropped off a party of six and returned when Cindy told him of Diana Corrigan's phone call. "I told her you'd get back about three."

Abe looked at the clock. It was ten after.

"She said she'd be home all afternoon."

Abe dialed the four numbers and got Diana on the second ring. She told him the school allowed visitors on Sunday afternoon, and only between two and four.

"Even if someone dies?" Abe asked.

Diana said they would make an exception in that case, but only for immediate family.

Abe turned to Cindy. "What's Sunday look like?"

"Booked solid. Dawn till dusk."

What's between two and four? Anything we can move?"

Cindy shook her head. "Two flights out of Blindfold Lake. These people have connections to make."

Turning back, Abe spoke into the mouthpiece. "Sunday's out for me." He wanted to ask Diana to go it alone, but felt that wasn't the right thing to do. He listened as she explained she'd only talked to a secretary. There were ways of working around these things. When was the soonest he could go?

"Day after tomorrow. The plane is scheduled for an inspection right after lunch."

Diana promised to pick him up. Abe suggested lunch. They agreed on the café in the Kenricia Hotel. He could walk up from the dock.

Two days later, Abe entered the Kenricia's dining room and found Diana seated at a table for two, a white sweater draped over her light-green dress. He walked over and sat down as a waitress approached with a couple menus and poured him a glass of ice water before leaving.

"I appreciate this," he said.

"Jack was a good man. He deserved better," she said, touching Abe's hand.

They ordered a light lunch, then over the meal talked about Jack, a little about Ted, but a lot about Diana. All Abe really knew was she came from a pioneer French Canadian family down on the Winnipeg River.

"I was the youngest of eleven kids. Well, ten really," she said in her slight French accent. "Franciene was adopted."

"How'd you met Ted?"

"Through Hector."

"Hector?"

"Ted's brother. One night three of us girls had taken a team of horses and had driven into town for a dance at the Rowing Club. Hector was there. Ted had been in Europe for over a year fighting the Germans. Kate and I were standing on the balcony when she spotted Hector coming our way."

"Oh, God," Kate said, "here he comes again."

Diana shoved an elbow in her ribs. "I think he's cute."

"He talks too much."

"Hi, Kate. Whose your friend?"

"She's my cousin."

"Hi. I'm Hector Corrigan."

"I'm Diana." her voice laced with a heavy French accent.

Hector turned to Kate. "I didn't know you were French Canadian."

"I'm not." Her frosty reply was lost him.

"Well, Diana, how come I haven't seen you around?"

"I've been away."

"She was attending a convent," Kate said.

"You're a nun?"

"Oh, no." Diana blushed. "My parents sent me to school there. I was studying biology."

"In a convent?"

"Well, yes. It's more of an academy school with residences."

"Like Saint Anthony's?" Hector asked.

Diana eyed him sharply. "It was not an Indian school."

Kate put her toe into his shin. "Hector, really."

He ignored the kick. "I'm sorry. I only meant it had dormitories."

"Yes."

"You finish your course?"

"No."

"She got booted out," Kate said, a smug look revealing her knowledge of a secret.

Diana shot her a fierce look.

"Oh, there's Patrick Reierson." Kate said, walking away.

"I don't pay any attention to Kate," Hector said. "It's not that she has a big mouth, her feet are small enough that she can get one in without trying. You dance?"

"Yes."

"May I?" he had asked. She took a sip of water, remembering he hadn't waited for an answer before leading her onto the dance floor in the middle of a song the musicians had been playing.

Abe watched Diana stare into the distance. "You fell for him."

"Yes." She paused. "Later that evening we stood on the balcony looking across the bay at the hospital lights. He told me he wasn't going to fight in any stupid war, even if his preacher gave him a white feather every Sunday." She stopped a moment and dabbed at the corner of one eye with her napkin. "He wanted to be a doctor, but said he'd probably end up working all his life for the railway, raise a family and be buried here."

"So, why didn't you marry him?"

"Well..." As Diana hesitated, Abe feared something bad had happened. "Shortly after we were engaged, he died in an accident on the railroad."

"I'm sorry." Abe touched her hand. "After his death Ted started chasing me. I thought I saw a lot of Hector in him. My parents wanted us to be married in the Catholic Church. Ted didn't care where the wedding took place. I think Hector would have. He was a lot like Nan."

"Nan?"

"His mother, she was very spiritual. As it was the priest wanted too much money for the wedding. Dad kicked up a fuss and the Presbyterians did it for half." She looked at her watch. "Goodness, we should be going."

TWENTY-SEVEN

The Corrigan's drove a 1936 Dodge sedan. It had few miles on it, and still smelled new as Abe settled into the front seat for the drive out of town. Diana pulled into the residential school and stopped in front of the main building, parking in an area of dirt, spotted with mud puddles from last night's storm. Abe looked up at the monotonous red brick architecture, then over to his right. Two sets of swings divided by a wooden fence were the only things in the playground. As Abe got out, he noticed grass growing under the swings. Any park he went to as a kid had a hollow of dirt underneath, always a lot more fun when it rained.

Diana led the way up the steps and waited while Abe opened the door then followed her in. They turned right along the hallway to a door with frosted glass. She knocked and walked in.

Father LaFrenier, seated behind the desk, stood up and came around to meet them. "Mrs. Corrigan. What a pleasant surprise." He held out the back of his hand. Diana took one look at the big ring, then reached out in a motion to shake his hand. The priest gave her an annoyed look. It didn't change when he acknowledged Abe.

"Father LaFrenier," Diana said, "we are here to see Jack Redsky's two boys. I presume they know their father was killed?"

Boy, Abe thought, this woman is really cutting to the chase.

The priest looked skyward as if seeking help from above. "There was an accident involving their father. They know, but we saw no reason to tell them how it happened."

"Well, on behalf of the family, we'd like to see them."

"Visiting hours are on Sunday..."

"We would like to see them now."

"That's not possible. Ah, they have chores and studies to attend to."

Diana opened her purse. The priest watched with interest. Taking out a check book, she asked him for a pen. He quickly got one out of the drawer and slid the inkwell across the desktop to within easy reach.

Diana inked the pen, then wrote in the date. "I'm sure your school could use some extra funds." She dipped the nib again and wrote in a figure that brought a smile to the priest's face.

"It is only by the generosity of people like you, madam, that we are able to teach the Indians to be Christians."

"I'm sure my gift pales into insignificance against the contribution made by the Federal Government." She dipped the pen into the ink a third time, then placed it on the signature line of her check. "We've gone to quite a bit of trouble to schedule this visit. I hope it's not in vain?"

"Oh, no. No, not at all. As a matter of fact I was about to suggest we find the Redsky children right now."

Diana signed the check and handed it to him. "I didn't fill in the pay-to line. I'm sure you'll know what to put there."

"Oh yes. I'll take care of it." Father LaFrenier put the check in a drawer on the side of his desk and locked it, then with a false smile, said, "If you will be so kind as to accompany me, we'll find the boys."

Black robes flowing around his feet, Father LaFrenier led them out of the building. Abe noted that all the classrooms were empty, even though it was early afternoon. The priest, stopping another man in brown habit, asked where the Redsky boys were and was directed to the barn. Sticking his head in the doorway, he called the stable master and had the boys brought outside. Abe sensed the priest didn't like being around animals as he moved away until the smell disappeared.

Pete came out first by himself, looking bewildered until Father LaFrenier called him over. The boy looked at Abe, then Diana, waiting for them to speak first. This wasn't the vibrant youth Abe knew. He greeted the boy in Ojibway. Before Pete could answer, the priest cut in,

"The children are not permitted to speak in their own language. We only allow English here."

When Father LaFrenier stepped forward, Pete backed away from him until he was against the barn wall. The priest, taking hold of his arm, had to drag him back to Abe and Diana. "These people are here to see you. Show some manners."

Abe reached for Pete, who moved to his side while always facing the priest. "Hello, Pete."

The Native boy glanced at Father LaFrenier, who nodded. "Hello, Mr. Williston."

Abe was about to speak again when Johnnie came through the doorway followed by the stable master, who hovered behind him.

"Johnnie," Diana said, reaching out.

The boy caught the priest's eye and remained still. "Hello."

All so formal, Abe thought. He'd heard Johnnie call Diana, Auntie Di. Both the boys were bundles of energy, always chasing around. Where had that gone? Everything here was so stiff.

"Father, please. Could we have some time alone?" Diana asked.

The priest looked at the stable hand. There was a negative shake of the head.

"We have a policy of..."

Diana stepped up to the two boys, her back to the priest. "Perhaps I should have put the church's name on my check."

Father LaFrenier cleared his throat. "Well, I can see they know you, so we can relax our rules. Ten minutes. These boys have work to do."

Once the two men had left, Pete's shoulders slackened. Johnnie stood behind him, looking sullen. Abe didn't know where to start. "We're here about your Dad."

Pete looked at the ground. Johnnie stared wide-eyed at Diana.

Abe hated what he had to say next. How did you tell a child his father was shot in the hallway of his school? He couldn't find the words.

Diana came to his rescue. She reached out and took one of the boys under each arm and looked down. "I'm so sorry." Kneeling, she spoke to Pete first. "You must be strong. Your father would have wanted you to look after your brother."

"Is he in the Land of Souls?" Pete asked.

"Yes. Yes, he is."

Pete stared toward the west. "Is he happy?"

She nodded. Johnnie started crying and she took him in her arms. "It's, okay sweetie, Auntie Di is here."

"I want to go home."

She hugged him. "I'm sorry. You can't. But your mother sends her love."

Abe placed a hand on Pete's shoulder. "She has a lot to look after Bethy and your brother. You will be strong for her, won't you?" Pete gave Abe a vacant stare. He felt he wasn't getting through. God, he wasn't good at this. "Your Dad was coming to see you when, when.., it happened."

Pete focussed on Abe. "What happened?"

Abe looked into the youthful round face that seemed to age before him. The boy deserved the truth. "He was shot by the police."

Pete slowly looked down at the ground, but not before Abe saw his black eyes blaze with hatred. Johnnie broke into a wail and clutched Diana who rubbed her hands on his back. Both hands stopped, then softly with her fingers, she traced a line diagonally across his twitching back. Spots of blood oozed through his shirt.

TWENTY-EIGHT

When Diana saw the colour red, memories long repressed came tumbling out of her past. Stepping off the train, she had been overwhelmed by the city's size. Buildings taller than she'd seen in Winnipeg surrounded churches that reminded her of Europe's cathedrals. Entering the convent through a wrought-iron gate in the high walls, she had felt like a peasant walking into a European castle. Inside was the brick and limestone academy, where she would study biology and work toward her degree.

During the months that followed she applied herself, attaining top grades in everything except catechism. She made new friends, particularly two girls from well-to-do families in Quebec City. An adventurous trio, they often snuck out after bedtime to roam the empty halls of the convent. With only a candle, they would sneak into forbidden areas. One night a door opened in the corridor. Diana blew out the candle and backed up, forcing the girls around a corner. Shadows, accompanied by voices, moved across the stone walls.

"Those were men," Diana whispered after two priests walked past.

"What are they doing in the convent?" her friend asked.

The third girl snickered. "It doesn't take much imagination to figure that out."

"I'd like to know how they got in," the second one said. "Let's follow them."

The three girls trailed behind in the darkness left beyond the glow of candlelight, moving ever deeper into the lower levels of the convent.

A door opened and closed. They were left in pitch dark with no way to light their candle.

Holding hands, they groped their way back, making wrong turns and running into dead ends and locked doors. Quite by accident they found the stairs leading upward. Daylight was breaking when they got back to their room.

Next evening, they decided to find out where the priests had gone. Tracing the previous night's route brought them to a square room with a heavy wooden door secured by great rusty iron hinges bolted to the planking. It opened into a tunnel. Beyond their candlelight was only darkness.

Heart pounding, Diana led the way in, following the flickering light reflecting off the stone walls. Her foot sank into something oozy and soft. She jumped back, almost knocking the other girls over as her shriek echoed in the black void. At her feet was a pool of dark green slime fed by water seeping out of the wall. Stepping around it, she pressed on, passing alcoves along the way. Her two companions crept along behind.

In the darkness ahead hinges creaked. Forty feet beyond them a sliver of light appeared as a door opened. Trapped, the girls ducked into the nearest alcove. One tried the door as footsteps entered the tunnel. It opened and they hurried through.

Diana, holding the candle, had been the last one in. What it illuminated had set all three of them to screaming. Scattered on the lime white floor were baby skeletons.

"Diana." She felt Abe's hand shaking her arm. Looking down, she saw Johnnie crushed against her, struggling to breathe she had been holding him so tight.

Abe let go. "Are you all right?"

"Yes." Then after a pause that Abe thought too long, she said, "I'm fine. Sorry." She released Johnnie, who, with eyes wide, turned and ran into the barn.

Abe and Pete watched as Diana took a hankie out of her purse and wiped the blood off her finger. Seeing it, the boy began to cry. Abe again placed a hand on his shoulder and drew him close.

As his weeping died down, Pete spoke between sobs. "I cannot stop them." He looked up at Abe, eyes fierce with determination.

"Who are they?" Abe asked.

Pete was about to answer when his eyes left Abe and settled on something behind. Pete stepped back and looked at the ground by his feet. Abe glanced back to see Father LaFrenier and the stable master approaching. "Who, Pete? Who does it?"

The boy's eyes darted to the priest then back to the ground, conveying an answer without words. Abe allowed his personal bias against the man in black robes walking up to him to interpret it. "Run along, son. I'll tell your mother you love her."

Pete turned and ran into the stables.

TWENTY-NINE

D iana had little to say on the trip back to town and Abe quit trying to make conversation. She dropped him off at the corner of Main and Second, letting him walk down to the seaplane dock. Driving home, she parked in the new garage built for the Dodge. Turning off the key, she sat for a while, then opened her purse and took out the hankie. It was only a tiny smudge of red, but what it meant brought tears and bad memories.

She remembered dropping the candle and all three girls had ended up screaming in the dark. One had fumbled open the door and run out. Diana and her friend followed, stumbling into strong arms that held them tight. The first girl's voice echoed in the tunnel as she disappeared into the darkness. Roughly the priests shoved Diana and her companion toward the convent and entered the square room just as a light appeared in the corridor ahead. The girl who'd escaped walked in followed by a nun holding a candle.

After a heated conversation, the nun sent the two men on their way, toward the convent. The three girls were led off into the underground labyrinth and locked in separate windowless cells.

Alone in the blackness, Diana's hands trembled as goose bumps ran down her spine. Her chest tightened and she couldn't help crying out when the screaming started.

Ten minutes later her door opened. Two nuns, followed by the Mother Superior holding a cane walked in. She smacked it in the palm of her hand while issuing an order in French. "Take off your dress."

Diana stood in disbelief.

"Off with it."

Diana fumbled with the buttons, ripping two of them loose before the dress fell to the floor.

"Your under things next."

"No!" Diana held both arms across her breasts. "You can't do this."

The woman nodded to her two attendants. Each grabbed Diana by an arm then turned her around. Twisting her arms, they bent her over. The Mother Superior ripped down her panties and laced the cane across her bare buttocks. Pain flooded Diana's eyes. She screamed continually for the ten minutes it took to administer her punishment.

Left to dress in the dark, she endured the screaming from the next cell as the third member of their group was beaten. After that, they were escorted back to their rooms. When Diana took off her panties, they were streaked with blood.

Opening her eyes, she looked at the hankie in her hand. A single smudge of red. The same colour that years ago marked the destruction of her faith in the Church. She was older now, and, like Jack's funeral a few days ago, had attended church only for social functions. Still, she believed in God, but looked for Him in a spiritual world of her own making.

Neatly folding the hankie, she knew another world was being destroyed.

THIRTY

Autumn turned into winter, light snow covered the fallen leaves signaling long months of loneliness for the Native children separated from their parents in the name of education. Pete missed his father. At catechism he was told that all good people go to heaven to be with God. He knew his grandfather was in the Land of Souls. His grandmother had told him that. Now that his dad was dead, he believed he and grandpa were together again. Maybe they would come to him in a vision.

One day, an older boy asked if Indians went to heaven. The hesitation in the master's answer confirmed Pete's suspicions that white people didn't want Indians in their heaven. That only left one other place for them, he reasoned, and refused to believe in a god who burnt people forever.

No, his dad was definitely in the Land of Souls. Unaware of the schoolmaster droning on, Pete daydreamed of going home. He'd see his father in Mother Nature. She was kinder than God. He would reflect her goodness in the forests, the animals, the skies, and birds.

In the following days, Pete's spirits dropped with the outside temperature. He lost all interest in learning. His thoughts centered on going home. Physically nobody touched him. Other than the severe beating after his father's death, he was never struck again. But he suffered inside. Two days after the incident, he was lying in bed when the lights went on and Father LaFrenier walked in. He made sure Pete noticed him, then turned and motioned Johnnie to come with him. The room was plunged into darkness as the door closed.

Pete lay awake until he saw the door open and close. Moments later he heard Johnnie crawl into bed and sob softly into his pillow.

"What is wrong?" Pete whispered.

"It hurts."

"What?"

"Go away."

"Did he beat you again?"

"No."

"What happened?"

"He hurt me."

"How?"

"I don't want to talk about it."

"Tell me."

"Go away."

Pete heard Johnnie turn over in his bed. "Johnnie?" No answer. "Johnnie?" Waiting for an answer that never came, he stared at the black ceiling. Sleep was a long time coming.

Once or maybe twice a week, the priest took his brother away at night. It was over a month before Pete found out what was happening. After that, the cold hard look he got from Father LaFrenier each time Johnnie was taken out began eating away at his soul.

One day, early in December, he could stand it no more. He was going home. Later, while working in the stables, he revealed his plan to Johnnie.

"We are going to run away."

"No."

"Yes. We can do it," Pete said, glancing around to make sure no one was listening.

"We will get caught."

"No!"

"How can you be sure?"

Pete wished he knew. One other boy had run away and was caught. What happened to him flashed in Pete's mind.

"I cannot go," Johnnie said.

"Yes. You have to come."

"No."

Taken aback by Johnnie's firmness, Pete just stared at him. A horse in the stall beside them stamped its feet and lifted his head as Tony Powless stepped out. "How are you going to do it, Pete?"

"Do what?"

"Escape. I heard you." His eyes shifted from Pete to Johnnie. "I know how to get out." He saw Johnnie's eyes look down. "You are not going?"

Pete felt torn between only wanting to do this with his brother and finding out how Tony, who was two years older, would get out of this place. "We were just talking."

"No, I heard you," Tony said. "You are going to try. I can tell. Let me come and I will show you how we can get away."

As Tony waited, Johnnie's downcast look decided for Pete. He realized his younger brother wasn't coming.

"Okay, so how do we escape?"

Tony nodded toward Johnnie. "Not with him around." Johnnie glared at him, then turned and shuffled away.

Tony explained his plan. They decided to make a break for it the next night.

THIRTY-ONE

Under a steady north wind, clouds in the night sky parted, then disappeared to display the stars as twinkling white on a backdrop of velvet black. Pete and Tony had been trudging through ankle-deep snow alongside the road leading into town. The bitter wind, which had sprung up after they fled the school dormitory, cut through their woolen coats. Pete wished he had a pair of mitts. Both hands, tucked into his coat pockets, were stinging from the cold. Walking along the road was easy but twice, when cars came by, they had dashed into the trees. Pete had used his hands to ward off branches, and, after falling a couple of times, the snow on them had turned to water. Now the insides of his coat pockets were wet. His fingers were starting to go numb when they came to the railroad tracks. Pete turned right.

"Where are you going?" Tony asked.

Pete, stopping so Tony could catch up, said, "To town."

Looking down the black ribbons of steel, Tony hunched against the biting cold. "We have to find shelter." Pointing back to the dim outline of houses, he shouted in the rising wind. "We have to go over there and see if we can find a shed or something."

"I am not stopping. I want to go home."

"Pete, we live a day's journey by boat out on the lake. We cannot go on in this." Tony tucked up the collar of his coat against one ear. "Let us find a place to hide until morning."

Pete looked at the stars spread across the heavens. It was going to get a lot colder, but they weren't very far from the residential school and

99

he wasn't going back. He'd rather die first. "We need to keep moving. Come on, maybe we can get warm in the train station."

Tony, who'd also been watching the sky, turned back the way they'd come. The wind stung his face, freezing the tip of his nose. Covering it with his gloved hand, he swung around and followed Pete into the darkness.

They made it to the east end of the CPR yards before Tony's nose lost all its feeling. Pete's hands felt like two clubs in his pockets. They were walking between two rows of boxcars which broke the wind against their bodies, but blew wickedly below. Stiffening legs slowed both boys to a shuffle. The rapidly dropping temperature continued sapping what little strength they had left. Pete knew they'd have to find shelter soon, or freeze to death. Head down, he kept walking. There was no way he was going back.

The line of boxcars on their left ended. Beyond were the lights of the roundhouse. Silhouetted against yellow light from inside as it backed out an open door, a steam engine sent smoke from its stack billowing into the frozen night. Hope sprang to life from what was beyond the black hulk, the warm glow of interior lights. Thinking of only one thing, heat, Pete started running. Tony followed, close on his heels.

As Pete ran beside the moving engine, he could feel his face warming from heat radiating off its boiler. The door opening bathed in yellow beckoned. He'd made it.

"Hey, you! Stop!"

Pete looked up to see a tall husky man in front of him.

"Hold up there, boy."

Pete tried dodging him. A hand grabbed his coat collar, jerking him back about the time his feet ran into thin air. Looking down, he saw nothing but a black hole.

"You'll get yourself killed running into the turntable pit, kid." Andy Barrett, the CPR policeman held the boy off balance, then pulled him to safety. Pete collapsed at his feet.

Last time Andy Barrett looked at the thermometer hanging outside the roundhouse wall, it read twenty-one below zero. The wind, he knew, made it much colder. Kneeling beside the kid he'd yanked to safety, Andy saw he was Indian and half frozen to death. No wonder with the cold Arctic wind driving down from the north.

Hearing footsteps behind, he rotated on his knee and spotted another young Indian running away. "Hey! Stop, kid." Andy leapt up and started after him. "Hold on, kid. I won't hurt you."

Tony disappeared around the end of a boxcar.

"Dammit, stop!" Andy ran faster. He'd have to catch this one. If he was as bad off, he wouldn't last long. Rounding the boxcar he found only darkness. "Where are you, son?" Andy stopped, listening. Only the sound of a steam engine huffing into the distance carried on the wind. "You've gotta be cold. Come on, I'll take you where it's warm."

Nothing. Andy walked ahead a few paces, stopped and listened, called again, then turned and hurried back to the turntable.

Tony climbed to the top of a boxcar and lay still as the man below called to him. He waited, shivering in the wind. When he realized the man was no longer calling, he relaxed, closing his eyes. He was so tired. A gentle motion rocked him to sleep. The boxcar, thirty-seventh in a train of eighty-nine empty grain cars headed back to the prairies, carried the sleeping Indian boy west.

Pete could only lie in the snow, his cheek numb against a cold steel rail. There was simply no more strength he could call on. He twitched when two strong hands picked him up, but couldn't care less. His eyes closed. He was dreaming of a hot summer day when they laid him down.

It bothered Andy that he couldn't find the other Native boy. The temperature continued falling. By morning he figured it would touch forty below. With one of the boys safe, he borrowed a coal-oil lantern and walked back outside. The wind bit into his cheeks. His breath froze in his nose, forcing him to put a heavy gloved hand over his mouth.

Knowing both of these kids were near the end of their rope, he quickened his pace. Stopping by the boxcar where he last saw the second boy, he lowered his light to look for footprints in the snow. Few showed. Walking further, he discovered two sets coming from the east, but none going the other way. Crossing over the tracks, recently vacated by the empty grain boxcars, he searched in vain. Then it struck him. The kid had climbed aboard the departing train.

Not content to abandon the search, Andy walked the tracks west, past the yard office, past the depot, and through the rock-cut under the Matheson Street bridge. His lamp showed no sign of the boy getting off. Standing there, looking west across the lights of town toward the hospital, he let the lantern hang by his side. Shaking his head, he turned and started back to the depot knowing that if the boy hadn't hopped off in the yard, he'd never make it to Winnipeg.

In his office, he wrote up a report about the incident and missing boy, then, thinking back to the times he had put Frankie in the boiler room to survive winter nights, he crumpled the paper and threw it in the wastebasket. An Indian kid rides the train west. So what, they would say in head office.

So he took a trip to eternity, Andy thought.

"Damn." Lashing out with his right foot, he sent the metal trash can clattering across the room.

All the way back to the roundhouse, he couldn't shake a feeling of gloom. After checking on the kid sleeping in the boiler room, he gave instructions to the night watchman to look in on the boy. He'd be back in the morning and decide what to do with him then.

Pete woke up in a sweat. His brain told him he should be freezing to death but all he could feel was heat. I'm in hell, he thought, afraid to open his eyes. He could hear a fire roaring away somewhere close. Strange sounds filled his ears. A distant voice, a shout in return. At least he wasn't alone.

Opening one eye, all he saw was yellow flame. The priest was right. He blinked it shut. Something was missing. The pain. Father LaFrenier said he'd have eternal pain. All he felt was a slight tingle in his hands.

Then came a kind of a whooshing noise, followed by another. A steam engine. Opening both eyes, he found himself staring at the firebox of the roundhouse boiler. Little shafts of flame flickered through vents in the door.

Sitting up and looking around, he saw the boiler and felt its heat. Relieved, he lay back, knowing he was alive and let the warm room and its quiet rumble lull him to sleep again.

THIRTY-TWO

Throwing the last half-cup of coffee into the sink, Andy Barrett rinsed the ceramic mug, setting it upside down on the drain board. Before putting on his coat, fur hat, and gloves, he looked at the thermometer outside his window, then left for the CPR station. Stopping at the lunch counter, situated between the express shed and the depot, he ordered breakfast and, deep in thought, ended up picking at the scrambled eggs. He just couldn't quell the feeling of failure over last night. The unanswered question crossed his mind again. What were those kids doing out on their own?

"Hello, Andy."

"Ernesto, good morning."

The Italian section foreman slid into the seat beside him. "It's-a so cold, the Mona Lisa, she shiver."

"Thirty-seven below."

"No wind-a blow now." He waved to the waitress behind the counter. "Miss-a Mavis, one-a coffee, please." Swinging on the rotating stool, he took off his hat. "So, what's-a new, Andy."

"Spotted a couple of Indian kids in the east yard last night. I think one of them hopped the grain drag."

"He just-a ride to the station?"

"No, I walked the tracks. No sign of him getting off."

Ernesto's bushy eyebrow furrowed. "You think-a he go to Winnipeg?"

Shrugging his shoulders, Andy said, "Hope not. He'd freeze to death. His friend was about done in when I spotted them."

104

"What they doing out? Should-a be in-a school."

It all fell into place for Andy as he looked at the Italian: two Indian kids in thin clothes, sneaking through the night, running when he called. "Thanks, Ernesto." He patted the foreman on the shoulder as he got up and tossed two dollars on the counter.

"What I do?"

"Solved my problem."

Mavis placed a steaming mug in front of Ernesto and reached for the two dollar bill.

"Take that out, too," Andy said, pointing to the coffee. "Keep the change."

He caught a ride on the switch engine going east to the yard office, then walked to the roundhouse. Entering the boiler room he found it empty.

Earlier, Pete had awakened to find an old man in gray, bib coveralls shoveling coal into the boiler. Putting down the shovel, he kicked the door shut, at the same time noticing the Indian boy was awake.

"Hello, son. I'm Amos."

Pete nodded his head.

"Good. You stay right there. I'll get you something."

In the ten minutes it took the old man to return, Pete discovered a door to the outside, wiped grime off its window, and looked into the bright morning. Standing in the warm room, he could see sparkling ice crystals drifting to earth in the bitter cold. It didn't matter, he was going home.

Amos came in with a plate and a mug. "Best I could do." He set down the plate with two pieces of toast and handed him the mug of hot tea, laced with sugar. Pete ate it all and finished the tea.

"Good, lad," Amos said when Pete handed the empty mug back. "Fill the gap?"

Pete nodded his head.

"Sure not very talkative, are you? Oh well, now you stay right here until Andy comes. He told me to look after you. You gonna stay right there until he comes, okay?"

Pete nodded.

The old man eyed him, then left.

Pete watched a steam engine back out of the roundhouse onto the turntable. When it started to rotate, he opened the door and stepped out. Cold air pierced his clothing. Drawing tight shallow breaths, he thought of going back inside, abandoned the idea, and shut the door. When he let go, strips of flesh frozen to the knob, tore off his fingers.

He yelped, holding the bleeding fingers in his other hand, waiting until the pain subsided as he watched a man climb into the steam engine on the turntable. Putting both hands in his pockets he walked away.

Following the tracks west, he skirted the repair track and walked beside a row of boxcars. When it started to move, he climbed onto the ladder attached to its side. Seeing a building and another locomotive up ahead, he swung around to the end of the car and rode on the couplers.

Just before reaching the yard office, he caught a glimpse of the CPR policeman walking toward the roundhouse.

"Damn, I told you to watch the kid." Andy's voice drowned out the boiler fire in Amos' ears.

"He was there ten minutes ago. I made him some toast." The old man's head hung down. Andy was always nice to him. He felt bad letting the policeman down.

Andy knew it wasn't his fault. At least the boy had eaten. "I'm sorry, Amos. I know you did your best. Thanks for feeding him." Amos looked up at Andy who patted his shoulder before walking out of the boiler room. "He'll be okay."

Ice crystals glistened in the cold morning sunshine as Andy walked away from the roundhouse. Steam rose lazily from a parked locomotive.

"Where are you, kid?" he asked himself. "And where did your buddy get to?"

While scanning the azure sky, he became aware of the cold raising prickles on his bare face. Last night's gloom settled over him again. If the kid hadn't gotten off the train and found someplace warm... He didn't want to think of it. As for the other one, he had to be one tough little Indian heading out in this.

Andy wondered what was driving these kids. Looking back on his youth, he didn't think going to school was so bad. Mind you, he was home with his mom and dad every night.

One of the engines on the ready track let out a chuff of steam. Andy ran over and jumped on the coal tender's running board. He hopped off at the yard office.

"Morning, Ted."

The Yardmaster swung in his seat. "Andy." Turning back, he hollered through an open door to the switch crew. "Pull the paper mill first, then spot two gondolas at the coaling tower."

Andy was taking off his gloves when Ted Corrigan addressed him again. "You're out awfully early. Any excitement last night?"

"Found a couple Indian kids nearly frozen down by the roundhouse." He unbuttoned his coat and related the story.

"What's with these Indians nowadays?" Ted asked. "Letting their kids run around in weather like this."

The operator stuck his head in the door. "Number One's on time."

"Thanks, Al. At least something is going right." Ted looked at the clock, then Andy, who now had his coat off. "So, you figure one is dead, and the other you don't know."

"Yeah." Andy picked up the telephone, holding the earpiece in his left hand while dialing out with his index finger. He noticed Ted turn when he asked for Father LaFrenier, but gave up listening in when the car checker walked in and announced they'd lost a boxcar full of newsprint.

Andy hung up and sat back in an old caboose chair, drumming his fingers on the wooden arm.

"Well?" Ted asked.

"Seems two kids bolted from the residential school yesterday." Andy placed both sets of fingers together, index ones touching his mouth. He studied the ceiling. "One of them was Jack Redsky's oldest son."

Pete looped one arm around a ladder rung and stuck his hand back in his pocket. He wished he had some gloves, but when they left yesterday the weather was barely freezing. The fingers of his right hand rubbed against the lining inside his pocket, stinging his finger tips where the skin was missing. Ignoring the tingling pain in his hand and arm, he watched the yard office go by. The train continued at a crawl until it passed the station. Breaking out of the cut under the Matheson Street bridge, the land opened up and Pete could see the lake was frozen over. He rode the boxcar another couple hundred yards before noticing it was picking up speed. Looking at the ties and rails rush by, he panicked, unhooked his arm, and jumped off. Hitting the ground much faster than expected, his feet went out from under him and he tumbled down an embankment, his outstretched arms sending snow flying. Sitting up, he put his bleeding fingers into his mouth as tears of pain welled up in his eyes. Standing, he felt a bruise on one elbow and melting snow running down his back. Brushing off his face, he put both hands in his pockets and headed for the lake.

THIRTY-THREE

Jack Redsky. The mention of Jack's name brought a twinge of grief to Ted. Picking up the telephone Andy had just set down, Ted spun the rotary dial four times. On the second ring a voice filled with sunshine, answered. "Good Morning. Williston Air Services."

"Cindy? Ted Corrigan here. Where's Abe?"

"He's down at the plane hooking up an engine heater. Someone from the Hudson's Bay wants to go to Shoal Lake."

"Listen, have him call me when he gets back."

"Where are you?"

"The Yard Office."

"If it's important I can run down with a message."

"No. Well, yes. Tell him Jack Redsky's kid is missing."

"Which one? Oh, hold on a minute. Someone's at the door." When Cindy got up and opened it, a body fell inside. "Oh, my God!" She ran back to the phone. "Mr. Corrigan, Pete Redsky just came in half frozen. Gotta go."

Ted heard the line click dead. Setting the earpiece back on its hook, he looked over to Andy. "The kid's at Abe's winter base."

The big policeman let out a sigh. Well, that's one," he said, standing and putting on his coat. "Now where the hell is the other one?" he asked no one in particular while slipping on his gloves and walking out into the crisp morning air. Last thing Ted saw before answering the phone again, was Andy pulling the fur flaps of his cap over both ears as he started across the rail yard and walked down the track to the paper mill.

Pete's hands were ice cold to the touch when Cindy took hold of them to pull him inside. By the time she'd hauled his dead weight across the office floor she was out of breath. Closing the door shut out the frigid air. Kneeling down, she began rubbing the boy's cheeks, then his hands. Pete whimpered when she touched his raw fingers. Spotting white on his nose and ears, she ran outside, down towards the plane.

"Abe! Abe!" Waving her arms, she finally caught her boss's eye. "Come here. Hurry!"

Abe thought he heard shouts over the roaring engine heater and looked around. Spotting Cindy without a coat, waving madly, he dropped the wing cover he was folding and ran to the office.

Cindy dashed back inside. Abe entered the office to find her bent over someone lying on the floor.

"It's Petie Redsky." Abe knelt beside her. "Oh God! Look at him, Abe."

Reaching over, Abe felt for a pulse on Pete's neck. It was cold, but steady. "He'll be okay. Make some tea."

Cindy put on water to boil as Abe opened the boy's coat and took off his boots. She brought over a mug of hot tea, which she held under his nose, now flaming pink against his light brown skin.

They both watched as Pete opened his eyes. Looking from Abe to Cindy, then back to Abe again, he forced a weak smile and spoke in a croaking voice. "Hello, Mr. Williston."

THIRTY-FOUR

Abe's first trip to Long Grass Reservation on floats was April 27th. It had been a busy break-up, working with his mechanic to change over from skis to floats. They had sent the propeller to Winnipeg. Its tips needed to be smoothed out and balanced. There was new birch plywood to put on the floor, and last thing they did was replace the winter muffler with a short summer pipe. The first flight of the year was always exhilarating. Abe just loved hearing the big radial snapping out the short exhaust stack as the engine worked hard breaking the floats loose.

Outside of a trip to see his mom in a nursing home in Saskatoon, Abe spent the last few days before the ice went out reading *Doc Savage* novels and eating Mrs. Litynski's cooking.

Ted and Diana Corrigan had invited him over for supper with their two daughters. Shortly after, he and Ted ended up at J D Riley's, in the basement drinking whiskey and telling stories until all hours of the night. The next morning Abe ignored Mrs. Litynski's calls and slept in until ten o'clock.

Flying had started up on a limited basis at the end of April. Now, while he taxied to the dock at Long Grass, that cold winter day came back to him. Cindy had put some antiseptic salve on Pete's fingers and had bandaged them. The Hudson's Bay agent had chafed at Abe's explanation for the delay, but agreed to wait a couple more hours. Abe flew him to Shoal Lake first. The cargo hold was loaded with beaver skins and they took off for the return flight. Twenty minutes later he shut off the engine at Long Grass Reservation. Pete, who'd been sitting behind Abe, got up and moved between the two front seats.

"Well, there you go, Pete. Home."

The boy just stared out the front windows.

Abe tussled his hair. "Come on, let's go see your Mom."

"How long you gonna be?" the agent asked.

"I don't know. Half an hour, forty-five minutes, maybe more."

"I'll hoof it up and talk old times with Luther." The agent did up the buttons on his fur coat. "Stop on your way back." Opening the door he got out, and, breaking a trail through ankle-deep snow, set off toward the trading post. Abe wrestled the canvas cover over the engine and tied it shut. After putting on a pair of Abe's mitts, Pete climbed out. Covering his arms to the elbows, the mitts looked absurdly large, but Abe knew they'd keep his hands warm as Pete led the way home.

<hr />

Jenny Redsky had heard the plane land but thought little of it. Since Jack's death, life had become a daily ritual of existing, often ending in a night of tears, although this was happening less now that she'd started drinking to relieve her pain.

The baby began crying. Jenny ignored it until Michael tugged at her arm. "Mommy, Bethy's crying."

Jenny stood up and walked across the floor. She knew her daughter only wanted the bottle put back in her mouth. Right after Jack died her breasts had dried up and she now fed Bethy powdered milk, often watered down to go further.

Michael went back to the couch, sitting on it sideways and pretending to use a piece of kindling as a paddle. Looking over the end of the couch, he could see beyond the bow of his canoe. He was hunting ducks.

A knock sounded at the door. Jenny walked over to open it while Michael continued paddling. Cold air rushed in as she stood looking into the face of Abe Williston. Pete put his arms around his mother and squeezed tight. Jenny held her son until he let go.

Pete spotted his brother. "Hey, Michael!"

Abe waited a moment as Pete moved away, then asked, "May I come in?"

Jenny turned and walked back into the kitchen. Abe followed, closing the door behind.

"Where is Johnnie?" Jenny asked.

"As far as I know, he's still at the residential school."

"Why is Pete here?"

"He ran away." Abe paused when no reply came from Jenny, then he went on to explain what happened. Through it all he sensed an aloofness in the woman. Her eyes never met his until he finished and said, "I'm sorry about Jack. I know how you feel."

"Do you?" Her question cut the air. "Do you know what it is like to lie alone at night?"

Abe slept by himself every night but had to admit it must have been different for her. "Jenny." He placed both hands on the Indian woman's shoulders. "Jenny, what can I say? Jack's leaving has left a big hole in our lives. Nothing we do can bring him back, but he lives on in his sons. Pete's as tough as Jack ever was. He'll be a real help to you."

Jenny relaxed under his hands and looked in his eyes. He saw her sadness, and a need he couldn't fulfill. She felt a strength that had been missing since her husband's death. As it flowed to her she reached out and embraced the man Jack had always respected and treated as an equal. It was the only good day Jenny had that winter.

The left float bumped against the dock, bringing Abe back to the present. Looking out, he saw Pete, holding the Norseman's wing strut. After waving back, he opened the door. "Hey, Pete."

"Hello, Mr. Williston."

"The name's Abe." Turning in his seat, he said, "You call me Abe from now on, okay?"

"Yes, Mr.., uh, Abe."

"That's better, kid." Hopping down onto the float he tied it off then stepped onto the dock. Punching Pete lightly in the arm, he asked, "How's it going?"

Pete shrugged his shoulders.

"How's the hand?" Abe took it, turning the fingers upright. "Looks good as new. How's it feel?"

"A bit tingly when these two touch together. But it doesn't hurt anymore," he added quickly, looking at Abe.

"How's your mother?"

"Fine."

Abe wasn't satisfied with the answer. "You sure?"

"Yeah," Pete said, casting his eyes to the ground.

Abe sensed something amiss. "Care to tell me?"

Pete shook his head.

"Anything I can do to help?" Abe watched the young fellow shuffle his feet while still looking at the dock. Of all the things Abe found hard to accept in Ojibway culture, this looking at the ground was the hardest. He stared at his own feet, keeping Pete's face in the corner of his eye.

When the boy glanced up, Abe didn't respond until he spoke.

"I want to go fishing."

Abe looked up. "Great!"

"I will use my Dad's boat and motor."

"Good. How about nets? They okay?"

"Yeah."

"So, when you gonna start?"

"I cannot fish."

"Why not?"

Pete's eyes fell again. His words were indistinct mumble. "There is no gas for the engine."

"Luther's out of fuel?"

"No. He will not let me have any unless I can pay for it."

"What?"

"He says Mom owes him too much money."

114

I'll keep that in mind, Abe thought. "Pete," Abe put a finger under the boy's chin, lifting it until they looked at each other, "can you catch enough fish to pay for the gas?"

Pete stiffened, raising his head high. "I am as good as my Dad. He said so last summer when I worked with him."

Abe saw a lot of Jack in the boy. "Tell you what. I'll bring you a drum of gas and some oil. You have to ship out enough fish to pay for it, then the rest is yours."

Pete broke into a wide smile, teeth white against his light brown skin. "Thanks."

Abe reached out with his right hand. Pete took hold of it and held on as Abe shook it vigorously.

THIRTY-FIVE

Next morning on the way to Blindfold Lake, Abe dropped off a forty-five gallon barrel of gas and a case of two-cycle engine oil. Pete's face lit up like a Christmas tree. Inside, Abe felt a warm glow seeing the boy so happy.

"I will make it up to you, Mr..,uh, Abe."

"Your Dad would be proud of you."

Pete's smile vanished. His gaze fell to his feet.

Lifting his chin, Abe waited until coal black eyes caught his. "We both miss him, son." Then, with a gesture that swept the lake, he said, "He loved these waters. You just do your best. I'm sure he'll watch over you."

The smile returned, illuminating his face.

Abe pointed inside the cargo door. "That's your oil."

"Thanks, Abe."

Catching the boy's enthusiasm, Abe rolled the drum down a plank and with a practised flip, lifted sideways, pulling it upright on the dock. "One barrel of gas for Redsky Fisheries."

Pete stood beside the drum, holding his oil in both hands. Abe tussled the kid's long black hair.

"First fish, you take home to your mother. I'll be back at the end of the week. Keep your catch iced down. I'll help you load your tub."

As it was, Pete lifted the tub by himself. Abe guessed there was more ice than fish in it. Pete wouldn't catch Abe's eye, so he decided to let the boy deal with his own discouragement and shoved the tub further back in the cargo bay as others were loaded.

The following week, Pete's tub weighed the same, but had more fish than ice. Two weeks after that, Pete asked for another barrel of gas.

"You know you're a little short on the last one?"

Pete looked down. It annoyed Abe. "Pete!" The sharp address jerked the boy's head up. "You gonna do business with me, you look me in the eye."

Pete looked at him. "Yes, sir."

"Oh cut that sir stuff. Now I didn't say you couldn't have any more gas. I'm just letting you know where you stand."

"I will make it up."

"I know you will. But that's how we're going to do business, okay?"

"Yes, s..."

Abe's brow furrowed.

"Okay, Abe"

"Right. Have your empty here at three this afternoon. I'll trade it for a full one on my flight to Shoal Lake."

"Okay."

Abe had to help Pete load this day's tub. He guessed it weighed eighty, maybe ninety pounds. Two barrels of gas later, Pete turned a profit and by then was loading two tubs.

Later in the season, Luther, who ran the local trading post located outside of reserve land, offered to sell Pete gas and supplies on his own account. Abe told him to accept. "I'm in the transportation business, Pete. I'd like to get paid for all the fuel I bring in."

"I will pay freight."

"That's not the point. Luther sells stuff. I transport it. Understand?"

"Okay, Abe."

"Be careful with Luther. Don't get to owing him too much. Your Dad always kept his account paid up."

Pete ended the year with enough money to buy two new nets for the following season.

A tub of iced fish weighs one hundred, maybe a hundred and ten pounds. When Pete lifted one by himself into the plane at the start of his second season, Abe knew the shy kid he'd flown home a year and a half earlier had grown into a man. A young man maybe, but his drive reminded him so much of Jack.

Pete made money that second year and used it all supporting his family. Little Bethy had put on weight since Pete started buying her real milk Abe flew in for Luther once a week. Abe noticed Michael following Pete everywhere, walking in his older brother's shadow, forever asking questions. That fall when Father LaFrenier came to take the kids to the residential school, Michael was among the nineteen Indian children Abe flew to Kenora.

THIRTY-SIX

His mother no longer cried at night, but Pete noted more and more his account with Luther listed wine and liquor. Through the winter, Jenny spent most evenings alone in her bedroom and slept late. One day, when the ice was melting and Canada geese were swimming in the lake, Pete tried to talk to his mother about her drinking. She flew into a rage, told Pete it was none of his business, and shortly after began drinking openly, often starting in the morning.

When Pete stopped paying for her booze, his account fell in arrears and Luther cut off his gas. Pete paid up the account but made excuses to be away from home more. Later when Michael came home for the summer, he spent a lot of time with Susan Two Bears. Bethy ran around the house, often with only a dirty shirt on. Pete would dress his baby sister before leaving in the morning, but most often on his return he found his mother sitting at the table, Bethy half dressed, playing on the floor.

Early in the spring, Pete had dug the garden for his mother. By summer it was a patch of weeds and thistles. Often he had to cook when he came in tired from fishing.

One mid-summer day, after working long hours under a blazing sun and slicing his finger while cleaning the last of only seven fish, he walked in to see his mother drinking with men from the reserve. Their vacant expressions displayed lack of concern when he told them to get out.

Jenny put a wine bottle to her lips. Pete snatched the bottle from her hand, swung around, and smashed it against the stove. Wine and broken glass flew into the room. Holding the jagged neck in his right hand, he strode over to the closest Indian man seated on the couch. Jerking him up, Pete shoved the broken glass to within inches of his face, yelling at him to get out. The man's eyes grew wide. He wriggled out of Pete's grasp and ran for the door, followed by his two companions.

Jenny stood, her back to the sink counter, screaming at Pete, going on and on about the spilled wine. Bethy cowered in a corner, crying. Michael ran out of the house. Pete ignored his mother's ranting and packed his things, then without a word, left home.

Ignace Two Bears helped Pete build a tepee on a point about a half mile from the reserve housing. Susan came by with Michael who wanted to sleep in it that night, but with Susan's kind coaxing, he agreed to stay with her.

As the summer wore on, Pete built a small dock to tie up his boat and a shed for gas and supplies. Paying up his account with Luther, he cancelled it, explaining to the German that he'd buy only what he could pay cash for, and none of it was going to be liquor for his mother.

During the times when the sun set at his back, Pete loved to sit and watch the false sunset to the east, then see the lake turn black as night fell. The splash of small waves and frogs croaking in the bulrushes, set a melancholy mood in the warm evening breeze. He missed his father. Sometimes, when Michael was with him, he would wait until the first star appeared in the heavens, then, after pointing it out to his younger brother, told stories about their father. The boy usually fell asleep, leaning against Pete, who felt closest to him at times like this and would then take him inside for the night.

The old ones said that the father was represented in the Ojibway sky. There were times, when Pete was alone, that his father would appear to him in a vision. He never seemed to age. His weathered skin, brown against the dark sky hid his features, but Pete knew it was his father who was telling him where to fish. One night he appeared holding a baby instructing Pete to give this one an Indian name. It was the last time he came to Pete.

One day during blueberry season, when the lake was warm and high thin clouds streaked the sky, Michael stood waist deep in the water beside Pete's boat watching his brother fix the outboard. Every little thing he did brought a question which Pete patiently answered.

Hearing a paddle dip in the lake, Pete looked up to see Anna Quoquat and her mother in a canoe. Anna's eyes captured Pete. The trace of a smile radiated from her lips as she turned to look forward, holding her head high. Something inside made his spine tingle and his eyes followed the canoe as Anna gracefully paddled in the front seat. It disappeared around the point leaving Pete with the illusion of seeing a dream.

Anna Quoquat. He couldn't believe it! He remembered her only as a child, one of many he used to sing and play with. She was there when they went swimming, although now he found it hard to pick her out from among the other naked kids.

She had smiled at him, he was sure she did. The thought made him feel like someone dribbled ice water down his back. Her image haunted him all night.

After that, it seemed he came across Anna almost everywhere he went: Luther's store, on the dock when Abe's plane came in, walking on the lakeshore. She always watched him until he caught her eye, then forming the faintest of smiles she'd turn away and look down. It intrigued Pete.

The Pow Wow was already underway when Pete arrived. He'd bathed in the lake and washed his hair. After it dried, he combed and trimmed the ends until it hung just above his shoulders. Although this was a social event, he felt out of place. His mother ignored him. Michael, his brother, didn't bother coming over to him, he was having more fun playing in the bushes with children his own age.

Wandering through the crowd, Pete talked with relatives and other fishermen. Some were drinking. He refused their offers. As the evening wore on, he found himself watching the dancers, tapping his foot in time to the drum.

He became aware of a presence by his side, a space full of silence drowning his spirit. The beat of the *Tewiken* died in his ears.

He dared not turn, yet did. "Hello, Anna."

Her eyes looked up, engaging his, then fell. "Hello, Pete."

After that neither knew what to say until the drum stopped and dancers spread out into the crowd. She took his hand, holding it with a delicate touch. "The Blanket Dance is next. I would like to dance it for you."

Pete felt like a stream of water drawn to the crest of a hanging valley, before tumbling down a steep ravine. His mouth wouldn't work. He placed his free hand on Anna's and nodded. She smiled, then let go and walked into the dance circle with her blanket.

Someone threw wood on the fire and red embers rose into a night sky as the drum began its beat. Among the dancers, only one captured Pete's attention, Anna. Her body became one with the blanket as she began a slow graceful walk. Expressing more exuberance, her long braided hair bounced with the music, casting shadows on her narrow face as it occasionally swung across her small nose and soft high cheekbones. Her light-tan buckskin dress, decorated in beads, reflected the firelight shadows. For the first time Pete realized she had breasts.

Nearing the end of the dance, Anna switched to a bouncing double step, ending on the final beat of the *Tewiken* and casting her blanket to the ground in Pete's direction.

The spell remained as she walked over to him. "Did you like my dancing?"

"You were beautiful."

Anna held out both hands for him. Standing in the fire's glow, Pete held them in his as they looked into each others eyes and understood the universal message they sent back and forth. Squeezing their hands together, both knew they were falling in love.

Across the dance circle, Anna's mother jabbed an elbow into her husband's ribs, jiggling beer out of the bottle at his lips. Looking at his wife of twenty-three winters, he wiped beer off his chin as she nodded her head across the fire. Silhouetted against the night were Pete Redsky and Anna Quoquat holding hands. A smile spread over his face and later when the young couple, wearing the blanket over their shoulders, left the gathering, he did not object.

Anna was content to let Pete lead her away from the firelight. Entering the forest, he followed a trail that broke out on a high ledge overlooking the lake. Partially hidden by scattered clouds, a full moon painted the sky pewter gray as they stepped close to a cliff that dropped away into the water thirty feet below. The clouds parted, bathing the couple in the moon's silver glow.

"It is beautiful," Anna whispered.

"I come here when I feel alone. It is nice to have company tonight."

Anna smiled.

"Your dancing was beautiful."

"I was thinking of you."

Pete pointed along the shore. "I live down there."

"Yes, I know. Why are you not living at home?"

"My mother drinks."

"So does mine. And my father beats her sometimes." She paused a moment until he realized her eyes were beseeching him. "You will not beat me, will you?"

Pete could not imagine why anyone would want to hurt someone so delicate and tender. "Of course not."

"Make the promise in words."

Pete edged close and put his arms around her waist. "I promise not to hit you." Noticing her eyes soften, he asked, "Will you give me a son?"

"Only Kitche Manitou can grant such a wish. But I will give you my love." She stood on her toes and kissed the father of her future children.

Pete drew her to him, feeling for the first time the gentleness of a woman's breasts. It sparked a feeling both desired, yet knew was inappropriate until he spoke with her father.

THIRTY-SEVEN

The Ojibway Nation is a collection of family groups structured socially into seven clans. These tended not to denote status so much as responsibility. As a member of the Fish clan, the Redsky's had always taken pride in their role as teachers. The clan often acted as a mediator between the two Chieftain clans, the Loon and the Crane. Pete could remember his father's strength and wished for some of it now. Anna's father towered a head above Pete and he had never known him to smile. He'd have rather fought a wolverine than ask Alex Quoquat for his daughter.

After that first kiss under the moonlight, Pete and Anna had talked about their future. He had told her he'd build a house with a separate bedroom. The children they would have could sleep in the main living area. Anna wanted to grow a garden. Pete agreed to dig the ground in the fall so she could plant the next spring. Anna said he'd have to put the seeds in and look after it until she came back from school. When Pete objected, she stomped her foot and told him it was not open for discussion. She wanted her education. Pete's experience with the residential school had left him incapable of understanding her desire, but if she wanted it that bad, he'd work around it.

The moon grew small and was high in the night sky when Pete led Anna back home. She stood with her back to the door, waiting. When Pete kissed her for the second time that night, she wrapped her arms around him. "*K'zaugh-in,*" she had whispered in his ear.

"I love you, too," Pete had said as the night ended.

Once again he stood in front of Anna's door, calming himself, working up the courage to knock. Anna's mother, Gladys, broke into a wide smile and invited him inside. Alex stood up and greeted him. Pete wished he'd remained seated. Talking uphill to the man was daunting.

"How is fishing," Alex said, his voice filling the room.

Pete had been prepared for the question, although not so soon, as he knew Alex would only let his daughter go when he was satisfied she would be well looked after. "I send out two or three tubs a week."

"That is good."

"Is your tepee warm?"

"No."

"You need to keep your woman warm in winter." He winked. Pete had no idea why.

"Anna is going to school this winter."

Alex scowled. "She does not have to go to the school this year."

"I cannot look after her this winter. Let her go to school."

"Next year you will take her," Alex said.

Pete nodded. "On the day of Long Suns. I will plant a garden and build a house."

Alex slapped him on the shoulder. "That is good," his voiced boomed. "I like you Pete Redsky. You can have my daughter." For the second time Alex Quoquat smiled his approval.

THIRTY-EIGHT

Thats very good, Michael. Now run off the nine times table for me."

Glowing under Susan's praise, Michael started reciting the multiplication, "Nine times one is nine, nine times two is eighteen..."

He was at nine times seven when the drone of an airplane flying overhead drowned out his voice. Susan, recognizing the sound of Abe's Norseman, looked at the ceiling as it passed. Michael, who'd never stopped, completed the table with, "Nine times ten is ninety."

"Good. I think it's about time you learned how to divide." Michael gave her his attention as she began to explain division. "Two times two is..."

"Four," he said.

"Correct. So how many two's are there in four?"

"Two."

"How'd you figure that out?"

"I know two times two is four."

"Okay. How many two's in six?"

"Three."

"How many three's in six?"

"Two."

"There, you're doing division."

"I am?"

"Yes. Division is just multiplying backwards. Repeat after me. Two into four is two."

"Two into four is two."

"Two into six is three."

"Two into six is three."

"Two into eight is four."

"Two into eight is four."

"See the pattern?"

"Yes. Two into ten is five, right?"

"You got it."

Ignace walked in the front door. "Father LaFrenier's here."

Susan looked at the calendar. She hadn't expected him for another couple of days, at least. Glancing back, she noticed her husband looking at Michael. Inside she flooded up, wanting to give him a son, but children hadn't come along and since Jack Redsky's death he'd taken Michael under his wing, treating him as a son, or at least his favourite nephew. "I won't let him go to the residential school again."

Ignace nodded his head in silent agreement. Michael had returned the previous spring quiet and sullen. Throughout the summer, Jenny only fought and yelled at him when she was drunk, or ignored him when she was sober. Michael had sought refuge at their place. Ignace had watched his wife as she worked all summer to straighten the boy out. "The Indian Agent will want him to go to school."

"I know." Susan's voice betrayed the painful decision she was making.

Ignace looked out the window. "I will go trapping this winter."

"You're not angry, are you? Please tell me that's not the reason you're going." She rose and started toward him.

Turning, Ignace waited until she came to him, then, taking both hands, rubbing her fingers with his thumbs, he looked into misty-brown eyes. "I could never be angry with you. I would come to Winnipeg, but it is not good for me."

"Daddy would..."

He held up a hand. "I know, but I would not be happy. I will go trapping."

His words were soft, but behind them Susan detected a finality that made her accept his decision. Rubbing his shoulder, she asked, "Will you come for Christmas? I'll have Abe fly you out."

"Maybe."

"Please."

"Okay."

Susan wrapped her arms around him and laid her head on his chest, content beside the man she loved. When a knock sounded at the door, Ignace unwrapped his wife's arms. Susan moved to answer the door, knowing full well who it would be.

Father LaFrenier walked in. "Thought I'd find you here," he said, looking at Michael. Bolting from his chair, the boy scooted behind Ignace as Father LaFrenier tried to grab his arm. When the priest found himself facing up to the big Native with chiselled features, he backed away and turned to Susan. "He has to go to school."

"He will," Susan said, "but not to yours."

"That's where he's supposed to go."

"Doesn't have to."

"He was with us last year. I was counting on having him again."

"Well, un-count him. He's not going."

Furrowing his brow, the priest allowed a pained look to cross his face. Loss of revenue, Susan thought.

Ignace spoke up. "He is going to Winnipeg."

Father LaFrenier wheeled on him. "They don't have jurisdiction here."

He turned back as Susan replied. "He's going to public school. He'll live with my parents."

"They'll take in an Indian?"

The urge to gouge the priest's eyes out seized Susan. "I'm going with him." Her words carried a high pitch and she told herself to calm down.

"Ah! You're leaving this man."

"Get out!" Susan hauled open the front door, banging the priest in the back. "Out!" Holding up her right arm, she pointed through the door. "Right now."

Father LaFrenier opened his mouth to speak.

Susan didn't afford him the opportunity. "Out of my house. Right now."

When the priest noticed Ignace move toward him, he turned and scurried out in rustle of black robes.

Susan slammed the door behind him.

⁂

Pete stood with Anna and Johnnie as they waited for Father LaFrenier to round up all the kids going to the residential school that year. Anna's mind, he knew was made up, but Pete once again appealed to his brother not to leave. Johnnie refused to listen, leaving Pete to wonder why his brother, knowing what lay in store, kept going back year after year.

The priest arrived with a crowd of kids and loaded everyone on the plane. Abe came running down from Luther's. "Untie me, Pete," he hollered, getting into the pilot's seat. As Pete slipped the ropes off the float and turned the plane, Abe fired up the engine in a cough of blue smoke. The Norseman inched forward in the water until Abe opened the throttle. Propeller spray blew out from between the floats as Abe rocked the plane back and forth until it rode up on the step.

Pete watched the silver and red Norseman rise into a clear sky. His love was strong. It would not wither like the leaves before winter. Yet it hurt to know that he wouldn't see Anna again until life returned to the trees next spring.

THIRTY-NINE

Having flown three trips in three days with Father LaFrenier, Abe was thankful to find the booking schedule on the fourth day filled with commercial work. He'd flown a total of fifty-seven Native children into Kenora. By rights, he should have done it with a DC-3 to be legal.

When the door opened behind him, Abe turned to see Orville Peterson walk into the office.

"Abe! Long time, no see."

"Orville." Abe glanced at the book on Cindy's desk. "You the first flight out?"

"Yep. Me and Willy Jones. He's loading our stuff."

"Lac Seul, right?"

"Near there," he said, glancing at Cindy. "I'll let you know exactly when we're in the air."

"Might as well tell me now. I'll only let Cindy know when I get back. In case I make that trip to the big airport in the sky."

"Hah!" Orville let out a hearty laugh. "Never happen. You don't know how to land at an airport."

Come to think of it, Abe couldn't remember the last time he had touched down on wheels. "Maybe he has a lake I can use."

"Not until you come and get me and Willy, then I'll put in a word for you." He slapped Abe on the back.

"Okay. You can square up with Cindy. I'll help Willy load." Abe dropped the two prospectors off at some nondescript point on an un-named lake a hundred miles north of Lac Seul. The extra hour and a half flying, which Cindy already knew about because Orville told her to bill it, put him back the rest of the day.

Luther's order was weighed and waiting on the dock when he taxied in. Cindy helped him load while their mechanic fuelled up. An hour later the supplies were either loaded on Luther's wagon or sitting on the dock at Long Grass. Abe was about to leave when Ignace Two Bears hailed him. Abe waited as he and a boy walked to the dock, followed by two women.

"Ignace. Good to see you. Susan. Jenny."

Susan smiled back. Jenny looked at the ground. Abe paid it no mind as he tussled the boy's hair. "Hey, Michael. Going for a trip?"

"To Winnipeg," he said, handing Abe his little suitcase.

Ignace put a larger one in the plane as his wife spoke. "We're taking the train. We just want a lift to Kenora."

"That's where I'm headed." Abe shoved both suitcases to the back of the cabin.

"I am not going," Ignace said, stepping back, "but Jenny is."

"You ladies can ride in the back. Michael and me will fly this thing, okay?"

The boy's eyes lit up and a smile crossed his face. Abe noticed the patch of white hair behind his ear as Michael climbed into the cabin. After waiting for Susan to give Ignace a parting kiss, Abe took her arm to help her in, but held back for a moment. "You're not taking him to the residential school, are you?"

"No. We're going to my folks place for the school year."

That was a load off Abe's mind. He'd flown Michael home last spring. Although the other kids were excited about seeing their parents again, Michael had sat beside his older brother and stared at the cabin wall. Through the summer, he'd seen how Susan had brought back the happy little kid he had taken to town a year ago. A touch of envy ran through his heart for the big Native man standing beside him. Ignace had married a gem by anybody's standards. "Catch ya later, Ignace."

"Thank you again, *needjee*."

Abe shook his hand, then climbed into the cargo door and slipped between the seats. He always felt honoured when an Indian called him his friend. "So, Michael, you're going to school in the big city."

"I know how to divide," the boy said.

"Really?"

"What to hear me?"

"Sure." Abe buckled his seat belt and looked back as Michael started.

"Two into four is two. Two into six is three."

Abe only half listened as he went on. Glancing back his attention fell to Ignace who was standing on the float. Susan knelt on the birch floor, taking his face in both hands, she kissed him once more. "You will come for Christmas?"

Ignace didn't respond.

"Please. I do love you. It will be unbearable being away from you the whole winter."

Still the man said nothing. He just stared into her eyes.

"Oh, please, Ignace. I'll have father get us some furs for the bed."

His stone face softened, mischief glittered in his eyes. "Good. Then I will not have to bring green beaver pelts to sleep on."

Susan slapped him on the shoulder. "You leave those stinky things at home." She kissed him again. "And make sure you have a bath before you come."

"I will cut a hole in the ice and wash with pure winter water."

Abe figured he would too. "Hey, we going or not?"

"*K'zaug-in.*" Ignace stepped off the float.

"I love you, too," Susan said before closing the door. She sat up on the bench seat and put on a seatbelt while her husband untied the plane. As he turned it, Abe started the engine. Ignace remained standing on the dock waving as Abe took off and banked toward Kenora. Picking up the microphone, he called Cindy.

She had a taxi waiting to take his passengers to the train station. Susan and Michael packed their suitcases away as Abe helped Jenny from the plane.

"You need a ride back?"

"No." She looked at him, then bowing her head looked down. "I will stay with friends."

In that brief moment Abe saw sadness mingled with despair, no, it was more like hopelessness. He pondered her future, Michael in Winnipeg, Johnnie at the residential school, Pete moved out. "Where's Bethy?" he asked.

"With friends."

That meant her daughter could be anywhere. "Jenny, if there is any way I can help..."

The Native woman shook her head, then shuffled off toward the taxi.

Images of Jack came flooding back. Abe felt his heart hang heavy while his eyes moistened. It tore him up to see Jack's family falling apart. Blinking forced a small tear to form as the taxi drove away. While wiping it, he recalled Jack's wish. *"Of all my sons, Michael is going to get a good education."*

Thank God for Susan.

FORTY

Pete had no idea building a small log house involved so much manual labour. Using a new Swede saw and axe he bought from Luther, he cut down and peeled logs between fishing trips. Each night when he finished for the day, he'd sit by the lake waiting for the first star to appear. It reminded him of Anna. Looking toward Kenora, he tried to picture her in his mind. He hoped she'd like the cabin. It was small, but he'd make it a home.

Anna's father, Alex, showed Pete how to notch and lay the logs, pointing out to Pete that the door should open to the east, for the sun infuses life into all things. Often spending a whole day helping, Alex would sip from a bottle of whiskey he occasionally brought along. Whenever this happened, Pete noticed the quality of his work deteriorate, and as the day wore on, he would lose interest in working. Pete invariably found Alex sitting with his back against a tree, making intricate animal carvings with a small knife. Once, when Pete told him how good it was, Alex scoffed and tossed the work away. Pete later recovered it. He was thankful for the help and by snowfall the logs were all placed.

Pete wanted to put the roof on but needed to buy traps for the winter. Alex had invited him to join his group for the winter, trapping beaver. With Susan and his brother, Michael away in Winnipeg, Pete had wanted to spend the winter trapping with Ignace, but if he wanted Anna as his wife, he was obligated to her parents. Pete suspected Alex wanted to see if his future son-in-law could support his daughter.

Luther took all his money and advanced him credit for the traps and supplies he'd need for the winter. Luther was packing items in a box and Pete was counting traps when his mother walked in and asked for two bottles for wine. Luther told her no, she still owed him from last month.

"Put it on Pete's account," Jenny said.

Pete, now half a head taller than his mother, standing with shoulders broadened by working the logs for his house, shook his head.

"You buy all this for a schoolgirl and you will not help your mother?"

Pete had learned to ignore her when she got into one of these tirades and stared at a point off in the distance. She slammed the counter. "Fine, then. I know someone who will."

Marching out, she pulled the door shut with a crash. Pete and Luther concluded their business.

FORTY-ONE

Public school in Winnipeg wasn't at all what Michael expected. Susan walked with him along a straight path of hard stone. She told him it was called concrete. The road, which followed their stone path, was also hard. It was called asphalt. There was no dust from the cars going by and, unlike the wagon trail on the reservation, it didn't have grass growing on it.

Many roads crossed one another. Where this happened Susan instructed him to stop, look both ways, and walk to the other side only if no automobiles were coming.

Earl Grey School looked similar to the residential school Michael attended last year, only this one had four stories. High stone archways leading into the red brick building brought back memories, none of them good. Later he found out nobody lived here. All the rooms were for classes and the students went home every night.

Something was different about this place. The sounds. Children were laughing and yelling. Michael could see a group of boys playing by the swings. Beside them a line of boys, and girls too, he noticed, waited for their turn on the slide. As Susan led him through the school yard he saw two girls swinging a skipping rope. One was Indian, who along with her white partner and the girl skipping, also white, chanted in unison to the rope, "Cinderella, kissed a fella..."

Inside Michael followed Susan down a hall similar in every way to the residential school, except this one was full of kids, boys and girls. He found his fear of the place disappearing. They entered a classroom where a bald man, who looked like he had a bad sunburn, sat at a big desk dressed not in black robes, but a grey suit coat, white shirt and tie. Michael noticed the books, lots of them, piled up on a ledge along the back of the room.

Susan moved Michael to stand in front of her. "This is Mr. Stodard. He's going to be your teacher for this year."

Michael looked at him, then down at his own shoes.

"Hello, Michael."

The Native boy didn't respond.

"Say hello, Michael." Susan nudged his shoulder.

"Hello."

"He spent the last year at a residential school. I suspect he'll be a bit shy. He speaks English reasonably well and I think you'll be pleasantly surprised by his arithmetic."

"I'm sure we'll get along just fine."

A bell rang. Michael jumped and clutched Susan's hand.

"It's okay." She gently removed his hand. Children started running into the classroom.

"No running. Walk to your desks," Mr. Stodard called out. Bending down he pointed along the second row of desks. Michael expected the man to touch him, but he didn't. "How would you like to sit behind that girl wearing the pink dress?"

Michael hesitated. He was used to sitting with boys.

"Away you go," Susan said. "Here are your scribblers." She handed him the books along with pencils, an eraser, and a ruler.

Although the room was filled with chatter, Michael felt every eye watching him as he walked to his desk. Following the example of the others, he put his stuff into the desk. Looking around, he noticed an Indian boy two rows over and one up near the front. Their presence helped calm his anxiety as Susan left the room.

"All right everybody, quiet now." Mr. Stodard waited until the class had his attention. "Today's Bible reading is from Saint John, chapter six." The room remained silent as all listened to Mr. Stodard read about Jesus walking on the Sea of Galilee.

Michael was thinking about the strong magic he must have had when, to the clatter of banging seats, everyone began standing. He followed and listened as the class recited the Lord's Prayer. When it was over, all sat without instruction from the teacher. Far different from the residential school where you never did anything unless you were told, or wanted a beating.

"Today," Mr. Stodard began, "we are going to start memorizing the multiplication tables." Michael found it all very boring and ended up daydreaming about the man who could walk on water.

At recess he went over to one of the Indian boys from his class. When he saw Michael coming, he turned and walked down the hall with a group of older kids. Adrift in a sea of strangers, Michael followed the flow outside to the playground where he stood alone beside the fence watching everyone play. It was so unlike the residential school. Most of the kids were running around, hollering and laughing. At the sound of girls singing, he stared in their direction, waiting for a teacher to come out and scold them. He was still watching when someone touched his arm. Beside him stood a skinny, redheaded boy with freckles. Through glass with thick lenses, Michael detected a spark of friendship as he looked down a little at the boy.

"Hi, I'm David. What's your name?"

"Michael."

"Wanna play marbles?"

"What is marbles?"

David reached into his pocket and took out a handful of little round glass stones. "These."

"I don't have any."

"That's all right. Here." David held out a half a dozen and dropped them in Michael's hand.

Rolling them in his palm, they felt smooth and cool. "What do you do with them?"

"Shoot 'em."

"With what?"

"Your finger or thumb. Here, I'll show you." David dropped to his hands and knees. Michael hesitated, knowing that if he got his pants dirty, his teacher would scold him. David waved him down, so he squatted as David drew a circle in the dirt.

"Put one of your marbles in the middle."

Michael took a pale blue one with green swirls and placed it in the circle. Holding one of his marbles between his thumb and fore finger, David closed one eye and squinted, taking aim at the lone marble sitting in the dirt. Michael watched with fascination as the marble squirted from David's thumb and finger, knocking his from the circle. David put one of his in the circle. Sitting back on his haunches, he looked at his Indian friend. "Your turn."

Unaware he was getting his pants dirty, Michael kneeled in the dirt holding the marble like he'd seen David do. When he tried to flick it with his thumb, it bobbled a few inches into the circle.

"Ah, try again," David said, letting Michael have three tries before he blasted the marble away. After that they took turns. Michael's shots were coming closer and he even hit the center marble once before the bell rang. He was down to one marble of clear glass with silver strands swirled inside. Holding out his hand, he waited for David to take it.

"You keep it. Want to sit with me at lunch?"

Michael nodded, curling his fingers around David's gift. Nobody had ever given him anything like it at the church school.

"Come on." David tugged at his coat. Michael followed, tightly holding the marble that cemented their friendship.

A bell, signaling the end of the school day, hadn't stopped ringing before kids began running out the doors. Michael followed in the rush, eager to get outside. Standing in the tower entrance covering the steps, he looked around the school yard for Susan. Not seeing her in the crowd of parents and kids, he felt his insides tighten. The urge to run seized him but he didn't know where to go. Then she was walking toward him, calling his name, waving her hand.

Michael bounded down the steps to her. "Look what I got!" Opening his hand, he showed her his treasure before she could say anything. "It is a marble."

"That's nice." Susan picked it out of his palm and looked at the swirls within the glass. "Where'd you get it?"

Michael, who looked down as soon as Susan caught his eye, replied, "From David. He is my friend. We ate lunch together."

Susan warmed to his wide smile as she handed the marble back. "Well let's take this home and show Opa." Watching the boy she'd grown to love as her own while his fingers carefully enclosed his prized possession, the trepidation she'd felt coming to get him vanished. Michael was coming home from his first day of school, happy.

FORTY-TWO

Susan made Michael wait until after supper to show her father the marble. Dr. Strombecker looked at it in Michael's hands as if he was studying a medical x-ray. Touching the marble, he rolled it a little. "Ah! A Spaghetti Swirl. May I?" he asked, picking it up.

Michael nodded, although he didn't want anyone else to have his marble, he felt he could trust the elderly man before him who studied it in the living room light.

"I haven't seen one of these in years." Holding it between two fingers and his thumb, he knelt down on the Persian carpet and squirted it across the thick pile. Michael ran and retrieved it. Dr. Strombecker stood up. "Show me how you do it."

Michael held the marble in his curled forefinger and flicked it with his thumb.

Dr. Strombecker watched the shot go crooked. "Here." Kneeling again, he showed Michael how to hold it between two finger tips and his thumb. After a few shots, he stood. "We need more marbles. Come with me."

Michael followed him into the basement where Dr. Strombecker reached up and took an old tobacco can off a high shelf. When he unscrewed the lid, Michael's eyes lit up. It was full of marbles.

"Haven't used these in years," Susan's father said. Leading Michael to an area of the basement with a dirt floor, he drew a circle. There on hands and knees, with long fingers trained to perform delicate surgery, he taught the young Indian boy how to shoot marbles.

Michael played with other kids at school, but he chummed around with David Croft. One day he looked through David's glasses to find the world all blurry and marveled how, when wearing them his friend was deadly at shooting marbles, winning pockets full from older kids. His skill deteriorated when he played with Michael. As a result the marbles he steadily lost were replaced by his winnings from David.

Autumn leaves littering the school yard signaled the coming end of marble season. David and Michael were two of only a handful of boys playing marbles when a big kid walked over.

"Hey, David, wanna play me?"

"Nope," he said, knocking one of Michael's marbles out of the circle.

"Why not?"

"I'm playing with Michael."

"He's an Indian."

"He's my friend."

The kid pushed Michael, who went sprawling to the ground.

"Hey!" David grabbed the big kid's arm. "What did you do that for?"

"I wanted to see if he'd fight. My Dad says Indians are scared to fight."

Michael stood up behind David as he faced the older boy. He didn't want to fight him, but he wasn't scared of him either. Indians fought all the time. His big brother Johnnie would have beat him good.

"Go away, Steven. We don't want you here."

"Scaredy cat." Steven Wright kicked all the marbles out of the circle, sending them in different directions. After shoving David back into Michael, he walked away.

"Why did he want to fight?" Michael asked.

"He's a bully." David picked up the scattered marbles. "He's not tough, only picks on smaller kids."

"And Indians?"

"Doesn't matter."

To Michael it did. White men at the residential school beat Indian kids, and here white kids beat Indian kids. An inner rage welled up against whites, then he looked at David: red hair, glasses that made his eyes look big, white skin. His own skin was brown, yet the two of them were best friends. What did skin colour have to do with friendship?

It would be a long time before he understood the answer.

FORTY-THREE

By mid-December the thermometer had dropped to sub-zero temperatures, not rising above twenty below during the day under cloudless blue skies. Abe lay on the couch in his winter office reading a *Popular Mechanics* magazine while a wicked north wind rattled the windows and whistled in under the door. Across the room, an oil heater glowed dull red labouring to keep the place warm.

The door opened. Arctic air gusted into the office. Abe sat up as Cindy, bundled up in a parka and scarf wrapped around her face, stepped in and stomped snow from her felt-packed boots. "Thank goodness." Unwrapping her scarf, she tossed a bundle of letters onto the desk. Abe closed the door behind her, shutting out the biting wind.

Removing her gloves, she held both hands over the heater. "Thought I'd freeze to death out there."

"I said you didn't have to go for the mail."

"Hah! You lie around here snug and warm, reading magazines while our bills pile up at the post office."

"Might as well. Haven't any money to pay them, anyway."

Cindy, knowing the healthy state of their finances ignored the remark. "Here." She fished out a window envelope with Canadian Pacific scrolled in red on the top left corner. Underneath, in block black was the word 'TELEGRAM'. "Picked this up while checking the Express. Your parts never showed."

Abe had ordered a new latch for the right-hand cargo door from Noorduyn in Montreal. Right now he was flying with it tied shut. Safe enough, but drafty.

"Who's it from?"

"Susan Two Bears."

Abe opened the envelope, unfolded a sheet of paper, and read the message.

'PICK UP IGNACE AT STONE POINT CAMP ON DECEMBER TWENTY THREE STOP FLY HIM TO WINNIPEG STOP WILL PAY FOR FLIGHT UPON ARRIVAL STOP SUSAN'

Cindy waited until her boss finished reading. "Well, shall I book it?"

"Of course."

"I won't be here to remind you." She undid the buttons on her parka. "I'm away the day before."

"I won't forget."

"Sure, like last year?"

Abe winced. There was a flight scheduled for December 24th, some people from the paper mill to Fort Frances and back. Trouble was, the night before he'd gotten all snarled up with Ted Corrigan, Reg Christie, Arnold Kincade, and a few more people over at the Forestry Building. The party turned into an all-night poker game. Good thing Cindy was around to re-book the flight with one of Doc's planes.

"I'm a reformed man." Abe watched Cindy roll her blue eyes.

The morning of December 23rd broke clear and cold, no wind blew to disturb the ice crystals forming in the morning air, now thirty-six degrees below zero. As dawn broke in the eastern sky, Abe sat at Mrs. Litynski's kitchen table enjoying a second cup of coffee. Picking up Ignace was his only flight and he wasn't going to try starting the plane before ten o'clock. It was a good thing because his old pickup truck wouldn't turn over and he had to call a taxi.

The clock read seven minutes after ten when he unlocked the office door and walked in. An hour and a half later he was circling over Stone Point, checking out the ice before landing. A lone figure walked out to meet him when the plane's skis touched down and rattled across uneven ice.

With the engine ticking over at an idle, Abe leaned across the cabin and opened the right side front door. Ignace threw in a bundle tied with rope, which Abe stuffed between the seats. Ignace shut the door and put on his seatbelt.

"Good to see you," Abe hollered as he opened the throttle and the instrument panel vibrated all the dials into a blur.

"You too, my friend." The big Indian took off his glove to shake Abe's hand.

"We're off to Winnipeg, then?"

"Yeah."

The Norseman, responding to Abe's touch, swung around and started along the ice, skis rumbling beneath their seats. "Okay then, here we go." Abe pulled the control wheel and the plane pointed its nose into the frigid winter sky. An hour later, they landed on the frozen Red River at Western Canada Airways operations at the foot of Brandon Street.

Susan, her father, and Michael met the plane. Abe shut off the engine and climbed out with Ignace. Susan ran into her husband's arms. He scooped her up in a big bear hug, lifting her feet off the ground.

Abe walked over and tussled Michael's hair while addressing Dr. Strombecker. "Hello, Henry, new car?"

"Yes. A Buick this time. Straight Eight. Have a good flight?"

"Perfect weather for flying. And how's Michael?"

"Fine," he replied, quickly looking at the ground.

"Learn anything new in school?"

"Yes."

Abe waited for more. Finally, Henry spoke up. "Excellent at arithmetic. Reading needs some work, but Susan's helping him there. Turned out to be quite the marble player."

"Good." Abe patted the boy's shoulder as he looked up and smiled.

Susan and Ignace joined them. "Hello, Abe."

"Susan."

"Thank you for bringing Ignace." She looked at her husband with longing eyes then turned back to Abe. "You have a bill for us?"

"Cindy made one out. It's in the plane. I'll get it." He returned and handed the envelope to Susan who handed it to her father. Henry Strombecker, took out the bill, then wrote a check, stuffing the envelope and paper in his pocket.

"You going anywhere for Christmas?" Susan asked.

"No." Abe really had no place to go now that his mother had died. "I'll just hang around Mrs. Litynski's."

"You're welcome to join us."

"Thanks anyway, but it's my turn to be available for Christmas day." He and Doc had an informal agreement that they would alternate years on standby in case of a medical emergency. This was his year.

Henry handed Abe the check. "Always room for one more here."

"Thanks, anyway."

"Okay, more turkey for Michael and me."

Abe folded the check, unzipped his flight jacket and put it in his shirt pocket. "You have a return date?"

"Not really," Susan said, looking at her husband.

"She would have you come for me after you put floats on your plane," Ignace said. "But you would fly a crazy man home if I live in the city that long."

"Do I drive you crazy?" Susan asked.

Ignace wrapped both arms around his wife. "Yes," he said lifting her up. She kissed him as he set her down.

"We'll get in touch when he wants to go back," Susan said, unwrapping his arms.

"Good." Abe left to handshakes all around.

Loneliness set in on the flight home. Why hadn't he found someone to marry? Lots of other pilots were married, some with kids. Even if he did, would his wife be like Susan? He didn't think he could ever have the inner strength of Ignace. They were such a pleasure to be around. By the time Abe landed in Kenora, he wished he'd taken them up on their offer.

FORTY-FOUR

The Strombecker house, built before the Great War, exuded a Victorian charm enhanced by heavy fir mouldings and banisters stained to a deep wine red. As a light snow fell outside, Susan and her husband walked up the carpet-covered stairs to their bedroom.

"So, how is Michael doing?" Ignace asked, closing the door and walking toward the bed.

"Fine."

Ignace sat and waited.

Susan allowed the silence to linger, then added, "In arithmetic."

"Tell me," Ignace said.

"The boy amazes me. He picks up anything to do with numbers right away. I know he's way ahead of the other kids, but I can't slow him down." She raised her hands in despair. "Now he's getting into solving math problems."

"That is bad?"

"It puts him way ahead of the class."

"That is good, then. He is smarter than the others kids."

"It's not good"

Ignace frowned.

"His teacher says he gets bored."

"You talked to his teacher? No Indian parent talks to the priests."

"This is public school, Ignace. They have parent-teacher days." Her husband looked lost. "It's a day set aside for teachers to talk with parents about their children."

"You did this?"

"Yes. I know it must sound strange but I did meet with Mr. Stodard, Michael's teacher and talk about how he was doing." Susan reflected back to their meeting. Mr. Stodard had been forthright and kind. He'd mentioned how good Michael was in math but expressed grave concern about his reading and writing.

It hadn't surprised her. She noticed his numbers were precise and well formed but his printing was barely legible.

"He doesn't say much in class," Mr. Stodard had said, "yet I see him talking with other children, particularly David Croft. So I know he can speak. Is there some problem I should be aware of?"

She remembered thinking, how can I tell him his father was shot to death in a school hallway? "Not really," she replied. The look in Mr. Stodard's eyes told her he thought there was more to it. All she had said was, "Perhaps I can help him at home more."

Ignace broke into her thoughts. "So, what did he say?"

"That he needs help in reading and writing English." She picked up a comb off the dresser, then turning to the mirror, lifted her long brown hair over the back of her shoulder.

"Good." Ignace lay back, settling into the soft mattress and feather tick. Holding his head with both hands clasped together behind it, he watched her run the comb through her long hair.

Looking into the mirror, Susan caught her husband's eyes, full of excitement. "Did you miss me?"

"I would not have come if I did not."

She swivelled around to face him. "Honestly, Ignace, you can be so Indian at times. I'll bet you were too busy skinning beaver to think of me."

"There are not enough beaver in the country for that. My hands were busy but my heart only waited for you."

"That is so poetic."

Ignace smiled.

"How many beaver?"

"Twenty-seven."

"Your heart had a lot of time to wait."

His grin widened. "Between eight mink, fourteen foxes, twelve ermine and seven marten."

Susan threw the comb at him. "You fit me in between skinnings?"

Ignace sat up, gesturing across the ceiling. "Every night I would step outside and look to the stars. I would see your eyes as they twinkled in the black sky, then in a vision you would come to me."

Susan knew why she loved her man so.

"Once you were holding the hand of a little boy." The woman's smile vanished. She looked away as he stood up. "I am sorry." He moved to her, taking both hands. "It was a bad vision."

Reaching up, Susan embraced him. "You won't ever let that come between us, will you?"

"It was only one vision. When it appeared I turned away and walked inside." He drew her to him, feeling his wife relax in his arms.

"I love you," she whispered.

His reply was a tender kiss before he picked her up and carried her to the big four-poster bed. She squealed with delight as they both fell into the soft feather-filled quilt.

FORTY-FIVE

Winter trapping was good to Pete. It wasn't his favourite type of work, but he did it for Anna. When she came back from school, he was determined to have the cabin finished. After settling his account with Luther, he had enough left over to put on the roof and cover the floor with wood. All he needed was a stove.

Digging the garden where Anna's mother showed him, turned up good soil. She put the seeds in and told Pete to water them. By the time Anna came home, it needed a good weeding.

June 20th was the longest day of the year. Pete, dressed in a pair of buckskin leggings his grandmother made for him, and bare-chested in the summer heat, walked over to Alex Quoquat's house to ask for Anna's hand in marriage. First there was a big feast and much drinking by Anna's parents. As the sky darkened, Pete took Anna outside to watch the first star appear, then, holding hands and carrying Anna's few possessions, they walked through the reservation to his cabin. There on a bed of furs, they made love for the first time.

FORTY-SIX

The past two days had been hot and muggy, heralding the incoming storm. Ted used to look forward to these final weekends in August when Jack Redsky and his family camped nearby and picked blueberries. He and Jack spent the evenings smoking while the kids played and women cleaned berries. Once or twice they'd make a run to town with full baskets. Ted could still see his friend driving the *Foxey*, excitement blazing in his eyes, long hair blowing wildly in the wind. He was good male company, not to say that Diana and the two girls weren't fun to be around. Janice might as well have been a boy, the way she acted, though it wasn't the same. He wondered what life would have been like with a son.

Approaching the south end of Devil's Gap, Ted felt a few spits of rain. To his left, the thunder clouds that had been building all afternoon, now blotted out the setting sun. Reaching down, he turned on the navigation lights, their green and red glow reflecting in the chrome horn mounted on the front of the *Foxey's* long bow. Turning into the gap, Ted saw the wide spray of an oncoming boat. It wasn't leaving him much room to pass the black buoy marking a reef on his right.

Ted recognized the town's police boat about the same time it moved over, crowding him out of the channel. He had no choice but to run over the submerged rocks.

Sergeant Farnell roared by, mouthing obscenities Ted couldn't hear. He returned them, scraping the buoy to avoid ripping the bottom out of his boat on the reef. Killing the throttle, Ted swung around in a vicious turn. Feeling a vein pulsing in his neck, he opened up the engine, and took off after Farnell.

The pursuit developed into a straight line race between the two fastest boats on the Lake of the Woods. Farnell ran for ten miles as darkness fell.

Ted gained very slowly. God, he hated that man for what he did to Jack. Ted recalled the year before Jack died when a few Indian families with kids in school had camped on Coney Island. One Sunday morning, while they were visiting their children, Farnell, with nothing better to do, went over and shot all their dogs. Ted hammered the throttle, already wide open. A year later the bugger shot Jack.

The police boat's white stern light crept closer as darkness engulfed the lake. Lightning lit the sky electric-arc blue as the storm broke. Rolling thunder, loud enough for Ted to hear above the *Foxey's* engine, echoed through the angry clouds as air filled with rain so heavy it cut visibility to a few yards. Farnell swung left, disappearing from view. Ted rolled the *Foxey* left, turning inside of him, knowing he was gaining. Another bolt of lightning illuminated Farnell, making a turn in the opposite direction. Ted wiped water dripping in his face and followed around, keeping him in sight. Two more wild manoeuvers found the *Foxey* off his stern. Farnell cut in front of Ted. The two boats touched before Ted could turn and run beside Farnell. The big cop kept working Ted toward the island they were passing. Ignoring the shore a few feet to his right, Ted swung the *Foxey* hard into the sleek Hacker-Craft, knocking Farnell off balance. Rain, mixed with spray, cascaded over the two men as they rammed their boats against each other. Ted hit Farnell twice more before Farnell pulled out his revolver. Flame spat from the gun as the shots died under rolling thunder. Ted backed off, then pulled up once more.

Unable to out run Ted, Farnell waited until the two boats were once again side by side, then he began a gradual turn to the left, forcing the *Foxey* to run a wider arc on his right. Ted lost ground. Farnell looked back as lightning flashed silver-blue in the night. Ted hauled back the throttle, dropping the *Foxey's* nose into Farnell's wake and spinning the wheel hard left. Farnell turned his head around, opening his mouth in shock the moment his boat slammed into the darkness.

Thunder echoed above as the Hacker-Craft disintegrated and caught fire, briefly illuminating a sheer rock face. Ted slowly circled back, soaking wet from the rain, water streaming down his face and into his eyes. He watched the wreckage sink. "Stupid bastard. That's for Jack."

FORTY-SEVEN

By the time Luther Vogler had seen fourteen winters, he was painfully aware that he didn't fit into Canadian society. His father was a German who'd run away from an abusive father and after working as a sailor for two years, jumped ship in Montreal and made his way west. His mother, a Cree woman from northern Manitoba, had died giving birth to him. Memories of his youth centered around beatings from his father and constant harassment from school mates for being either German or Indian.

All his facial features he inherited from his mother, the broad nose, thick lips and tan skin. Indians may have accepted him except for his blonde hair and blue eyes. The Metis had no use for someone who didn't speak French and the whites, particularly after the Great War, hated Germans.

Running away from his father at age sixteen, Luther Volger took up trapping around Shoal Lake and eventually set up a trading post on land adjacent to the Long Grass Reservation. Abe flew in a plane load of food and dry-goods once a week for him with instructions to fill out the load with gas or liquor.

As hot as the Norseman was in summer, winter would see frost inside the cabin on very cold days. This day, the thermometer tied to the wing strut read twenty-three below zero. Not all that cold for a January morning. Still he had to fly with his gloves on.

Touching down, Abe felt the skis jolt and rattle along the ice as his plane slowed. Swinging around, he parked on the frozen lake beside Luther's horse-drawn sled. It always took two trips to transfer the goods to the trading post and, as usual on the first unload, after covering the engine, Abe went along to help. He was growing numb by the time Luther pulled up in front of the log building.

Abe hurried inside, took off his gloves and stood with both hands over the wood stove. Luther followed, cartons of goods stacked to his chin, kicking the door shut. He wasn't halfway across the room when it opened again. Jenny Redsky walked in. A five-year old girl followed.

The quick glance Abe got from Jenny was as cold as the snow outside. He ignored it only to look down on a young child by her side who stood shivering while watching him with big black eyes.

Little Elizabeth Redsky. How she'd grown in the years since Jack's death. Dressed in a tattered coat and thin pants, she clutched her mother's coat, looking up at her.

"Mommy?"

"Not now, Bethy."

"Mommy." She took hold of her mother's sleeve and began tugging it.

Jenny pushed her assistance check across the counter. "Just wait." Slapping the girl's hand away, she looked down. "I'm busy?"

"But..."

"No, Bethy!" Jenny turned to count the money Luther's wife had placed on the counter. After leafing through the bills, she calmed down.

"Mommy."

"What is it?" Jenny never looked down but pointed to two bottles of wine. "I'll take those."

"Please buy me a new pair of boots."

When Abe looked at Bethy's feet he could have cried. A pink sock showed on the left sneaker through a tear in its side. The other, although it didn't show the blue sock on that foot, was badly worn and had no lace. Both were soaking wet from melting snow.

"You don't need new boots."

"But Mommy, my feet are really cold."

Jenny rounded on the girl. "No. I need this money."

The little girl broke into tears which Jenny ignored while picking up both bottles of wine in one hand and heading for the door. Still sobbing, Bethy followed. Abe wasn't far behind, but Jenny was off the porch before he caught up with her.

"Jenny!" The Indian woman kept walking. "Jenny, wait." Abe grabbed her shoulder, dragging her to a halt.

"Let go of me." She twisted in his grip.

Abe turned her to face him. "What would Jack think of his little girl running around in this weather with worn-out summer shoes?"

"Jack's dead. He doesn't care."

A hard landing in the dark flashed through Abe's mind. "Well, I care. There's no reason why you can't go back inside and buy Bethy some boots."

"I won't."

"Why? You have the money right now."

"I need it for myself."

"To buy booze. You don't need that."

"Yes I do." She was screaming and shaking her head. "Without Jack what have I got to live for?"

"Bethy needs you."

"I needed Jack. You white people shot him and took my sons away." Her face hardened, her narrow eyes almost closed. "You don't care what happens to us." She turned and walked away. Bethy started to follow, but Abe took her hand and walked back into the store.

"Luther."

"It won't help."

Abe pointed to the liquor rack. "Why do you sell that stuff here?"

"Why do you fly it in?" He waited for an answer that never came. "If I don't sell it, bootleggers will, and charge twice as much. That leaves a lot less for food."

Abe knew all too well. He'd flown plane loads of Indians to Kenora where they got drunk and used to run afoul of Sergeant Farnell. These people were caught in a vicious cycle of the white man's making. He felt like shit. Turning to Luther's wife, he said, "Give Bethy the best pair of boots you have." Pulling on his gloves, he opened the door. "Take it off my freight bill."

Abe worked up a sweat he wanted the Norseman unloaded so fast. Without waiting for Luther to sign the bill, he took off and flew to Kenora at full throttle.

***

"Cindy!" Abe threw open the office door, bouncing it off the wall. Slamming it open a second time, he walked in. "Cindy!"

"What?"

"We have an emergency," he said pulling off his gloves.

"Calm down, Abe."

"Dial the hospital and give me the phone."

One look at her boss and Cindy did as told.

Abe held the receiver to his ear and talked into the mouthpiece. "Kate O'Brian, please."

A pause.

"I don't care. Tell her this is an emergency."

Another pause. "It will be a medical emergency if she doesn't come to the phone."

Abe waited on the line for five minutes, pacing the floor as far as the line would allow.

A voice sounded in his ear. "Hello."

"Kate, Abe here. You have to come out to Long Grass."

"Slow down. Why me?"

"Because you're a nurse."

"Is someone injured?"

"No."

"Then why do you need a nurse?"

Abe told her about Bethy.

"The poor girl. I'd come but I'm the only one on staff to help with an operation that's about to start."

"She'll die."

"Don't over-exaggerate, Abe."

"I'm not. I saved that little girl once, I'm not going to let her die a second time."

"Look, I'd come, you know that. But I can't. Call Diana. She knows Jenny."

"We have to get Bethy out of there."

"Abe, listen. We have agencies to handle this sort of thing."

"They take days. Bethy has only hours."

"You're overreacting."

"I am not. Dammit, Kate, there's a little girl out in the freezing cold with wet sneakers. How long do you think she's going to last?"

"Call Diana. Go get the girl. I'll see what I can do. Now I really have to go."

Abe said nothing.

"Abe?"

"Yes."

Kate lowered her voice and spoke slowly. "Go get Bethy. I'll fix things on this end."

"Thanks."

"Just go."

There was no answer at Diana's. Abe tried three times then phoned the hospital back.

Kate was on the line in a minute, listened to Abe, then told him to hold on. She came back on after what to Abe seemed like an hour wait. "Okay. Doc Payton says if you're that upset then I should go. We have a trainee that he says can help him with this operation. I'll be there as soon as I can."

For the second time that day, Abe landed at the Long Grass Reservation and taxied his plane across the ice. Opening the door let in twenty below cold air, stinging his nose and biting his lungs. Kate climbed out her side as Abe walked around to help her to the ground. Dressed in an ankle-length fur coat, she followed him up the snow path to Luther's store.

"She won't last long if she's out in this." White breath drifted away from Kate's words as she struggled to keep up with Abe's long strides.

"I told Luther to keep her inside." Opening the door for Kate, he followed her in, stomping snow off his boots.

Luther stepped from behind the counter. "Hello, Miss Kate. Abe."

"Where is she?" Abe asked.

"Who? Oh, the Redsky kid." Luther motioned out the door.

"What?" Abe threw up both hands. "I told you to keep her inside."

"No you didn't."

Kate noticed Abe's face getting red as he spoke. "You sent her out in this?" his right arm pointing outside.

"Kids come in and out of this place all the time."

"Not with wet sneakers in forty below."

Kate stepped between the two men, facing Abe. "It's not forty below out. Calm down." She turned to Luther, "Both of you. How long ago did she leave?"

Luther shrugged his shoulders and looked at his wife.

"Well," she said, "it took sometime to find a pair of boots that fit. She walked around the store a few times then wanted to try them outside. She went out and hasn't been back since."

"How long ago?" Abe asked with deliberately slow words.

"Fifteen, maybe twenty minutes after you left."

Two hours. Abe's heart sank.

"She's probably home with her mother," Luther said. "This happens all the time. Kids come and go." As if to prove him right, three boys pushed open the door against Abe and ran in, stomping their feet.

Grabbing Kate's hand, Abe dashed out the open door. She stumbled after him, quickly recovering and trying to keep pace as he headed into the reserve. The trail that led to the opposite end of the reserve from

Jack's house, for some reason Abe continued to think of it as Jack's, was a ten-minute walk from the store. He left the beaten path to cut across country, dragging Kate behind. Breaking trail in knee-deep snow, Abe marched on with a fervour Kate was unable to match plowing through loose snow.

She yanked her hand from Abe's. "Abe! Slow down."

He pushed on with a vengeance. Kate waded through the snow, falling further behind until they reached the wide beaten path between two rows of houses. Kate ran to catch up, her bulky fur coat trailing out behind. She caught his arm as he walked up to the door. "Take it easy, Abe. She'll be alright. Just calm down."

Abe beat on the door and was told by a slurred voice behind it, to come in.

He entered, unprepared for the sight that greeted him. Jack's place, the one always so clean and tidy, now looked like a garbage dump. Clothes, boots, and empty bottles were scattered about. The couch he'd sat on with Jack was torn, sitting crooked on the floor because of a broken leg, a cushion missing. Two men were sprawled on it, one passed out, the other took a disinterested look at the white couple in the doorway, then went back to drinking whiskey from a bottle.

Jenny sat on the only chair at the table, head cradled in her crossed arms. Abe kicked boots out of the way and made his way over to her.

"Jenny!" He shook her so hard her head bounced off both arms. "Jenny, where is she?"

The woman's head turned to the voice. Uncomprehending eyes stared into the distance. Abe grabbed a handful of hair and lifted her head. His voice filled the room. "Where's Bethy?"

When all he got was an abject smile, he let go. Jenny's head fell sideways on the table with an ugly thump. He didn't care. "Check out the two bedrooms," he told Kate.

She looked in one. It was empty. The other had three men and a half-dressed woman on the bed. Kate slammed the door, shaking her head.

"Damn!" Abe turned and went outside not bothering to close the door. Kate stood beside him as he searched the houses to his left, then looked right.

"She could be in any one of those houses," Kate said.

"She's not. I feel it."

Kate put her gloved hand on his arm. "You don't know for sure."

Abe turned to her. "I just know."

"Well, where do you suggest we look?"

Abe looked left, then right, then left again. "This way." They worked their way to the end of the road, calling at each house. Few people answered. Those that did hadn't seen Bethy. They walked back toward Jack's house. The door was still open. Abe didn't feel sorry for the people inside. If they wanted to freeze, that was their business. He and Kate continued walking, his eyes searching.

Kate bumped into him when he stopped.

"What is it?" she asked.

Abe pointed to fresh tracks in the snow leading behind the house. Bending down, he touched them with his mitt. They'd been made by a child's boots. The imprint showed they were brand new.

Followed by Kate, Abe ran behind the building only to come up short when the tracks disappeared on frozen bare ground.

"Damn. Where would she have gone?" He scanned the countryside.

"Abe!" Kate elbowed him in the ribs.

He turned to see her pointing to the far side of the house. Curled up in the snow was a big shepherd-type dog, her head turned back, covering the body of a small child. Seeing new boots, Abe rushed forward. The dog lifted its head, curled back the side of it lips, and growled.

Just out of reach, he could see Bethy lying on her side, face snuggled into the dog's belly. One arm was tucked underneath her body, the other clutched a small doll with one leg missing, the fingers holding it waxy white. Abe looked at Bethy's blue lips. "She's dead."

He tried approaching the dog again. Once more it snarled, baring it teeth. Abe stepped back.

"I'll try." Kate took off a glove and extending her bare hand, approached. The dog waited until she touched its nose, then after sniffing her fingertips, allowed Kate to feel its muzzle. "Good girl." Kate's voice was soft and gentle. "Good girl." Reaching down, she touched the cold body. No response.

Closing her hand over Bethy's fingers, she tried to loosen them from the doll. Under her hand the frozen fingers tightened around the doll.

"She's alive!" Kate rolled her over and slipped an arm under Bethy's neck as the dog got up. Under its watchful eye, Kate lifted the child. "We need some place warm."

"Luther's. Give her to me."

Holding Bethy in his arms, Abe ran all the way to the trading post. Inside, he laid her on the counter as Kate took off her gloves. "We have to get her to the hospital. Luther, lend us a blanket."

The German, who hardly tolerated the Indian kids in his store, reached up and took down a new Hudson's Bay blanket.

Kate shoved Abe toward the door. "Go warm up the plane. I'll be down in a few minutes."

With the engine idling over, Abe waited for Kate as lukewarm air from the heater blew into the cabin. Luther came down the path carrying Bethy bundled in the blanket. Kate ran through the snow to get ahead and open the cargo door. Cold air rushed in as Abe waited for Luther to place the girl inside and Kate to climb aboard.

"Thank you," Kate said.

"Will she live?" Luther asked.

"Yes." Kate's eyes said otherwise, and he closed the door.

"You'd be better off up front, Kate. There's no heat at all back there on days like this," Abe said.

Kate picked up Bethy and moved into the front seat. Abe took off. Five minutes into the flight the cabin was cold.

"Can you turn up the heat?" Kate asked.

"This is it." Abe put his hand over the vent on the floor. Hot air as usual. "In the summer this 'old girl' will cook you out, but in this weather, well," he said, feeling the cold draft seeping in around the doors, "I'm afraid this is it."

Kate pulled back the blanket. Abe caught her look as she felt the frozen fingers. "Still cold. And she's not shivering yet. That worries me. I thought it would be warm in here."

"Sorry."

Kate shifted Bethy's dead weight so she could undo the buttons on her fur coat. Flipping it open, she started undoing the front of her nurse's uniform.

Abe glanced over.

"You just keep your eyes on your flying."

Releasing the last button, she moved the material aside exposing her panties and brassiere, then unwrapped Bethy. She laid the girl against her warm skin and covered her with the uniform and coat as best she could.

Bethy's cold body drew the warmth from Kate as she struggled with the blanket. Abe reached over and lifted it to her shoulders. Halfway into the flight, Bethy began shivering. Kate's tummy was freezing, but she sat back and relaxed for the remaining twenty minutes of the flight.

Abe radioed Cindy to call for an ambulance, and to make sure it was warm. He landed and taxied right up beside it. Two attendants helped Kate out of the plane with Bethy still bundled next to her. As she was getting into the ambulance, the blanket slipped away and the little Native girl's head rolled to one side.

It was the last time Abe ever saw Elizabeth Redsky.

FORTY-EIGHT

Spring came early, warming the land and returning life to the forest. Late in May, after washing clothes and hanging them on a line out back, Anna gave birth to a daughter that Pete said looked like her.

They called the baby Ruth, after Anna's favourite Bible character, and somehow never got around to the naming ceremony. To Pete, it didn't matter. He was aware that his wife knelt and prayed each night to a god he didn't understand, but in which she found comfort and peace.

During the next winter, when she was pregnant again, she'd spend a few minutes each night reading by a coal-oil lamp from a Bible she'd bought in Kenora. Pete, who could barely read, knew nothing of what it contained. When she'd start to read aloud some passage to him, images of the residential school would come back and he'd hold up his hand to stop her. It was the only little thing of contention in their marriage, until Father LaFrenier came along.

Anna refused to believe that they were not married in the traditional Indian way, and didn't believe Father LaFrenier when he told her she was living in sin. Out of respect for the God of the Bible, whom she'd come to love, she asked Pete to let the priest marry them in the church.

Pete refused. It was the first of many arguments that always ended with Anna crying. Two or three days would pass before things settled down. It wasn't that Pete didn't love Anna, he did, deeply. What upset him was the arrogance of the priest to tell him his Indian wedding wasn't valid.

Pete felt he needed to bridge the gulf that was opening in their marriage. He took the initiative and brought up the subject one night after Ruth was asleep.

"That man was responsible for the death of my father."

Anna listened as he related the details.

"He abused Johnnie."

Anna was horrified by what Pete told her.

"When Tony and I escaped, he never even tried to tell our parents. Tony froze to death that night. When his body was found in the spring, that priest never bothered to get word to his folks. They only found out when school ended and he never came home."

A tear slipped from Anna's eye. Pete touched her hand. "It's not your God I blame, so much as Father LaFrenier. Every time he touches my life, something is ruined."

Pulling his wife close, he held her in both arms with his chin over her shoulder. "I love you so much, Anna." Tears flooded his eyes. "I do not want our lives ruined."

Pete held her a moment more, then released her. "But I am not setting foot in his church."

Anna drew him to her, kissed him, and said, "I understand."

FORTY-NINE

The Redsky cabin that winter was a happy place. Johnnie, now out of school, came over once in a while. Michael, who was staying with Susan's parents and going to school in Winnipeg, visited on long weekends when she brought him home.

Pete adored his daughter, Ruth. She slept through the night now and kept him entertained during the short winter days, smiling and laughing as she played. On a rare moment, while holding Ruth, Pete would wonder about his sister, Bethy. Since the Children's Aid Society had taken her away, they'd heard nothing, except that she'd lost a couple of fingers from frostbite the day Abe found her in the snow.

Anna's belly swelled as the months passed and the days lengthened. Pete realized their little cabin was becoming crowded. Their next child wouldn't be the last, so Pete decided to ask the Indian Agency to build them a frame house, one with a separate bedroom. By using their treaty money and what he earned from fishing, they could just manage until Anna had a couple more babies.

Little John Mark came along when the ice was going out. Because the cabin seemed to shrink to the size of a tepee with his arrival, Pete went to see the Indian Agent about a new house.

He returned in a rage. Anna, having just got John Mark to sleep, cowered when he barged in. "That damn Father LaFrenier. Damn him! Damn him to the Land of the Dead."

Ruth ran to her mother's side. As Anna put her hand on the little girl's shoulder, John Mark began to howl. "Pete, please. Not so loud." She picked up the baby.

169

Hearing his son crying took all the starch out of Pete's anger. He walked over and softly cooed at him. The baby wailed for a bit, then settled back to sleep. Anna sent Ruth back to the homemade doll she was playing with, then seated herself at their small table and beckoned her husband to take the other chair.

Pete sat with his hands on the table. Anna reached over and placed a hand on his. Her eyes asked the question.

"The Indian Agent says he can only build a house for married families."

"So, what's the problem?"

"He says he has no record of us getting married."

"What!"

"According to the government, you've had two children without being married."

Anna knew before God, and Kitche Manitou, and by all that was holy, they were husband and wife. "But we are married."

"According to Ojibway tradition, yes. But unless we're married in the church, they won't build us a house."

"We have to be married to buy a house?"

"It has to do with the way the Indian Department figures out if we can afford to pay for it."

"That's silly."

Pete looked at his wife. After two babies she looked more beautiful than at the festival. He wanted so much to please her. "I'm not going to be married in Father LaFrenier's church."

Anna squeezed his hand. "I understand."

They sat in silence.

"Mommy, pee."

"Good girl." Anna got up and took Ruth to the little potty she used. Looking back, she asked, "We just have to be married, right?"

Pete nodded. "By white people."

"Let me see what I can find out."

FIFTY

Three weeks later, Abe had finished delivering a plane load of groceries, supplies and gas to Luther's trading post, and was checking the waybill when Pete and Anna Redsky came down the path. Luther signed his X then handed the papers back to Abe. He stepped aside as the young Native couple, dressed in buckskins, walked onto the dock.

"Let me know about next week, Luther."

"Ya, Ya, Abe, I will." The German waved a hand then climbed aboard his wagon, yelling foreign words to get his horses moving.

Abe turned to the couple. "Hello, Pete. Anna."

"You on your way back to Kenora?"

"Yep," Abe replied, looking over their handmade clothes.

"We catch a ride?"

"Sure."

"Can you put it on my account?"

"No problem. Hop in."

Abe untied the plane and was airborne within five minutes. He throttled the engine back to cruise in a vain attempt to cut down the noise, but still had to raise his voice. "What brings you two to town all dressed in your Sunday best?"

"We're getting married," Anna shouted from the bench seat behind Pete, who'd sat up front.

Abe looked over at the Indian man. He was so much like his father. "You are married."

Pete spoke above the engine. "Your government does not think that is so."

Abe ignored the 'your' in front of government. "What?"

"We need to be married to buy a house."

"Sounds like bureaucratic bullshit to me."

"It's the way they do their accounting," Anna moved closer to Abe's ear. "Unless we have a paper saying we are married, the government thinks it never happened."

Abe spoke over his shoulder. "You could have got married at Long Grass, in the church when the priest is there."

Anna looked away. Abe stared at Pete. "Costs too much," he said, looking straight ahead.

Abe had an inkling of what the real reason was but kept it to himself. "Well, hell. This is a honeymoon flight. I can't charge you for it."

Pete began to protest.

"Forget it. Luther paid the freight. Anyway, he can afford it."

Kenora appeared on the horizon. Abe swung right a little to line up on the bay. Fifteen minutes later one of Doc's pilots looped a rope over the left float as Abe shut off the engine.

Cindy jumped in her chair as Abe barged into the office, slamming the door against the wall. "Don't do that to me!"

Abe grinned. "Guess what?"

"I have no idea," Cindy said as the Native couple stepped in behind Abe.

"Pete and Anna are getting married."

"Again?"

"Just for the government."

Cindy shook her head. Nothing the Indian Affairs Department did even remotely made sense in her mind. "Where?"

"At the Justice of the Peace," Anna said.

"Not a church?"

"No," Pete said.

There was such finality in his voice that Cindy decided not to pursue the matter. "Who's standing up for you?"

"Standing up?" Anna asked.

"Yeah."

"I read about witnesses," Anna said, "but nothing about standing up."

"Same thing. Just like a church wedding."

"Who can do this?" Pete asked.

"Anybody that knows you," Cindy said.

"Can you?" Pete asked Abe.

"Sure." Abe turned to his receptionist. "Do you want to work this afternoon or be a bridesmaid?"

"Can't be today. We have two more flights, and don't say cancel them. We can't."

"Okay." Abe looked out the office window. "Doc's got planes sitting. We'll get him to do it."

Cindy threw up her arms. "You're the boss." Looking at Anna's long buckskin dress with fringes and beads, she stood and tugged at her blouse and slacks. "I'll have to change. I can't go to a wedding like this."

"We have to find the Justice of the Peace and ask him to marry us," Anna said.

"You haven't made arrangements?" Abe asked.

"No."

Cindy looked at Abe. He knew what she was thinking. "Give me the phone." He dialed out. "Harry, Abe Williston here. You busy..?

"Good. Can you do a wedding on short notice..?

"No, not mine...

"Later today? Good....

"Pete and Anna Redsky..."

Abe rolled his eyes. "Ojibway. Married two years already...

"They want to comply with the nation's laws, Harry...

"Okay. I'll see they have it. Four o'clock, your office...

"Right, bye."

Abe put the phone down and hung the receiver on it. "He needs some paperwork."

"I have it." Anna produced an envelope. "Everything he needs is in here."

Abe did a short flight while Cindy re-booked the others before going home to change. She returned dressed in a navy skirt, white blouse and an embroidered vest. They all crowded into the old pickup truck, Williston Air Services now owned, and drove uptown.

By four-thirty, Pete and Anna were officially married. Now the Government of Canada would treat them as husband and wife.

Abe drove onto the dock beside his plane. Cindy hopped out, followed by the bride, who wore a soft buckskin dress, then the groom, whose long black hair covered the collar of his denim shirt. As the couple ran to the airplane, Cindy threw rice at them.

FIFTY-ONE

School started in Winnipeg like any other year, kids chummed up with their friends and sat at any desk they wanted or could find empty. Michael had located David in the schoolyard and together they walked inside, found their new classroom then took two seats side by side, three rows from the front.

Their teacher was new this year. With sunlight shining off his carrot-red hair, he stood beside his desk waiting for everyone to be seated. After things settled down, his voice echoed throughout the room, commanding attention. He spoke with a funny accent that Michael later learned was Irish.

"Everybody stand up! Move along to the walls."

There were always those who jumped to it right smartly, but most gathered their things and were bunching up in the aisles, waiting for those ahead to make room along the wall. The teacher's voice boomed again. "Move along, there. When I tell you something, I want it done right away." To emphasize the point, he smacked his right hand on the desktop. Everyone moved a little faster.

"All right," he said, surveying his class, now standing along two walls. "My name is Mr. Donovan. I'll be your teacher for the year." He stepped away from his desk, holding both hands behind his back. "I have a few rules in here. No gum. No running. Anyone talking when they shouldn't gets a detention. You are here to learn." He scanned the sea of faces, stopping briefly on each one. "I expect everyone to pass. Are there any questions?"

No one dared raise their hand.

"Good. Let's get started. I'm going to assign your seats. Atkinson, here." He pointed to the front desk on the window row. A girl in a yellow dress Michael had never seen before, hesitated, then walked over and flipped the seat down before sliding behind the desk.

"Benson, here." Mr. Donovan tapped his finger on the front seat, second row, and so it went until a boy named Wilson was assigned his place.

"The rest of you fill up the last seats." He gestured across the back of the room and five Indian children sat at random as the teacher turned his back and walked up to the front of the classroom. During the first week, a few changes were made. From his desk at the very back, Michael noticed it was the smart kids who got the front-row desks.

Although seated apart, David and Michael were always together on the playground, often with others; running, laughing, shouting, or playing games. Sometimes good-natured teasing would turn serious and a little shoving and pushing happened. When it came to David, who was skinny and the butt of jokes about his pop-bottle glasses, even the older kids tread lightly when they noticed Michael beside him. Fishing with his brother Pete during the summer, and good meals Susan's mother made were showing up. Michael, although not as tall as the older boys, still commanded respect. David walked in his shadow.

"How come you don't answer in class?" David asked, looking through his thick glasses.

"I try." Michael looked at the ground. "I have my hand up when nobody else does for a math question."

David bent over to catch his friend's eye. "He won't ask you?"

Michael looked up. "No."

David straightened up. "Then I'm not going to answer, either."

As the days wore on, it became clear to both boys that Mr. Donovan was teaching the smart kids while five Indians made up an audience in the back.

FIFTY-TWO

Report card day; Michael stood with his head bowed as Susan read his grades. What normally would have been A's and B's were now C's and C-'s.

"This is not like you, Michael."

He said nothing. Susan looked at him. A twinge of nervous emotion spread inside. She knew he could do better. Was he destined like so many other Native kids to be relegated to a life of failure? Not her Michael. She would move heaven and earth to make sure he never ended up like that. Crouching down, she asked, "Care to tell me about it?"

Michael shook his head.

She wanted to scream. He was slipping away, but she knew better that drive a wedge between them. "Maybe later. School can be tough." But not for you, she thought while patting his shoulder. Standing, she resolved to get to the bottom of it.

Next day as the final bell rang, Susan walked into Michael's class. One glance around confirmed her fears. How could the Native kids be expected to learn when they were shunted off to the back seats? Walking over to the teacher, she introduced herself.

The man remained seated. "Surely you're not his mother?"

"I'm his guardian." Her icy reply was lost on him. Damn Irish, she thought, Canada would be better off without them.

"So, what is your business here, Mrs..."

"Two Bears. Susan Two Bears."

"Well, Mrs. Two.., ma'am. What can I do for you?" Disdain dripped from his words.

"I'm here about Michael's grades."

The Irishman stood up, towering above her. Living among the Ojibway, she wasn't intimidated by big men and never gave an inch when he spoke.

"Look, Mrs. Bear, I have a full class of students and there is only so much time to teach them. Those that want to learn get my attention."

"And the others?" Anger crept into Susan's voice.

"They pick up what they can."

"Well let me tell you, sir, learning ability has nothing to do with skin colour. Michael has had very high marks since starting school, my concern is the drop in his grades this year."

"Surely you don't question my ability to teach."

"Not in the least. It's who you're interested in teaching. I don't think Reginald Huntington would be impressed knowing he has segregated classes in his district."

"Don't threaten me."

"Then do something about it." Susan turned and strode out of the room, clenching both hands as her blood boiled.

That evening, she pounced on her father the moment he walked in the door.

"Whoa, girl. Hold on," he said, hanging his coat on the rack. "Come into the living room and talk about this calmly."

Susan followed, controlling herself while he poured a glass of sherry.

"Now, then," he said after seating himself in a velvet-covered, wing-back chair, "what's this all about?"

"Michael's teacher is an Irishman."

Her father's eyebrows raised as he sipped his glass.

"Yes, he's that type of Irishman; big pompous ass."

Henry Strombecker set his glass on the chair arm, holding it by the stem. "Susan, if you have something to talk about besides running down people of different nationalities, then say it. Otherwise let me finish my drink in peace." He closed his eyes lest he convey acceptance. Certainly she had reason to hate the Irish.

Susan sat quiet. What was her father thinking? She knew closing his eyes was something he did to hide his true feelings.

It had all been Timmy O'Neil's fault. She didn't even know what sex was back then. He'd talked her into the bushes at the park one summer evening when she was fourteen. A few weeks later when she told her mother about missing a period, the woman dropped the dish she was wiping. Four weeks later, she told her husband about their daughter's condition. Henry did the abortion himself.

In the years that followed, Susan had fallen into a world of darkness and only the love of Ignace Two Bears had brought her back from the brink of suicide. If it weren't for the Irish she would be able to give her husband a son.

Willing herself to calm down, she drew in a breath and spoke. "As you know Michael's grades have fallen."

Her father nodded.

"I went to the school today. Know what I found?" her voice rising before catching her father's eye. "All the Indian children sitting at the back of the class. Donovan isn't interested in teaching them. They're in his way."

"You know this for certain? You asked him?"

"No, but he said they'd have to learn on their own."

"Michael doesn't have to."

"What do you mean?"

"He has you to help him." Sitting back in his chair, he watched the attitude of his daughter change. When comprehension flashed in her eyes, he smiled and took her hand. "We spent a lot to put you through college. Now, maybe you can't be a mother, but you are a teacher. Do us proud with Michael."

"Oh, Daddy." Susan threw her arms around him, nearly spilling his sherry.

FIFTY-THREE

Imposing as it was, the long division question on the blackboard proved a snap and Michael had the answer worked out in his head even before Dick Mathews made his mistake. Michael wasn't surprised. Although Dick was the smartest arithmetic kid in the class, and therefore Mr. Donovan's favourite student, he had a problem carrying if a nine was involved. Michael had recognized the pattern shortly after the teacher had moved the Indian kids from the back seats. None sat up front, and few were asked for answers, but at least now they felt part of the class.

Dick finished working the problem and placed his chalk on the ledge at the bottom of the slate blackboard. Smiling, he walked to his desk and sat down.

Mr. Donovan got up and wrote the correct answer above Dick's. The boy's smirk vanished. "Anybody know where the error occurred?" He scanned the room for hands. None went up.

Michael looked around, waiting for someone to answer. Sally was as good as Dick. He waited for her.

"Come on, children, it's not all that hard to find." Mr. Donovan folded both arms in front of his chest and waited.

Michael edged his hand up. Mr. Donovan saw it then looked at Sally. The moments dragged on. All the kids behind Michael watched as their teacher ignored his hand.

With a look of exasperation Mr. Donovan pointed. "Okay, Redsky. Where's the mistake?"

"Row three, sir. The six should be a seven."

"Correct." Picking up a brush, he erased the offending figure, then reworked the calculation in white chalk. "Simple subtraction. Good long division requires accurate subtraction." Pointing the brush in Dick's direction, he touched the corrected line. "Keep that in mind."

The recess bell rang. "Tomorrow you'll write the test for the school math contest. Come prepared. I expect someone from this class to win." He dismissed the class with a wave of the hand and thirty-three boys and girls tried to rush out the door at once.

The test was two pages long. Michael finished and put his pencil down. Everyone else had their heads down working the complex arithmetic before them. Even Dick Mathews was still working about the middle of the last page. Michael reviewed the two answers he wasn't sure of, then waited until the papers were collected.

A week later the results were announced.

"Who had top marks?" Susan asked of Michael.

"Dick."

"What did you get?"

"I don't know."

"What do you mean, you don't know?"

"My paper got lost."

Thinking back on her teaching days, Susan could never remember a test paper getting lost.

"I didn't want to be in any stupid math contest, anyway."

Susan could see disappointment through his words. "I'm sure it will show up." In fact, I damn well know it will, she thought.

This time when she found herself standing before the Irishman, she liked him even less. "How can you lose a test paper?"

In response to her question, Mr. Donovan looked pained. "I have many papers to look after. Some are bound to go astray."

"Don't hand me that. I taught for seven years. You don't lose test papers."

"I did these."

Convenient, Susan thought. "You misplaced them." She held his stare until he looked away. "I think a little searching will locate them." Turning to leave, she said, "I haven't seen Richie since college. I think I'll stop by and pay him a visit."

While knocking on the door, Susan read the name plate; Richard Russell. Richie, as she called him, invited her right in. They talked old times, about her life on the reserve, and then Susan brought up her problem.

"Doesn't surprise me. Donovan's a good teacher. Brings smart kids along real well."

"Not all of them."

"I know." He held up both hands. "His class average is no better or worse than any other."

"Richie, he doesn't give one hoot about the Indian kids."

"He has trouble reaching them. We all do."

"I don't."

"Susan, I admire you. We've always got on well, but you know how the system works. We have trouble getting most of the Native children to grade eight. I've still to see one in a graduating class."

"Taking away opportunities like winning a math contest, doesn't help."

Richie Russell sat back. "Dick Mathews got ninety-eight percent. That's only two questions wrong. You think Michael got better than that?"

"Find the paper, then we'll know."

A knock at the door interrupted them. The school secretary stuck her head in, announcing Mr. Donovan.

"Send him in," Richie said.

The Irishman strode across the floor, glared at Susan, then tossed a test paper on the desk. "Found this with some English I was correcting. Thought you might want to see it." Without waiting for a reply, he walked out.

Richie picked up the papers and smiled. "Here."

Susan took them. The name on the top read, Michael Redsky. Beside was his mark. Susan scanned the pages to find the incorrect question. Third on page two. The math was correct, but Michael had carried the decimal one place too many. The mistake left him with a mark of ninety-nine percent.

FIFTY-FOUR

Eatons in downtown Winnipeg had a whole floor dedicated to women's clothing. Diana Corrigan wandered the aisles looking at the latest fashions. What she really wanted was a blue floral-print dress to go dancing in. Ted didn't like her in blue, but that was the least of her worries, he never went dancing with her.

Foolishly she'd already picked out a yellow silk scarf and was now searching for a dress with flowers to match. She'd come close, finding one the right colour blue with a touch of orange in the print. She wasn't fussy about the orange but threw the dress over her arm, anyway.

Another half an hour passed before she found two more she liked on the same rack. Laying the scarf beside them, she decided to take both and tossed the one with orange on top of the rack. The sales people would figure out where it belonged.

After trying on both dresses, she paid for them, bought a pair of silk stockings, then, setting off with her dark-blue Eatons shopping bag, she headed for the elevator. Diana was the only patron, and the operator took her directly to the main floor.

Stepping outside, she was surprised to find the sun low in the western sky. Looking at her watch she could hardly believe it was four thirty-five. Hurrying along Donaldson Street, she had just enough time to slip into a jewellery store and buy a pair of earrings before it closed.

Long shadows lined the streets as the sky turned to evening red. Spring was such a nice time to be shopping in Winnipeg. During the last few winters she'd felt down, nothing she could put her finger on, just a general feeling that life was drifting along. She'd taken up round

184

dancing to break the monotony. Ted wouldn't come and it had only widened the gulf between them. Walking the busy streets she felt alive again.

After eating at a Chinese restaurant, another thing Ted didn't like, she decided to walk to the CPR station. With her train to Kenora not due out for another couple hours, she strolled along different streets, window shopping as the evening air cooled. Such was the state of downtown Winnipeg that within the space of two blocks she found herself passing seedy hotels. Two rowdy drunks stepped out of a beer parlour in front of her. One whistled as they staggered by. The other gave her a good looking over. It was nice to know she could still turn a few heads, then felt ashamed for thinking she was attractive to drunks.

Coming to the end of the block, she rounded the corner and almost tripped over an Indian lying on the sidewalk.

"Hey, lady! Watch it."

Diana detected a familiarity to the slurred voice. Backing up, she was about to go around him when he rolled over and sat up, leaning against the building.

"Johnnie! Johnnie Redsky!"

The Indian looked at her through one eye. The other was swollen shut, the skin puffy from the forehead to the top of his cheek. "Ma'am."

"Gracious. What happened to you?"

"Got into a fight." The words spilled out in a mumble.

Diana bent down and touched Johnnie's eye. He winced. "That's going to show real purple, even against your brown skin." She tugged at his collar. "Get up, for heaven's sake."

He obeyed, and when fully erect, recognized the white woman in front of him. "Auntie Diana!"

She brushed his clothes off as he wavered before her. "What are you doing here?"

Johnnie looked at her blankly then shrugged his shoulders.

"How long have you been in Winnipeg?"

"Three, four days."

The smell of booze drifted into Diana's face. She ignored it. "Where're you staying?"

"No place. Do you have any money you could lend me?"

She waved a hand in front of her nose. "Not for more liquor. When did you eat last?"

"Long time. Couple days ago, maybe." He tried to stand straight and nearly fell into her. "Please, even a dime for a cup of coffee."

"I'll buy you a coffee." Diana grabbed the young man by the arm. "Come along."

As she led, he followed, keeping his arm hooked in hers while they made their way to Higgins Avenue and turned right. It was strange how she felt comfortable walking arm in arm with this Native youth, as old as her son. The son she never had. Grief rushed over her, heavy as the day she had suffered the stillbirth. That was between the two girls. Strange how she'd always wanted a son since her second daughter was born. Somehow, the youth at her side calmed that feeling.

Turning into the train station, they walked between four massive pillars set on bases as high as their heads. Inside, Diana sent Johnnie to the men's room to clean up. She'd finished buying a ticket to Kenora for him and was waiting outside the door when he re-appeared.

Ignoring the looks from passers-by, she took him into the restaurant and bought him a decent meal. She sat sipping tea while filling him with coffee until the train arrived. Boarding the day coach, they took two seats close to the back of the car. Fifteen minutes later, their coach jerked as the steam locomotive up front started the train out of the station.

A sign for St. Boniface flashed by outside as the conductor asked for their tickets. Johnnie looked bewildered as the uniformed man jabbed him in the shoulder. "This man bothering you, Ma'am?"

"No." Diana took a ticket out of her purse. "This is his."

The conductor tore off his portion, punched the stub and stuck it in the window blind. Diana handed him her company pass.

He glanced at it, then, while returning it, said, "Thank you, Mrs. Corrigan." He nodded sideways to Johnnie whose head was dropping forward in rhythm with the coach wheels clicking over the tracks. "If you need any help..."

Diana snatched her pass back without replying. The conductor turned away after giving Johnnie a disgusted look.

Too bad, Diana thought, having another Indian ride on your train. If he was white you'd probably have gotten him a pillow. If he was white, he'd be my son.

She sat back, waiting for the grief that didn't come this time. Johnnie's head rolled against her shoulder and she cradled it with her hand, feeling his smooth skin. She ran a finger down his nose and her world turned back in time.

When she and Ted were first married they had all but lived at her father-in-law's lodge on the lake during the summer months. By the time she was three, Janice kept her grandfather entertained exploring the island. Her mother-in-law Nan, bless her soul, had tried to help her over the blues, but that summer never seemed to end as each day dragged on.

It wasn't until the middle of July that she finally went swimming when a blazing sun in a sapphire-blue sky slowed everyone to a crawl. After much begging, Janice talked her mother into the water. Holding her daughter's hand, she followed as the girl pulled her into the lake. It felt good on her legs. Splashing water on her arms, she walked in until the cold water touched her swimsuit. She could go no further. From deep below, the pain of that dreadful day rose into her heart.

Doctor Payton and Kate had been with her. Sadness, etched onto their faces, whirled into a blur as her baby son was laid on a table and a blanket pulled over him. Only when they covered the tiny face did she realize the horrible truth and scream.

Still screaming, she ran from the lake, up the path and into Nan's arms. Having suffered two miscarriages herself, Nan held her with a tenderness that softened the pain. Diana cried while Nan stroked her hair. It was another week before Diana went into the water, walking along the shore with Janice, finding it difficult to explain again why her baby brother would never come home. After a while Janice stopped asking. Late in the month of August, Diana finally went swimming one evening by herself. The next day, Johnnie Redsky came into her life.

Jack and Jenny had spent the last weeks of summer camped around the point from Charlie Corrigan's lodge. Jack always announced their arrival by bringing his wife and son Pete to Charlie's, along with a Walleye that Nan would cook up for everyone.

Pete jumped out of the boat and fell into the water when Janice called him. Getting up, he ran out of the lake soaking wet to join her and they dashed onto the dock where Charlie shooed them off. Running back, they splashed in the lake under Diana and Jenny's watchful eye.

Jenny remained seated in the flat-bottomed boat as Ted tied it off, and Jack tilted the motor forward. Diana remembered the tikinagan Jenny wore in front of her. Jack helped her onto the dock. As the two women stood together, Diana lifted the flap. Bright eyes looked at her and the beginnings of a smile started to form on the little one's lips. "He's adorable."

Jenny's eyes caught hers briefly before slipping off the straps holding the tikinagan and cradling her son. In that brief moment, the glow of motherhood overshadowed both women.

Diana was so happy for her Indian friend. "May I?" Jenny handed her the baby. "What's his name?"

"We haven't had the naming ceremony yet, but we call him Johnnie."

Running a finger down his wide nose, Diana felt a shiver of excitement. "He's so cute."

Jerked back to the present by train wheels clattering over a set of switches, Diana looked at the sleeping boy beside her. Strange, she thought, that when she first held him in the hot August sun so many years ago, her heart warmed from the cold loss of her own baby.

Why hadn't it made her envious? Maybe it was Jenny's willingness to share her son so freely when hearing of Diana's loss. The evenings they had sat together on the chairs at the camp or on the ground by Jack's tepee. When Diana held the little one to her and closed her eyes, Jenny understood.

Diana's heart healed over the next two years and Johnnie was running around trying to keep up with the older kids when her daughter Rebecca arrived. The disappointment that it was a girl showed when Diana first held her in Ted's presence and a silent chasm opened that, looking back on it now, never closed. Her desire for a son was fulfilled in Johnnie and she lost all interest in having any more children.

⚜

"Next stop, Keewatin." The conductor continued through the coach repeating the same refrain. During the short run from Keewatin to Kenora, Diana woke Johnnie, gathered her things and walked him to the vestibule at the end of the coach. After the train stopped she stepped off the stool placed at the bottom of the stairs and took a deep breath of the night air.

The Corrigan's Dodge was still parked behind the depot, Ted always walked to the yard office from home. He was sitting in the kitchen when they walked in. Diana dropped her shopping bag on the table.

Ted glanced at it before pointing at Johnnie. "Where'd you find him?"

Diana detected a touch of malice in his voice. Well, too bad for him if he couldn't give her a son. "Winnipeg."

The Native youth stepped beside Diana. "Hello, Mr. Corrigan."

Ted acknowledged him with a nod, put his glasses back on and went back to reading his latest *National Geographic* magazine.

"Upstairs, young man." Diana pointed the way.

Walking in front of her along the hallway, Johnnie passed the bathroom. "Oh no you don't." Diana grabbed his shirt and steered him toward the door. "You get yourself cleaned up before you crawl between my clean sheets."

Johnnie obeyed, closing the door behind him. Diana stood outside until she heard water running. He was singing an old Ojibway song when she finally walked along the hall to her room.

What little tenderness there was between her and Ted had died after Rebecca was born. Gradually, Ted's insensitivity, aggravated by his drinking, drove them apart and she moved across the hall into her sewing room. Opening the door, she looked on its single bed. The chasm it symbolized had now grown too wide to bridge.

Next morning, Ted was gone when she woke Johnnie and fed him breakfast. "I phoned Abe Williston. He said he'd fly you home when he went down for the fish. We have to be at the dock by ten o'clock."

Johnnie grunted while finishing the oatmeal she'd made him.

"More coffee?"

"Yeah."

"Yes, please."

He looked at her, then away. "Yes, please."

She filled his mug from the stoneware pot and poured herself one before sitting opposite him. "Why aren't you in school?"

"I do not go to school any more."

"But you need an education."

"Why? Only white kids get jobs."

"Now, you know that's not true."

"Where do Indians work?"

"You tell me."

"They hunt and fish. Some are trappers or guides."

"That's because they have little education."

"If I learn and become smart, will Mr. Corrigan get me a job on the railroad?"

They both knew the answer to that. Diana touched his hand. "Your great Chief Saskatcheway gave up land so you could have an education. You owe it to him to learn. Even if you don't fit into the white man's world you'll still be better prepared to raise a family."

"No woman will want me."

Diana studied the youthful face, finding its Native features quite attractive. "Why ever not?"

"Because I lived at the residential school. All I learned was pain." He thumped his chest with a fist.

"They beat you, didn't they?"

"Yes, but I do not let that bother me."

"What does?"

Two tears slipped from his eyes. "It is the pain Father LaFrenier caused that would make women ashamed of me."

As his head dropped onto both arms, Diana felt a pounding in her temples. She understood the meaning of his words. Men. They were always destroying a piece of her world.

FIFTY-FIVE

Lumber for Pete and Anna's new house arrived by barge, and two white carpenters were hired by the Indian Agent to build it. The fact that they were related to him went unmentioned.

A touch of frost nipped the air one mid-September day when Pete and Anna moved out of their little cabin into the new frame house with a separate bedroom.

Many were the memories the log cabin held. Pete stood in the doorway looking at the lake, remembering the day he'd made a little pail for Ruth out of a tin can. After punching holes near the top, he'd tied a piece of string through them for a handle. She played for hours on the beach, shoveling it full of sand with an old spoon.

He'd miss the view and the gentle sound of lapping water. His new place faced north at the end of a row of houses clustered together on a flat plain, well away from the lake. Cold winds blew from the north. It was not good to face a house north, but others beside them did, so Pete accepted it, reluctantly.

Ruth toddled over to him. Bending down, he picked her up. She squirmed in his arms while he nuzzled her with his nose. Anna came out of the cabin to stand beside him. He put Ruth down and wrapped an arm around his wife.

"I will miss this place."

"Every time you bring your boat in, you will still see it."

Pete patted her bottom. "That is not what I meant."

Anna thought back over the two summers, visualizing the good times: the winter blizzards when they snuggled under warm furs, lying

192

naked and uncovered on hot summer nights, their midnight swim under a full moon. She loved the man standing at her side, loved his confidence, his tender touch. "Time to go," she said softly.

"Yeah."

Anna bundled up her son, resting him on her hip with one arm. Pete put little Ruth on his shoulders, while she giggled and laughed, they walked to the new house. That night Pete and Anna made love in a separate bedroom.

⁂

Nine months later, as spring flowers blossomed under a warming sun, Joseph Paul Redsky came into the world. After Anna's mother had washed the baby and wrapped him in a blanket, she handed the little bundle to her son-in-law. It warmed her heart to see him coo and cuddle his son.

Pete ran his hand over Joseph's dark brown hair, still wet to the touch. Gently he placed a tiny hand between his thumb and forefinger, surprised at its strength. Touching the flat little nose, Pete drew his finger over the two broad lips which opened to let out a wail.

"He has good strong lungs," Pete said.

"Must take after his grandfather," Anna's mother said. "He is always bellowing about something."

Pete stepped over to Anna, propped up on their bed. She radiated a glow he'd seen only twice before in his life.

That night while Anna nursed Joseph, Pete walked outside and after the first star appeared, stretched out his hands and thanked the Great Spirit. In the morning, he bundled his nets into the boat and went fishing.

⁂

During the coming weeks sunlight warmed the earth, heralding planting season. With no garden behind the new house, Anna continued to use the plot behind the cabin by the lake. For one thing it was close to water. While baby Joseph slept in the tikinagan, she spaded the soil.

Ruth came running over with a worm. Anna noticed dirt around her mouth and was about to say something when she looked over to see the girl's brother putting one in his mouth.

"John Mark, stop that!"

The boy paused, looked at his mother, then went back to stuffing the worm in his mouth. Anna walked over and lifted him off the ground. Ruth followed and watched as John Mark started chewing.

Anna put a finger in his mouth, prying open his lips. "Spit it out."

He shook his head, trying to get away.

"Spit it out! You do not eat worms." Anna wiggled a finger into his mouth and scooped out dirt and the half-eaten worm, now a mush of pink flesh. Ruth stomped it into the dirt with her bare foot. Baby Joseph woke up and began to cry. Setting John Mark down with the command, "No more worms," Anna went over, took her baby out of the tikinagan, and breast fed him while the other two splashed around in the cold lake water.

Blueberry season was a washout. Berries were few and small. One night Pete speared a hundred-pound sturgeon by torchlight that made up for the lost blueberry money. Life was good as summer turned into autumn. Winter snows arrived early and when the first cold snap came in December, Pete was prepared for it with a pile of wood cut and stacked outside the back porch of his new house.

FIFTY-SIX

Trapping beaver had been an Indian occupation for as long as Pete could remember. He didn't really care for it, especially skinning the animal. A deer was different, they ate the meat. Stripping the hide off these industrious little animals so some white man could wear it as a hat, Pete felt, must offend the Great Spirit. He apologized for each one he took, which lately, were few and far between.

Instead of spending the winter trapping with his in-laws, Pete decided to place a few traps within a days journey of the reservation. He'd probably only catch a couple beaver, and maybe a mink or marten. He'd be happy with that because what he really wanted to do was make his own fishing net.

Luther had ordered the twine, which now sat in the house begging to be knotted into a three-hundred foot gill net.

Anna didn't go with Pete to visit her parents on the evening before they were to leave for the winter trapping grounds. She'd spent the day helping her mother pack and was dead tired. After putting the children on a bed that lay along one wall of their single-room living area, she sang lullabies until they were asleep, then lit a coal-oil lamp with a match and fed the baby. When he was asleep, she got out a needle and began sewing beads on a dress for Ruth.

Pete should have known better. He'd often had a few beer while visiting or working with his father-in-law Alex. On the rare occasion he drank whiskey, he always ended up drunk. It wasn't really a crime on the reservation. People still got up the next day and carried on with their lives, although with the splitting headache Pete always got, he wondered why they kept doing it. Then he thought of his mother.

When Alex brought out the bottle of whiskey, he should have left but about that time his brother Johnnie walked in with a second one. Pete decided to stay for just one drink.

Whereas Johnnie got sullen when he drank, Pete found himself becoming angry and violent. His father-in-law, on the other hand, was a happy drunk and in the words of his wife, "Kept making a fool of himself all night."

Pete began talking with Johnnie about their mother when they were well into the second bottle.

"What do you care?" Johnnie's tone carried overtones of malice.

"I care. She is my mother, too."

"So why do you not come around?"

"I am busy."

"Doing what?" Johnnie shouted.

Pete wasn't sure of the real reason he didn't often visit his mother. He hated the constant drinking, but that wasn't it. Through his foggy mind, the thought that she blamed his father for all her troubles kept rolling to the fore.

If Pete was going to blame anyone, it had to be, "Father LaFrenier," he said out loud.

"What about him?" Johnnie asked, his words slurred.

"He is to blame."

"For what?"

"You know." Pete's voice rose. He looked into his brother's eyes, half shut, but spiteful. "He killed our father."

"The police did, and you do not talk about Father LaFrenier that way."

"After what he did to you?"

Johnnie rose out of his chair. "Shut up."

Pete stood, steadying himself with one hand on the couch.

"He is a man of God," Johnnie shouted.

Pete's head went light and began spinning. "Look what he did to our mother."

"I hate him," Johnnie yelled, running at his brother. "I hate you." He swung a fist at Pete. "And Anna. She thinks she is better than our mother."

"Leave Anna out of this." Pete drove Johnnie between the eyes. "You deserve Father LaFrenier," he shouted as his brother dropped to the floor. Pete tried to kick him, but missed and fell beside him. Getting up, he tried again and put a boot into Johnnie's ribs. "And this is for your god." He kicked him a second time and felt the satisfaction of hearing a rib crack.

Alex pulled him away. Pete stumbled backward and they both fell over the couch. Pete punched his father-in-law, then crawled to the door. Reaching up, he opened it and fell down the porch steps into a pile of fresh dog shit.

Anna heard the door open and looked up from her Bible. Seeing it was only Pete, she went back to reading. When the door slammed loud enough to make baby Joseph stir on the bed across the room, she sensed something terribly wrong.

A hand grabbed her Bible. She hung on, refusing to let go as Pete shouted, "Give me that."

"No, Pete!"

"Give it to me."

Anna felt the book being ripped out of her hands. "No!" she screamed, looking in horror at the torn pages she was holding in her left hand.

"Here is what I think of your god." Pete held the book in one hand and lifted the cover on the stove with the other.

"No! Please, Pete, no!"

Staggering to one side as Anna rushed at him, he swung a fist at her and collapsed in a drunken stupor. Anna reached down and picked up her torn Bible.

Morning sunlight streaming into the small kitchen window hurt Pete's eyes. His nose twitched as a revolting smell drifted from his body. Rolling up on one elbow, he saw Anna, her back to him, sitting at the table. There was no sign of the children.

"Ooh," he groaned. Anna's head moved to one side, but didn't turn around. Standing up, Pete held his head. His hands stunk. Looking down, he saw his shirt covered with dog dirt.

"Anna." He felt embarrassed calling her name. Taking a step forward, he brushed the lid holder on the stove, sending it to the floor. The pounding in his head as he bent over forced him to squat and pick it up. Setting it back into the metal cover, he turned to his wife and froze, staring at her puffed up face and darkened eyes.

Anna's soft voice cut him down. "You broke your promise."

Tears welled in Pete's eyes as he fell to his knees. "I am sorry." Covering the tears streaming down his face with stinking hands, he kept repeating, "I am so sorry," until Anna could stand it no longer and went over to comfort her man.

FIFTY-SEVEN

Diana picked up the ringing telephone expecting to hear the French voice of her sister Genevieve. The call came a little earlier than usual, she had just put water on to boil for tea. Genevieve, four years older, had retained a lot more of her French Canadian heritage than Diana, who, after living with Ted and his parents for twenty years, had acquired a taste for English things, Nottingham lace and Earl Grey tea in the morning. Her French conversation with Genevieve to catch up on local gossip usually lasted through two cups of tea.

Placing the receiver to her ear, she switched on the stove and said, "Hello."

The voice at the other end spoke English. "Hello, Mrs. Corrigan. It's Cindy." In the background the sound of an airplane engine drowned out her voice. "Hang on a moment." A door slammed, muffling the noise. "There, that's better. Abe radioed, he wants you to meet him here at the dock when he gets in."

"Did he say why?"

"No. He just said for you to be here when he lands on a flight from Long Grass in about twenty minutes."

"Okay, tell him I'll be there."

Diana hung up. Abe wanted to see her. Something deep stirred within until she remembered he was coming from the reserve. Reaching out, she turned off the stove and ran upstairs to change into a dress. Silly thing to do, she thought, he's probably bringing in some baskets of blueberries and wants me to have the first pick.

Putting on a light cotton dress, she smoothed it over her flat tummy, then reached for a bottle of perfume and dabbed a little under her left ear. As she grabbed her purse from the kitchen table and dashed out the door, her phone rang again. Genevieve would have to wait.

At the foot of Second Street where the float planes docked, she squeezed her car in between an old beat-up truck and a concrete wall. Abe's silver and red Norseman was taxiing in from the lake, its spinning propeller a blur in the bright morning light. Hurrying to the spot where he would park, she stood under a warm blue sky, cool breeze brushing her face, the scent of lake water drifting on the wind.

Seeing Abe's face behind the windscreen, she waved as he turned the plane and reached over to shut off the engine. Diana watched the floats bump against the dock. She could almost taste the blueberries.

Mid-morning air blew the dress against her legs as Abe opened his door and jumped down onto the float, took a rope, and tied it off. Diana reached out and held the wing strut while he secured the rear of the float. Standing up, he walked over to her, his brown wavy hair reflecting the sunlight until he stepped under the shade of the wing where Diana waited.

"Hello, Diana." He gently lifted her hand off the strut. At that moment Diana looked into his eyes and felt a twinge in her heart. It turned to the stab of a knife when he spoke.

"Johnnie Redsky is dead."

Her hand went limp in his. As she fell against him, he encircled her waist with both arms. She'd fantasized being here, but not like this. Her head settled on his shoulder, the fragrance of perfume faint in the air. Her cheek lay against bare skin where his shirt opened.

Abe felt a trickle of warm tears between them, and Diana's arms drawing tight around him. When he stroked her black hair, she looked up at him.

Diana stared into his hazel eyes. Eyes she'd almost forgotten. Hector's eyes. Turning her head sideways, she leaned on him again. "How?"

Abe drew a breath as the woman he held pressed against him. "He took his own life."

Diana stiffened. "Oh, Lord!" Relaxing in his arms, she was content to be comforted by the man whose eyes so reminded her of Hector, her only true love. And now this. Why was it the men who meant so much to her were always dying? At that moment she hated God for taking them.

Abe continued stroking her hair. "You okay?"

"No." She let her arms drop.

He released her, then guided her into the office. Cindy, sensing something wrong and seeing Diana's tears, brought some tissues. They sat in the waiting chairs.

After wiping her eyes, Diana spoke first. "How did it happen?"

"You don't want to know," Abe said.

Diana rounded on him. "Tell me. I want to know."

Abe resisted. Cindy reached to touch her shoulder.

Diana withdrew her arm. "He was the closest thing I had to a son. I have a right to know."

Abe looked away, out the window into the near perfect morning, pale-blue sky, slight breeze rippling wavelets on the water, reflecting sunlight in a dazzle of dancing diamonds. It was all too beautiful to be ruined by this. "He shot himself."

"How?"

"He's dead, Diana. It doesn't matter how it happened."

"It matters to me." Digging her nails into Abe's arm, she saw him looking at her with comforting eyes and the rage inside subsided. "Please," she said, releasing his arm.

"If you have to know, he put a shotgun in his mouth and pulled the trigger."

Cindy gasped.

Diana settled back into the chair. "Well, at least he didn't suffer."

"Here, Mrs. Corrigan." Cindy offered her the glass of water.

"Thank you." After taking a sip, Diana handed it back. "It wasn't his fault."

Cindy looked at Abe, who gestured her to remain quiet.

"The church killed him, or more precisely, Father LaFrenier," Diana said.

Alarmed at the allegation, Abe took hold of her hand. She turned to him. "I'm sorry. I shouldn't have said that." Standing up, she smoothed her dress. "I should be going now."

Abe stood. "You sure?"

"Yes," she said putting her hand on his. "I appreciate you telling me. I'll be fine."

"I can have Cindy drive you home."

"No, thanks. I'll be fine, really." She started outside. Abe followed her to the car and opened her door. Diana stepped into the opening.

Abe took her elbow. "You will be all right, won't you?"

That deep feeling she hadn't felt in years swelled in her heart. She leaned over and kissed Abe on the lips. Did they feel so much like Hector's or was it just her imagination? Getting in, she inserted the key in the ignition and turned it on as Abe closed the door.

"If there's anything I can do..." His hand rested on the open window.

She ran her fingers along his. "You're so kind. Thank you."

As he stepped back, she pushed the starter pedal with her right foot. Driving up the hill, she saw him in the mirror as he turned and walked back toward his office. When he disappeared, a rage welled up inside she couldn't control.

FIFTY-EIGHT

On the day Johnnie Redsky was buried, Abe flew a plane load of people to Long Grass for the funeral. Diana sat beside him in the front. Kate, and six relatives from Manitoba filled the bench seats along each side of the cargo area. Father LaFrenier looked out of place among them and was still seething about having to give up the front seat to Diana when Abe taxied to the dock at Long Grass. Pete Redsky came running down to meet the plane. Two of his cousins got out and helped an old Native lady down the ladder. When she turned and stepped onto the dock, Pete wrapped both arms around his paternal grandmother.

Diana remained seated, watching through the window as a family gathering assembled on the dock. When Father LaFrenier appeared in the plane's doorway, the commotion died down. They opened a path for him to walk through, then followed as he led them to the church.

Still inside the plane, Kate jabbed Diana in the shoulder. "You coming?" She climbed out.

Diana reached over and took Abe's hand.

"You'll be fine," he said.

She nodded and opened the door. Pete met them at the church entrance and escorted Abe and Diana up front to a pew behind Jenny. Abe sat down and watched as Diana went up to the casket. Although he didn't know the whole story, Abe understood Diana's need to see the young man. Ted hadn't been much help. Since Jack's death, he'd pretty much abandoned any of the Indians he knew. It was a disturbing trend.

Abe could see a chasm developing as the older generation of Natives and whites died off.

⊰⊱

Diana stood in front of the open casket looking at the youth she had so loved, yet not really known. Cradled deep in pillows to hide the shotgun damage, Johnnie's skin, which should have been tan, looked ashen grey. She reached out and touched his hands clasped together. All that came to her was the coldness of death. He was asleep she told herself. In spite of what the priest was going to say, she knew his soul wouldn't flit off to heaven, but would become one again with the earth. She let go, knowing Mother Nature welcomed him in a way no earthly woman could.

Turning, she walked over to Jenny. How the sands of time had worn away her youth. Once long hair, brilliant in the sun and flowing over her shoulders, now, but for a few strands of silver, lacked luster as it hung limp and unkempt. Harsh lines, etching her leathery skin, revealed lonely nights spent with a bottle. Dull eyes, that caught Diana's for only an instant, brightened when she leaned down to give her an embrace.

"I'm so sorry, Jenny."

The Native woman said nothing, although she returned the hug.

"We'll talk later."

"Yes."

Diana squeezed her, then sat in beside Abe.

True to her prediction, Father LaFrenier eulogized Johnnie Redsky then sent him to heaven. Diana preferred to remember him here on earth: young, smiling and laughing, playing with her girls while she and Jenny had picked blueberries, the times at Charlie's lodge when they had made heaps of crepes with the fresh berries. Nan always had a bottle of real maple syrup hidden that she brought out for such occasions. By the time it was empty, the kids had purple tongues and sticky faces.

Ted and Jack had smoked with Charlie on the front veranda as she and Jenny washed dishes. Nan dried and placed them in the cupboards. Later, as the sun set in the western sky, they watched the kids fish off the dock. Diana caught herself smiling as she sat in the church picturing the four of them casting their hooks into the lake. How nobody got snagged with treble hooks was a miracle.

First time Johnnie fished he was four. Diana had given him a little kid's rod and reel for his birthday. She remembered his eyes growing huge with excitement and his teeth, white in a wide grin on his tan face. She patted him on the bum as he turned and ran onto the dock. Imitating his older brother, he swung the rod back and flung the lure over his head. It landed at his feet. Diana could still see him fiddling with the reel, then, picking up the lure, and running off the dock.

"Auntie Diana, Auntie Diana." He handed her the fishing rod, its line snarled into a tangle.

Sitting on the veranda steps, she took the reel off the rod. "Well, let's see what we can do with this." Johnnie watched as she untangled the line and rewound it. "There you go," she said, finishing the task and giving the rod back.

As he started to run back to the dock, his mother called him. "What do you say?"

"Thank you, Auntie," he replied without breaking stride. Two minutes later he was back, tears in his eyes and the line snarled again. Diana dried his eyes with the tail of her blouse, then undid the line once more.

Handing him the rod, she took his hand. "How about Auntie shows you how to cast?"

"Yes!" He tugged her toward the dock.

She could see herself leaning over the little boy, holding his hand as she had helped him cast when those gathered for his funeral knelt down to pray. She hated this part but knelt anyway, pretending to pray to a god who allowed her to be beaten, took her beloved Hector away, and charged too much to bury her father. Surely Mother Nature wouldn't act like that.

Jack's only surviving brother and three of Jenny's relatives carried the casket to the grave. Afterward, Diana and Abe walked over to Jenny. Detecting the faint smell of alcohol, Abe held back as Diana embraced the woman whose son had so comforted her over the years. Jenny took her by the hand, and after giving Abe a wicked look, led her away.

<hr />

Long Grass Reservation has seven miles of shoreline bordering the Lake of the Woods. Occasional steep cliffs fall into the lake, but in many places brush and trees grow to the waterline. Scattered between are beaches of sand running into small bays full of cattails. Following a well-worn path, Jenny and Diana broke out of the trees to stand on a crescent-shaped beach with rushes and reeds along the shore. Here in the solitude of nature, broken only by the odd cry of a Redwing blackbird, Jenny unloaded the emotional burden she'd been fighting since Jack's death. Diana kicked her shoes off and stepped into the cool water up to her ankles as Jenny spoke.

"You must hate me."

"Why ever would you think that?"

"I am a drunk. I lost my daughter, and could not look after my sons."

"It's not your fault, Jenny."

"Yes it is. Jack would never have left to get the boys if he did not trust me to look after the babies."

"Jack planned on coming back."

"I knew he would not. The spirits showed me in a dream the night of Pete's naming ceremony."

Diana felt the waves lap at her feet. Visions and naming ceremonies, Indian traditions she could see disappearing. Was it good or bad? Was it any different than the church with its christening? She concluded they were the same thing. "You still have Pete and Michael."

"Do I? Pete was so much like Jack before going to the residential school. What he went through there made him bitter. I thank the Great Spirit for Anna."

"What happened to them at the school?"

Jenny shook her head.

"Please. Don't let Johnnie's death be in vain."

Jenny took a small bottle of whiskey out of her coat pocket. Diana was about to protest until she caught the warning look in Jenny's eyes. After taking a long swallow, the Indian woman revealed how the church was stripping the Native children of their culture and desire to work. Pete's strength kept him safe, but it had alienated him from her. Her words devoid of emotion, she confided the personal secret Johnnie took to the grave. By the time she was finished, the bottle was empty. Sitting on a rock with both hands between her legs, Jenny let her head drop forward and started leaning sideways. Diana moved to catch her.

"Do not touch me!" Jenny's voice was loud and slurred. She slapped Diana's hand away.

"Jenny, please." Diana moved toward her.

The Indian woman tried to get off the rock and fell in the sand. Diana bent down and took hold of both shoulders. Jenny swung an elbow in her ribs, broke loose, and rolled onto her back.

"You white people killed my Jack." She broke down sobbing.

Diana took a step forward. Jenny kicked her in the leg.

"Abe took Bethy. The church killed my boy."

"Jenny, please..."

"You did nothing while your white priests destroyed Johnnie's life. He should have died like your son."

"You can't mean that!"

"Get away from me." Rolling onto her hands and knees, she crawled across the forest floor. "Go away. I do not need you." Getting up, she staggered into the trees.

Diana's heart felt like stone. Looking up into the sky, she cried out, "Why did you let this happen, God?" Falling to her knees, she sobbed, unaware of the water caressing her legs.

FIFTY-NINE

After the funeral, Abe found Kate at Singing Dove's house and that's where he learned what happened to Bethy. He'd been told the old Indian woman was over ninety. It was beyond his ability to fathom someone being born in the mid-eighteen hundreds still alive today. The years had not been kind to her. What white hair she had was thinning and still streaked with grey. Deep lines crisscrossed her face, vertical ones marked her upper lip and chin. When she smiled at him, brown stubs showed where teeth used to be. Raising a hand gnarled with arthritis, she beckoned him to approach.

"Come, young man." Taking his hand, she held it between both of hers.

With two fingers, Abe touched the wrinkled skin covering the back of her hand as he spoke. "I'm sorry it has to be on such a sad occasion."

"Johnnie is still with us. We watched his body for three days. He will do us no harm. Look into the rocks, or the trees and birds. You will find him there."

Better than being in heaven with a bunch of white people, Abe thought in a macabre moment.

The old woman released his hand. "You did the right thing taking Bethy. I worried about her."

Only then did Abe realize he hadn't found out what happened to the girl. Why? Too busy? Poor excuse. He looked across to Kate, a woman exuding confidence. Things always turned out well around her. Still, he should have inquired before now. "How is she?"

"Fine," Kate said. "We got her just in time."

"Good. I should have asked. Where'd she get to?"

"The Children's Aid Society placed her in a foster home. Doc Payton had no trouble signing the papers after amputating the tips of two fingers."

Abe winced. "I'm surprised it wasn't worse."

"Us too."

"She is with white people?" Singing Dove asked.

"Yes."

"They are good people?"

"I think so. They want to adopt her."

"She is gone." The old woman closed her eyes. "I see no vision for this child."

"Are you saying she will die?" Abe asked.

Opening her eyes, Singing Dove reached up and touched the side of his face. "We all die." After a moments pause, she went on. "Bethy has left our Indian world, but I feel her happiness. It is long." She made a sweeping gesture toward the sun.

That was good enough for Abe. He waited while Kate fussed over Singing Dove and trimmed her nails. "I can give you something for the pain if you like."

"Save it for white people." She pointed with a crooked finger to the shelf beside her sink. "I have good medicine from the forest."

Kate put her things away then took the woman's hands in hers. "I'll see you on my next visit."

"I will not be here when you come."

"You're leaving?"

Singing Dove gestured skyward with both hands. "I will be with my ancestors."

Kate believed it, and bent down to embrace her old friend. "God be with you," she whispered, then walking to the door, waited for Abe to open it.

He followed her out. "This is getting to be a depressing place," he said, stepping beside her.

Kate took his arm. "We're slowly destroying these people."

"Why?"

"Nobody cares."

"We care, Kate."

"We don't count, and when the bureaucrats do, what happens? They tear their social fabric apart." She kicked a stone down the road. "I send their kids to white families. You fly booze in, and their kids out to schools that are systematically ripping away their Native tradition. What dignity do they have left?"

Diana hoped she was on the right path. With the lake visible on her left, she felt certain the reserve lay ahead, but the return trip seemed to be taking too long. Her shoulder stung where a dead branch snagged her dress, ripping open the material and scratching the skin. Blood seeped through the fingers of her left hand as she held the torn cotton over her arm.

Jenny's words couldn't have hurt more if she'd cut her heart with a filet knife. All the memories, gone. The times at their summer camp around the point from the lodge. Their kids, speaking two different languages, playing together as she and Jenny cleaned blueberries and put them into baskets Jenny later sold in Kenora.

Breaking out of the trees, she saw the houses. Kate and Abe were walking down to the plane. She called his name.

Abe turned as she approached. "What happened to you?" Diana collapsed in his arms.

"Where are your shoes?" Kate asked.

Diana looked at her feet, dirty, scratched, and bleeding. She hadn't realized she was barefoot. "I don't know. I must have left them at the beach."

"Where's Jenny?" Kate picked pine needles from Diana's hair.

"I don't know?"

"What do you mean, you don't know?"

"She ran off into the bush."

"Why?" Abe asked.

"She hates me."

"That's not true," Kate said.

"She hates you too, Abe," Diana said, pulling him closer. "She hates all of us white people."

"Well, can you blame her?" Kate said. "We've pretty well destroyed her world."

Diana knew she should let go of Abe. It wouldn't take long for Kate's suspicions to be aroused. But she couldn't. "We haven't wrecked it, the church has."

"Be serious," Kate said.

"I am. She told me why Jack wouldn't let his boys go to the residential school." Letting go, she moved away from Abe. "It's horrible, and I'm going to do something about it." Diana looked at Abe. "Can we go home now?" She stared daggers at Father LaFrenier, sitting in the front seat. His smug look told Abe he wasn't moving. Abe guided Diana toward Kate, who helped her in the back of the plane.

When the Norseman lifted off the water and climbed into a sky billowing with thunderclouds, Diana vowed she'd never return to the reserve again.

SIXTY

Pete Redsky fell into depression after striking Anna, but her forgiveness was kind, and she helped him feel worthy of her again. He never drank after the incident. Wouldn't have liquor in his house, and refused to let Anna's family in if Alex, or anybody else, carried a bottle or even smelled of drink. Visits to his mother were limited to times when she was sober, as a result they became quite rare.

When flocks of geese flew north the following spring, Anna announced she was pregnant again. Ruth was in her terrible threes, John Mark was walking, and Joseph crawled around trying to catch him.

Pete enjoyed playing on the floor with his kids before they went to bed. Anna moved the curtain aside and looked out her window as she finished the dishes. She could see the new garden plot waiting for warmer weather. The western sky turned a soft red then increased in intensity as orange took over, casting shadows inside. Life was good.

Letting the curtain fall back, she dried her hands and walked over to the stove. Taking the kerosene lamp down, she removed the glass. Striking a match, she held it to the wick then, once the flame had taken, blew out the match and dropped it in the wood box.

Together, they put the children down on the bed across the room, just out of the lamp's glow. Anna read her Bible while Pete worked on a little pair of moccasins for John Mark. When Anna finished reading, Pete blew out the light and followed her into the bedroom, shutting the door behind him.

When he awoke, his heart pounded fiercely in his chest. Strange sounds came through the bedroom door. Then he smelled it. Smoke.

"Anna!" Tearing the blankets off, he leapt for the door. Smoke curled underneath, crackling sounds came from the other side. Grabbing the hot knob, Pete yanked the door open. Clouds of noxious fumes billowed into his eyes and nose. Anna screamed.

Pete took a step forward. "Ruth!" he hollered as fresh air crept under the smoke.

Pete choked. "John Mark! Joey!" He couldn't believe the smoke stinging his eyes was so hot.

"Mommy," a little girl's voice called.

At that moment, the room ignited into a fireball that roared out of the smoke, singeing Pete's hair and burning his bare chest.

Anna cried out for her babies as flames engulfed the kitchen, driving Pete back. Anna rushed to the open door and the flames beyond. Pete caught one arm, throwing her off balance.

"Let go!" she screamed, trying to shake loose her husband's grip. "No! God no. Please, not my babies."

"Anna!" Pete's voice was lost in the roar of flames, now burning into the bedroom. He dragged her to the window, but when he let go to smash the glass, she ran back to the flames. Chasing her down, he picked her up by the waist.

"Let me go." She beat him across the back. "My babies. Please, Pete. No!"

Afraid to let go, Pete held her with both hands and kicked out the window with his right foot. Blood flowed from a gash in his ankle. Anna, choking and crying, struggled against him. Smoke stung his eyes. He could feel the heat burning his back. Holding Anna with one hand, he smashed out all the glass, and while shoving Anna through the opening, he looked around to see flames eating at their bed, then jumped out to see Anna running beside the house. Glass cut his feet as

213

he took off after her. Rounding the front corner, he saw flames burning through the front door.

Anna ignored them, trying to open it. "My babies! Oh God, not my babies. Ruth!" Pete reached her side. "John Mark! Joseph!" She left seared flesh on the doorknob as Pete pulled her away from the burning house.

Once safely away, he stood watching orange flames flare in the smoke that curled from under the eaves. Cradling his wife as she cried on his chest, he remained immobile as the roof collapsed, sending a shower of red embers ascending into the night sky.

Church bells ringing in the distance signaled the village of a fire. One by one, the walls fell into the inferno. People started arriving, some with buckets of water.

One woman placed a blanket over Pete and Anna's shoulders. There was nothing else she could do except stand beside her daughter as the fire consumed her grandchildren.

SIXTY-ONE

A be was whistling Yankee Doodle off key as he pumped out the floats. Looking through the cross braces he noticed the Coroner, and a Mountie, followed by the Fire Chief, walk onto the dock. Whenever those three were together, tragedy wasn't far behind. Hopefully they'd walk across the seaplane base to Doc's.

They didn't, entering his office instead. Sighing, he replaced the float cover, stood up and stored the pump, then walked over to the office. Inside, Cindy was booking their flight.

"Abe, these gentlemen have to go to the Long Grass Reserve."

"Right away, I imagine."

"Yes." She put her pencil down.

"You can drop us off and come back later," the Coroner said.

"How's that work, Cindy?" Abe asked.

"You'll have time to fly them out now, you've got a short break around four."

Abe turned to the Coroner. "Four-thirty, five, sound okay?"

The official nodded. On the flight out, he mentioned they were investigating a fire involving three deaths. Abe remained in his seat at Long Grass as the men got out.

It was an ideal day for flying, not too warm, not too bumpy. Alone in the cockpit on his way out to pick up two prospectors he'd dropped off before break-up, he rested his hand on the controls and let the plane fly itself.

Looking down, Abe saw a bald eagle soaring about three hundred feet below, its white head and tail brilliant in the sun. Watching it angle under the left float, he knew why he'd taken up flying. There couldn't be another job in the world that offered the exhilaration and freedom he had. Two loads of supplies to Blindfold Lake Lodge, followed by a flight north for the Fisheries Department filled out the day. After refuelling, he flew out to Long Grass, landing there well after five.

His three passengers stood waiting on the dock. He didn't bother getting out after shutting down. The RCMP Officer turned the plane after his two companions climbed aboard. When he was inside, Abe fired up the engine, taxied out, then lifted off for Kenora.

During the flight home, Abe learned the details of the fire. It turned an otherwise beautiful day rotten, and he fell into a melancholy silence, wondering how to break the news to Cindy. She'd take it hard.

Cindy knew something terrible had happened when her boss walked through the door. She rose from her chair as he walked over. "What?"

"Pete Redsky's place went up in flames."

"Anybody hurt?" Her eyes searched for the answer.

Abe looked at his secretary. Where would he be without her? She was tough with flight schedules, easy going with customers, and, what would he say, soft? Yes soft, displaying a human touch in what was a very demanding business.

Cindy found herself reading Abe's message. She'd seen that look on rare occasions, always accompanied by heartache.

"They lost their three kids."

"Oh God, no!" She fell against his chest, allowing Abe to wrap her in his arms. "How's Anna taking it?"

Cindy would ask about Anna. Abe wondered how Pete felt. Poor kid. He'd worked so hard for everything. Jack came to mind. Why didn't those men get the breaks they deserve? He stroked Cindy's hair. "I don't know. Hard, I guess."

Cindy reached her arms up under her boss's and tried to imagine the grief Anna was going through. "Any idea what caused it?"

"The Fire Chief figured it started in the wood box. The story is that Anna lit a lamp and threw the burnt match into the box."

"Oh, God," Cindy said as her eyes misted over.

SIXTY-TWO

Abe flew in a priest for the funeral. Someone must have passed along word that it not be Father LaFrenier. The young man in brown habit sent to do the service sat on the bench seat behind Abe. He never spoke on the flight out. Cindy sat in the front, holding flowers she'd bought.

Waiting at the dock was a crowd of mostly older women. They followed the priest as he walked to the church looking a little apprehensive.

"I'll bet this is his first Indian funeral," Cindy said, waiting for Abe to tie off the float.

"One funeral is much the same as another," he replied, without thinking. He stood up to see her glaring at him.

"This one is for three little kids."

"I'm sorry. It's just that..." He let it trail off.

Taking Cindy's arm, Abe walked her to the church where she placed the flowers beside three small coffins, hand-built of rough wood. After offering condolences to Anna, she walked down the aisle to join Abe in the back row. A bell rang in the steeple, and soon after the church was filled with mourners.

The young priest began reading his sermon from notes resting on his Bible. To Abe it sounded devoid of emotion. At least Father LaFrenier spoke with feeling. In fact, he thought, the only thing he did respectfully for the Indians was bury them. Abe half listened as the priest droned on about good people, and mansions, then said God needed three more angels in heaven.

"No!"

All eyes turned to Anna.

Jumping up, she shouted, "I needed them." Pete reached for her arm. She shook it off. "No! He can't have them." Breaking down, she ran from the church, tears streaming down her cheeks. Following her out, Jenny Redsky hurried to catch up. Abe watched as the young priest, more annoyed than shocked, went back to his manuscript sermon.

Jenny caught up with Anna as she dropped to the ground in front of the church, rocking back and forth on her knees, scraping up dirt and rubbing it in her hair. Crouching down, Jenny put one arm over her shoulder. With the pain of Johnnie's loss biting into her own heart, she understood how Anna felt. Taking the grieving mother in her arms, Jenny held her daughter-in-law close. Anna's face was wet with tears against Jenny's neck. She felt them hot on her skin before Anna looked at her.

"Why? Why did God need more angels?" Jenny had no answer. Anna looked up to the sky, raising her voice to heaven. "I would have cared for them, Lord. Didn't you know how precious they were to me?" She fell to heaving sobs as singing started inside the church.

Moving around, Jenny held Anna's face in her hands. Softly she spoke. "They're with their grandfather."

Anna looked at her mother-in-law. "In heaven?"

Jenny shook her head. "In the Land of Souls."

Anna broke into a wail as the church bells rang. When the coffins were brought out, the two women stood. Anna kissed each one as it passed on the way to the graveyard, then allowing Jenny and Pete to help her, followed the three men who each cradled a little coffin in his arms.

They were all placed in the same grave. The priest, seeing Anna stare at him, said a quick ashes-to-ashes phrase and left. Pete reached down and put Ruth's tin-can pail on one of the coffins, not knowing if it was hers, but it didn't matter. The pail was the only thing that escaped the fire. Ruth had left it in the garden.

SIXTY-THREE

Pete and Anna stayed with his mother. Two days later, Jenny and a bunch of relatives spent the night drinking and fighting. Pete gathered up what few possessions people had given them and moved to Anna's parents place. Next night the same thing happened there.

Getting up early, Pete took Anna to their little cabin by the lake. He fixed a few holes in the roof, covered the tiny broken window, and re-hung the door. Inside, Anna cleaned out the cobwebs and mice nests, then spread out the blankets Luther and his wife had given them. Pete brought in two blocks of wood for chairs.

After lighting a fire in the rusty airtight heater, Anna boiled water and made coffee. Pete looked around. It wasn't much, but it was a start. Love would make it a home. Anna reached over and took his hand, placing it on her belly. He felt the baby kick.

A boy, Anna was going to call Luke, was born in the middle of a cold winter night. The little cabin was cozy warm and filled with joy as Anna's mother washed the baby, wrapped it, then handed it to Pete. Folding back the blanket, he touched its nose, getting a wail in response. Standing with his back to the stove, Pete silently thanked Kitche Manitou for a healthy baby. Later, when Anna first nursed him, she tried to thank her God, but couldn't find the words.

Pete refused to let the boy be called Luke. At his naming ceremony Ignace Two Bears gave him the name, High Elk.

Pete was kind and Anna no longer poured out her grief, yet, he could feel the guilt eating inside her. He went fishing in the spring and life in the little cabin settled into a routine.

Looking out her window one early summer day, Anna could see two white women making their way along the path to her cabin. They each carried a handbag. High Elk was sleeping, so when they knocked she opened the door. Both radiated a friendly smile putting her at ease. The taller of the two ladies spoke, introducing themselves and asking Anna what it would take to make her happy.

When she replied that having back the three children she lost was what she most wanted, the short woman spoke up saying she understood. She'd seen her youngest son swept away in a flooding river.

"Where is he?" Anna asked. "Did God take him to heaven?"

Reaching in her bag, the woman took out a book. "Let me show you what the Bible says."

Anna touched the book, her fingers drawing comfort from its cover. She hadn't seen a Bible since hers was lost in the fire.

Kindly, the woman opened it to St. John, and told her about Jesus weeping over his friend, Lazarus. Anna knew the story, that Lazarus was a good man, and no doubt went to heaven when he died, but was surprised to learn that he was only sleeping. Turning back a few pages, the older woman handed the Bible to Anna, asking her to read a few verses. It was the story of Jesus raising the widow's son. "The Lord brought both these people back to life here, on earth. When your children awake in the Land of the Living, which Jesus called Paradise, you'll hold them again, my dear."

Anna felt an inner peace she had not known since the fire.

SIXTY-FOUR

Michael Redsky was not the first Native to graduate from Earl Grey School, but he was the first boy to do so. The previous year an Indian girl whose parents lived off the reservation had passed grade eight. This year another girl had passed, but it was Michael's graduating that warmed the heart of Richard Russell, Earl Grey's principal.

Susan had faithfully tutored and guided Michael through elementary school. Each winter, Ignace had gone trapping before coming to Winnipeg for Christmas. As the years went by, he stayed later and later, until this year, when he had not returned. He'd become involved with a small group of Native people helping the increasing population of Indian men at the Stony Mountain Federal Penitentiary. As he poured out the misery his Native brothers suffered to Susan at night, she was encouraged by his positive view toward a problem with few rewards.

Today she sat beside him in the gymnasium waiting for the graduation ceremonies to begin. Susan squeezed her husband's hand, now turning soft as the calluses wore away. "I'm so glad you're here."

"Jack would be proud."

Susan looked to the woman seated beside her. What did she think? Did she share Jack's desire to see Michael educated in a real school. Jenny Redsky, her short hair now streaking gray, skin drawn, eyes tired, displayed no emotion.

Once it was certain Michael would pass grade eight, Susan went back to the reservation and made arrangements for Jenny to come to

Winnipeg for Michael's little graduation ceremony. As much as Susan loved the boy, he was still Jenny's son.

Since arriving at Susan's parent's home, Jenny hadn't touched a drop of liquor. It now showed with a subtle tremor in her hands. She sat through the first rounds of applause until Susan nudged her in the side. By the time Richard Russell's homemade diplomas were given out, Jenny had shed some of her shyness and when Michael's name was called, she was the last to quit clapping. Susan's heart filled with a comfortable feeling of contentment.

People milled around the gymnasium after, congratulating their sons and daughters, and visiting with other parents. Ignace, Susan, and Jenny, stood by themselves, waiting for Michael to arrive. Richard Russell, working through the crowd, spotted them and came right over. "Congratulations, Susan. You must be proud. We've waited a long time for this."

"He's only the first, Richie. There'll be more as the years go by." Taking Jenny's arm, she moved her forward. "This is Michael's mother."

Richard's eyes brightened. "This is a pleasure, Mrs. Redsky. We really wanted to see Michael succeed. I think we all owe a debt to Susan for her hard work in helping your son through the difficult times."

Jenny allowed her hand to be held by the tall white man before her as she listened to his words politely, all the time looking at the hardwood floor. "He is a good boy."

"I'm sure he'll do well in high school," Richard said, turning to Susan. "He is going, isn't he?"

"Oh, yes!" she said, rising on her toes, looking for Michael. Spotting him, she jumped a little while waving and calling his name.

Michael, standing with David Croft, waved back but waited until Mr. Croft had finished speaking. David's father then ushered the boys along and they came running over.

Michael beamed with delight as he reached for Susan. She quickly kissed him on the cheek before steering him to his mother. Michael stood before her, not sure of what to say. As conversation continued to fill the gym, mother and son stood, waiting for the words to come.

"This is my best friend, David," Michael said.

"Hello," David said, a beaming smile crossing his freckled face.

"He passed grade eight, too. Next year we're going to the same high school."

"That is nice. Hello, David."

"Hello, Mrs. Redsky. My Dad said I could visit Michael on the reservation this summer."

"Can he come? Please." Michael turned to Susan who motioned her head toward Jenny. Looking again at his mother, Michael asked, "Please?"

She nodded an agreement.

"Great. See," Michael said to David, "I told you she'd say yes."

"Let's go tell my Dad."

The two boys left, spoke briefly to Mr. Croft, then disappeared into the crowd.

SIXTY-FIVE

"You have to come with me." Diana placed her hand on Kate's wrist. "I can't handle that man alone."

Kate didn't answer.

Diana sat back. In the subdued lighting of the Kenricia Hotel's dining room, much of Kate's concern was hidden, but, Diana knew, in the end her lifelong friend would help.

Over a lunch of chicken salad, she'd told Kate of the abuses going on at the residential school. Talking around, she was now convinced the government was trying to wipe out the Indian way of life using the church-run schools. It was common knowledge that the Native children in these places weren't allowed to speak in their own language, or dance, or sing.

"You've been out there, Kate. Have you ever seen one of those kids laugh?"

"No."

"You know why?" Diana asked. "I'll tell you why. They've been robbed of their childhood. They go to church twice a day and work the rest of the time."

"That's a bit of an exaggeration."

"My foot." Diana banged her fork on the table. "These kids go to school for years and they can't read. They know how to cross themselves, but," she leaned forward, "they can't read."

"Calm down. I'm on your side, remember?"

Diana took a sip of water. "I really need your help, Kate."

225

"Okay, okay. What do you want from me?" Kate asked, stabbing at her salad.

"Medical proof of sexual misconduct."

Kate spit out a mouthful of half-chewed lettuce, catching it in her hand. "Good God, Diana! I can't give you that." Dumping the mess on her plate, she wiped both lips with a napkin. "Those records are personal and confidential."

"I don't need records. I need to know if I have medical backing for my allegations."

"You do," Kate said, without hesitation.

"Can you get me Johnnie's medical file?"

"You have to be next of kin."

"He was a son to me."

"In your mind, maybe, but not according to the law."

"You know how I felt about him."

"Do I? I'm a nurse, not a mother. Medically speaking, I'd say you're becoming unbalanced."

Diana started to interrupt. Kate put up her hand. "But as a friend, I'd say you're strong minded and you have a cause."

"Sounds like a dangerous situation."

"You don't know the half of it. You're going to need someone to back you up, gal."

"You'll do it?"

"Was there ever any doubt?"

Diana paid the bill, and they drove out to the residential school. Father LaFrenier was in his office.

"Come in, ladies. Please sit down. To what do I owe this visit?"

"Business," Kate said.

The smile disappeared from his face. "Oh." He sat behind his desk.

"Some of the children at this school are showing signs of unnatural behaviour."

The priest's eyes narrowed. "I'm not following you."

"This is the boy's section of the school with priests as teachers, is it not?"

"What's your point, Miss O'Brian?"

"The boys are being sexually abused."

"I'm not aware of that."

You liar, Diana thought, then said, "Johnnie Redsky carried proof of it to his grave."

"Well he's dead, isn't he?" A faint smile crossed the priest's lips as he placed both elbows on the desk, touching the tips of his fingers together.

Before Diana sat a man who exuded the confidence of someone untouchable. "Don't you hear his spirit talking?" she asked.

"I don't believe in ghosts."

"This ghost says he was beaten severely the morning Abe Williston and I arrived to talk to the boys about their father's death. His shoulder was laced open and bleeding."

"You have no proof of that."

Diana opened her purse and took out a white hankie. Carefully unfolding it, she displayed the dried blood stain. Kate leaned forward to look at it.

Father LaFrenier only glanced at it. "So?"

"So, do you want to know why you beat these kids? Does it take two women to tell you what you do to little Indian boys?"

The priest jumped up, his face flushing crimson red. "Out!" Pointing to the door, he ordered, "Get out!"

Diana slowly folded the hankie and placed it in her purse. "This is only one of the pieces of evidence I have. Do you think you can leave a trail of broken kids behind and no one knows?"

"Don't threaten me."

"We're not," Kate said. "We're here to give you some advice." She opened the door and Diana walked out. "Have your people tested for venereal disease."

Father LaFrenier picked up an ink bottle. Kate ducked out just before it smashed against the door frame, spreading black ink everywhere.

SIXTY-SIX

David Croft waved over the conductor's shoulder when he saw Michael on the station platform. While the boys made plans of all the things they were going to do during the summer, Ignace went inside to claim David's baggage. The trio walked across manicured grass surrounding the station's flower garden, cut over to Main Street, then walked down to Second Avenue, and onto the seaplane dock.

David couldn't believe he was going fly in an airplane. The flight ended all too soon at Long Grass when Abe taxied up to the dock, crowded with a dozen or so kids. David followed Michael out of the plane. Everyone tried to get his attention, calling out his name and saying theirs. A couple of the older girls giggled while touching his red hair. As this was going on, Ignace turned the plane.

David watched as the engine came to full power, spinning the propeller and sending water spray between the floats. As the plane roared across the water, shivers ran down his spine. David decided he was going to be a pilot when he grew up. Before Abe even had the Norseman up on the step, most of the Indian children, who'd seen the plane hundreds of times, were already leaving the dock.

"Come on," Michael said.

David refused to budge, watching the plane until it disappeared in the sky, then following his best friend up the path.

Ignace took them to his house.

"My Mom doesn't have room," Michael said.

David shrugged. "Okay."

He got a big hug when Susan met them at the door. "Hi, David."

228

"Hello, Mrs. Two Bears."

Susan looked at him, a crease forming between her eyes. "It's Susan. Everybody here calls me Susan, young Mr. Croft. So you can, too."

"Okay."

Scooting the boys inside, Susan told Michael to show David their room. David took his suitcase from Ignace and followed Michael into a small room Ignace had made by hanging blankets from the ceiling. A single bed took up all the space.

"We're both going to sleep in that?" David asked.

"Why not? When I was little, I slept with my two older brothers."

"Can we go fishing with your brother Pete?"

"Sure."

"Great." David set his suitcase down.

"Want to go swimming?"

"Yeah!"

"Okay, come on." Michael left the area by swinging a blanket aside. David followed after getting his swimsuit.

The favourite place to swim was a rocky beach that had a cliff along one side and a bit of sand on the other. Michael led the way through the trees. The sound of kids yelling and playing got louder until they broke out of the woods. Michael took off his clothes and headed for the water.

David was looking around for a place to change when he realized all the kids were naked. "Michael!"

His friend stopped at the water's edge.

"Don't we wear swimsuits?"

"Nah."

Seconds later, all David saw was Michael's brown butt as he dashed into the lake. Sure that the girls were watching him, he hesitated. Seeing he was ignored, David took off his pants and shirt and ran into water up to his neck. No amount of coaxing could get him to come out and jump off the cliff, even if the girls were doing it.

In the coming days, none of the Native kids noticed his skin was lily white, or that it burned to the colour of his red hair. He was Michael's friend, and that meant he was their friend, too.

SIXTY-SEVEN

There was no place to park in front of the *Daily Miner and News* on the hot, muggy day in August, so Diana drove around the corner and walked back to the newspaper office. Gary Kirkland, the newspaper's editor, wanted to see her. His phone call came three days after she wrote a letter to the editor outlining the abuses taking place at the Rabbit Lake Residential School. She had a very good idea what he wanted to talk about.

Diana had known Gary since he was a fair-haired kid with pimples. Like everyone else from her youth, grey had crept into his hair. He'd also put on considerable weight. Seeing Diana through his glass door, he waved her in before she could knock. Smiling with his lips closed as he'd done since high school, he offered her a chair.

"Good of you to come. How are the girls?"

"Janice's in Ottawa working for the government. Rebecca's starting high school. And your mother?"

"Still the same. Hasn't moved out of bed since her stroke. The doctor says there's no hope for recovery."

"I'm sorry."

"I see Ted at the train depot occasionally. He still running the big boat?" A faint grin came to his lips.

"Yes." Diana made her voice sound cool knowing Gary had been on the occasional boat-bash in the *Foxey* with her husband, usually in the company of his young secretary. "He bought me a small run-about." Diana shifted sideways, crossing her legs. "This a social visit, Gary?"

Leaning back in his chair, he swivelled to his left, then back. "No, it isn't. Your letter came across my desk yesterday."

"Will you print it?"

"Of course not. We're not about to put those sort of allegations in our paper."

"They're not allegations."

"Whether they are or not is a moot point, but that's not the reason I asked you in."

Diana knew in a flash what was coming next. The Kirkland's owned a front pew in the church. It was expensive. Her family had inquired of it once. Gary was also well placed in several church auxiliary organizations. Obviously the letter wasn't sitting well with him. Well, she'd see just how much he valued free speech.

"This sort of thing," he said, picking up the letter, "can upset a lot of people."

"You don't think I'm upset?"

"I'm talking influential people."

"Your advertisers."

"The church. Father LaFrenier takes this personal."

"So he should."

Gary ignored the barb. "The mayor takes it personal."

Third row pew, Diana thought.

"The Chief of Police takes it personal."

Second row, right side.

"The Children's Aid Society takes it personal, and so do the medical people. You create a lot of enemies writing this stuff."

"Every bit of that is true."

"Even if it is, you don't print it in the newspaper," his voice filling the room.

"So, you won't print it."

"Absolutely not."

"I'll take out an advertisement."

"We have only so much room for ads. I think you'll find there isn't room for yours."

"Maybe I'll find a reporter to do the story for me."

"Not at this paper."

"I was thinking of Winnipeg."

"Think twice about that, Diana."

"Gary, you disgust me. There are kids whose childhood is being denied them, and you don't think it merits mention in your paper."

He leaned forward. "Indian kids. The government is providing them with an education. Do you seriously think it's going to teach them Ojibway and how to rain dance?"

"Don't be so facetious."

"I'm not. We teach them Christianity and English. What they believe and speak is of no use in our society."

"So you're saying they have to adopt our ways?"

"Or disappear as a people."

"They will, anyway."

He smiled, lips still together. "Now you understand."

"So why doesn't the government force the French to become English?"

"They're already Christians."

"I'm French-Canadian. Look at the colour of my skin, it's white."

Gary slammed his fist on the desk. "Dammit, Diana, I didn't ask you in here to argue about race discrimination. Here's your letter back." He threw it across to her while getting up. "File it in a deep drawer, better yet tear it up." He stepped around her and opened the door. "So nice of you to drop by," he said, loud enough for the office staff to hear.

"Bastard," Diana hissed in his ear as she walked out.

SIXTY-EIGHT

O n the south side of the rail yard, about halfway between the depot and the roundhouse, sat a Tuscan red building with a basement and a set of wooden stairs up the back leading to the main floor that opened to the north at track level. This was the CPR Yard Office. From here, twenty-four hours a day, 365 days a year, crews arrived and departed to move the trains east and west along the great trans-continental railway. Boxcars were reassigned and switched throughout the yard. Tank cars were spotted at the bulk plants, gondolas laden with coal, weighed and sent to the coaling tower. Steam locomotives coupled onto long strings of freight cars and hauled them to Ignace or Winnipeg.

At the center of all this activity sat Ted Corrigan, Senior Yard Master. After his brother Hector died under the wheels of a rolling freight car years ago, Ted had transferred to the non-operating side of things and now occupied the top seat overseeing Kenora's yard.

This night it was plugged solid. Ted was short on locomotive power, and the passenger train was late. Running a railroad certainly wasn't getting any easier now that the German's had started another war in Europe.

Burt Jensen, foreman of the switching crew, broke his thoughts. "Ted, where are we going to put this train load of grain Foster is bringing in from Winnipeg?"

"Where is it now?"

"Keewatin."

234

"Shit." He couldn't put it in the siding there, the Keewatin Transfer had the tracks tied up with cars for the two flour mills. He'd have to send Tom McCain out ahead of Number Eight. Ordering the grain drag to depart, Ted told the operator to get a hold of the dispatcher and send the train out.

Five minutes later, Tom walked into the Yard Office. "What the hell's this?" He waved the onionskin papers in Ted's face.

"You still here?"

"I'm not going."

"To hell. You're not staying in my yard."

"There's no way I can get to this siding before the passenger train catches me."

"Number Eight's late."

"There isn't time."

Ted knew there was, and felt his ears prickle. It was a wonder he didn't have high blood pressure. "Those are the goddamn orders you've been issued, now get out! I need the tracks your train is sitting on."

"Bugger you."

Ted jumped up, sending his swivel chair rolling back across the room. "The sun can roll up into a ball of shit and fall from the sky driving your caboose five-hundred feet into solid bedrock. But it's not going to happen in my yard." He walked past Tom into the operator's room. "Bring Foster through Keewatin. We'll have room for him in ten minutes." He looked up at Tom.

"One day, Corrigan. One day." He pulled on his gloves and stormed through the door.

As it worked out, Foster's drag contained some of the new steel cars and was too long for the siding. Seven cars had to be shunted onto the repair track. Ted caught a ride on the switch engine as it headed west. He stepped off while it was still moving and walked the rest of the way to the depot.

Spotting the seven cars delayed Number Eight's departure by nine minutes. Ted pressed a button, ringing a bell signaling the conductor, and any late passengers, that this train was leaving. J D Riley hollered,

"All Aboard," and picking up the footstool, stepped onto the vestibule stairs as the train started moving.

Bad enough she was now thirty-seven minutes late, but on top of that, Ted had no transportation back to the yard office. Walking through the snow past the freight sheds, illuminated only by night lights, he turned into the darkness and started across two sets of tracks leading to the coal sheds. Following a string of boxcars, he reached the last one, went behind it and stepped over the rail. Next thing he knew, his face was driven against the cold steel car as both hands were pinned behind his back.

"This is your only warning." Hot breath drifted against his right ear. He twisted in his captors' grip only to have his head pulled back as the voice spoke once more. "Tell your woman to stop investigating the residential schools."

The voice was coarse and low, but there was no mistaking who it belonged to. Ted's stomach started to churn.

"We mean business." To prove it, his head was dragged back then his face slammed into the boxcar. Ted could feel hot blood flowing down his cheek.

"Stop her, Corrigan, or the CPR will be looking for a new yard master and it won't be quick like Jack Redsky." A severe blow to the mid-section drove out all his air. Ted doubled up in the snow, gasping for breath.

He lay sucking short little gasps of air as three sets of boots crunched off into the snow. What had Diana gotten into? Well, he'd put a stop to it. When his breath returned, he hauled himself up, leaned against the boxcar for a moment, then made his way back to the yard office.

SIXTY-NINE

Diana woke with a start as her bedroom door flew open and banged against the wall. Light from the hall bathed her room, silhouetting a man in the doorway.

When he moved, she realized it was Ted dressed in his pants, suspenders hanging down each side. Curly black hair, which she'd always despised because it held the smell of sweat, stuck out of his undershirt, covering his shoulders and chest.

"How dare you..."

"Shut up." He took a step forward. Pulling the blankets up under her chin, she glared at him in the semi-darkness. She'd never allowed him to be with her in this room and wasn't going to start now.

Reaching out, Ted took hold of the blanket and her nightgown. She felt herself being dragged upright. "What have you dug up about the residential school?"

She shot him a fierce look. "What do you care?"

"See this?" He bent over her and touched the raw gash on his cheek. "That's what I care. Whatever you've found, get rid of it." He let go and shoved her away. "Stop looking."

"I'm not going to stop just because you..." Her head snapped sideways from the force of his fist smashing into her cheek and temple. Diana could feel her eyes watering, growing wide as fear rose in her stomach. They'd fought before, but he'd never struck her. She sat paralyzed, staring at him.

"I'm getting death threats and I'm telling you to quit looking into the residential schools."

"You don't care what happens to those kids."

"I care about me."

Anger replaced Diana's fear. "Oh, be serious."

"Look at this." He pointed to his face. "You think these people aren't serious?"

"So you want me to let these kids continue to be abused..."

"They're not our kids. They're Indians."

"Jack Redsky's kids are Indians."

Ted grabbed her by the arm and half lifted her out of bed. A button popped on her nightgown. "Listen to me." Spit flew from his mouth as the fingers of his right hand dug into her arm. "You will stop this business, period."

Diana felt the hand loosen. She fell out of bed when he let go and walked out. Then standing in the doorway, he turned. "I'll back it up with this," he said, showing her his fist. The door slammed and Diana found herself in darkness.

She was thankful for the dawn, knowing it was useless to stay in bed any longer. Sitting up, she felt the side of her face that had been throbbing all night. It was sore above the eye and down across her cheek to the jaw. While doing this, her diamond wedding ring that had turned sideways was digging into her finger, the pain triggering a flood of emotion under her heart. Taking hold of the ring, she began working it off her finger. Like a chain, tying her to a loveless past, she wanted to be rid of it.

Once it was off, she rubbed it between her fingertips. Maybe she had to put up with Ted, but she wasn't going to let his ring shackle her any longer. Flinging it across the room, she heard it tinkle against a perfume bottle and fall behind the dresser.

Rolling over, she puffed the pillow and laid her head on it. When a tear slid out of her eye, she knew it wasn't for Johnnie, or last night's fight. She missed Hector.

Sunlight streamed in through frost on her window, old man winter's designs on the glass diffusing the light, painting her room orange. Climbing out of bed, she stood in front of the dresser unbuttoning her nightgown, letting it fall. The figure reflected in the mirror had lost some of the firmness of youth. Only she would know as whenever she was with Ted in his room, the lights had to be out.

Reaching for the second drawer on her right, she pulled it all the way out and rummaged through some personal items at the back, finally locating a small dark-blue velvet box. She stood up while opening the lid. Coming alive in the sunlight was Hector's engagement ring. Without hesitation she slipped it on her finger, holding her hand out and rotating it in the light to make the facets dance. Beyond was the mirror. She was thirty-eight years old but felt like twenty and, except for the purple eye, made the naked figure in the mirror reflect it.

After a long bath and dressing, Diana made tea. Taking her second cup, she went into the living room and sat at her desk. Pulling the half-written letter out of her Underwood typewriter, she crumpled it up and tossed it in the wastebasket. Newspaper clippings, hand-written documents, and copies of letters she'd written followed. A search of all the drawers turned up a few odd items that she also threw out. Sitting back, she sighed. So this was where it ended: people's lives, children's lives destroyed, now the evidence she felt could bring justice was to follow.

Picking up the wastebasket, she walked over to the kitchen stove and after emptying its contents, placed the iron lid back in place as flames ate at the papers. Revealing the injustices and abuses perpetrated on Johnnie Redsky and his Native schoolmates would have to wait for someone else to expose.

SEVENTY

Stepping out into the chill of a late February morning, Diana held the collar of her beaver-skin coat up under her chin. Taking a deep breath, she allowed the bitter cold air to sting her lungs. Stepping off the porch, her feet crunched in virgin snow that had fallen overnight and squeaked under every footstep as she set out on a journey to nowhere. She just wanted to be alone with her thoughts and memories.

Crossing the bridge, she walked along the frozen edge of Laurenson Creek to Seventh Avenue, then followed the street south to Anicinabe Park. It was a popular beach, but with most of the summer spent at the Corrigan lodge, they hadn't come here much. If they wanted to be in a crowd, a visit to her parent's farm on the Winnipeg river for a family reunion would fill that bill. As a girl, she hadn't been allowed to go near the river. None of her sisters knew how to swim. Ted had taught her when Janice was born. They'd done a lot together as a couple, but then she'd felt their marriage beginning to drift. Today, they stood on opposite shores.

Alone in the expanse of white, she felt a sense of contentment, a feeling of purity conveyed in the snow. Low on the horizon a water-colour sun cast its light on her face, any warmth she felt came from inside as Hector's memory ran rampant in her mind: his smiling face, the gentle touch of his hands, his never-ending chatter in her ear. This day she only heard silence.

The left side of her face began to sting. Touching it, she realized Ted's bruise had swollen and was hurting in the cold. At least it would stop the purple bruise from spreading. Off in the distance, St. Mary's Residential

School came into focus through the trees. She felt unclean. Turning, she walked out of the park toward Fourth Avenue.

Skirting the forestry buildings, she came to Abe's winter base. Walking into the office, she found Cindy reading a *Colliers* magazine.

"Hello, Mrs Corrigan." Unsure how to respond to the black eye and swollen cheek Cindy stared at her. "You okay?"

Diana turned to hide the bruise, nodding her head.

"What brings you out on a day like this?"

"Just out for a walk. Is Abe around?"

"No. He flew up to Lac Seul." Looking at the clock, Cindy said, "I expect him back in forty-five minutes. Do you want me to call him on the radio?"

"Good gracious, no! Let the man do his work."

"Can I make you some tea?"

"Thank you. That's very kind." Diana took off her gloves, then on a whim, asked, "Does he have any more flights today?"

"No, just this one. When he comes back I'm going home. My folks are coming down from Winnipeg."

Once tea was made, Diana suggested that Cindy leave early. She'd watch the office until Abe arrived. Thirty minutes later, his Norseman roared overhead. While it circled to land, Diana put on her coat, went outside, and walked down to the ice.

Abe taxied up beside her and shut off the engine. Opening his door and stepping off the ski landing gear, he smiled and waved. Diana waved back. Feelings long suppressed began stirring inside.

"Hey, Diana!" He ran over to her. "Good to see you." Noticing the bruise, his eyes settled on her for a moment. She unconsciously covered it with her hand. Although he let it pass, his voice lost some of its cheerfulness. "Let's go inside."

Abe made fresh coffee as Diana told him about last night's fight with her husband. Diana couldn't understand why she poured out her troubles to him, but his kind listening ear encouraged her to relate everything: the destruction of Ojibway culture, their language and identity, even the burning of her research about the residential school mistreatment of kids.

"That's a shame." He placed his hand on her shoulder.

241

She never heard him say, "Somebody needs to tell the world," because blood pounded in her ears and a chill ran down her spine in spite of the warm room. Abe noticed her not listening.

"I'm sorry," she said. "I was thinking of something else."

"I said, it's a shame about your papers. Somebody needs to tell the world what these people are doing."

"It'll never happen."

"They can't threaten everyone."

"True, but with a war being fought in Europe, who's going to care about a few Indian kids."

Abe got the point. They sat for some time before he went over and poured another cup of coffee. With his back still to Diana, he set the pot down. "I've sold my plane." He turned to her.

"Why?" Deep inside, she felt dread curling into a knot.

"Well, a couple of reasons." He sat down beside her. "The war mainly."

"Oh, God! You're not going to sign up?"

"No, no. Nothing like that. The federal government is subsidizing a big mining company in Yellowknife to look for uranium."

"Uranium?"

"Yeah. I wondered about that too, but money seems to be no object. They paid me what I bought the plane for. I'm to fly it up to Slave Lake before spring break-up."

"How soon is that?"

"Three weeks. The paper work is done. I'm just waiting for the signatures and the money."

He'd be gone in three weeks. Diana's heart grew cold. Why? She searched the memories of long ago, then knew why. "Take me up for a flight."

Abe looked at her.

"Right now. Please. I'd like to fly with you alone. I've never done that, you know." She could see Abe thinking and willed him to say yes.

"You're right." He stood up. "Okay. I'll have to fuel up first."

She followed him outside and stood watching as he climbed up and filled both wing tanks. How he reminded her of Hector.

Diana hung onto her seat frame as the Norseman roared across the ice, skis hopping and dancing over its uneven surface. Twenty seconds later, Abe pulled back on the controls and she felt her stomach drop as the empty plane pointed skyward and lifted into the frigid winter air. She watched the ground fall away until Abe leveled off high above the frozen lake below. Settling back in her seat, she was content to let the world she knew disappear in the miles behind.

Abe was flying toward Long Grass Reserve. When Diana realized this, she told him to turn away. She just didn't want to go there. Dropping the left wing, he banked south and flew across Falcon Island toward the American border, then east over Aulneau Peninsula and gradually turned north. They came close enough to Sioux Narrows that they could see it in on the eastern horizon. Shadows were growing long when they turned for home.

Diana stared out the side window at the ground. Abe glanced her way occasionally, once he caught her looking at him. She smiled and reached over to touch his hand. Noise from the thundering radial engine and wind rushing through the struts faded to a whisper as she realized what the touch meant.

"Kate's cottage is below. Can we land there?"

"Is this what you want?"

"I know I don't want to go home, just yet."

Abe circled back and set down close to the snow-covered dock where wind had exposed the ice. Diana got out as he shut things down, then stepped out beside her. She took his hand and breaking through knee-deep snow on shore, led him toward the chalet-style log building.

"Kate's father built this himself," she said as they approached. "He cut down all the trees, peeled them and notched the logs without help. Kate said he was still working on it when she was little."

Abe looked up at the peaked roof as they climbed snow-covered stairs to the porch. Beneath a coat of clear varnish, the logs looked freshly peeled. Diana stamped snow from her boots and walked past the door. Reaching up, she felt along the chinking, found what she was after, and took down a key.

Inside, the living room opened beneath a vaulted ceiling. Stairs led up to a loft. Half the end wall was a massive stone fireplace. Soot above the mantle told of fires long dead. Stacked along each side were piles of split wood.

Abe lit a fire.

Not until after the sun went down did the room begin to warm, even with a large crackling fire burning away, it took another half hour before they removed their coats. Diana melted snow and brewed coffee. Abe brought in his emergency pack from the plane and, along with what Diana found in the cupboards, they put together a meal worthy of summer camp.

Sitting on the bearskin rug in front of the flames, they ate and talked and laughed until the wood burned down to glowing ruby embers. Abe placed more logs on the fire and soon it was a crackling blaze, warming the room. Diana leaned against him when he came back to the rug. Resting her head on his shoulder, she remained silent, staring into the flames, into the past.

Jumping up, she went into the bedroom and returned with blankets and two pillows. "It's freezing in there." Spreading the blankets before the fire, she undid the two top buttons on her sweater, kicked off her boots, and laid down. Abe slid in beside her. She nestled against him as he drew her close and kissed her.

Afterward they lay together, watching a fire that had again burned to embers. Diana, her bare shoulders above the covers, looked at the ring on her finger. Sensing Abe's interest, she said, "It's Hector's." As a satisfied smile crept across her lips, she settled under the blankets. After all these years, she knew what it would have felt like being with the man she truly loved.

Abe stared into the dark fireplace where embers glowed as little pinpoints of red light.

PART TWO

SEVENTY-ONE

Intermingled with shades of purple, red, and yellow, Northern Lights danced before a green curtain spread across the night sky as Abe Williston waited for the last passenger to board his flight. Slowing as he approached, the Native man stopped in front of Abe.

"Hello, Mr. Williston."

The stranger's voice echoed a familiarity from ages long past as the pilot studied the young man standing before him: black eyes, alive with fire, pupils surrounded by a fringe of gray. He should know them.

Wearing a buckskin coat, blue jeans, and hiking boots, the man remained motionless as Abe searched the recesses of his mind. Overhead, the aurora crackled.

Finally, he introduced himself. "Michael Redsky."

"Michael! Michael Redsky. Well, I'll be.., it's been a long time." Abe reached for his hand. "Last time I saw you was..."

"Winter of 1940." Michael responded with a firm handshake.

"Right." Abe thought back over the years. "You were still a kid. I sold my Norseman the following spring."

Michael nodded with a smile.

"What brings you to this part of the world?" Abe asked.

"Business."

Abe looked at his watch. "We gotta go." He stepped aside allowing Michael to board, and while following him up the aisle to his seat noticed the scar about an inch and a half long covered in white hair running above Michael's ear toward his neck. "I'm off tomorrow. Be nice to catch up on old times."

"Sure."

Abe patted Michael's shoulder then walked forward and entered the cockpit. Sliding into the left-hand seat, he scanned the instrument panel, then told his co-pilot to start the engines. Ten minutes later, the DC 3 was airborne and climbing into a clear sky lit by the aurora.

With an hour and a twenty minute flight ahead of him, Abe rested one hand on the control wheel, letting his memories wander the pages of time, staring beyond the airplane's windshield until the Northern Lights shrank to glowing embers of red light beckoning him from the night. He heard his co-pilot talking with the tower, then adjust the altimeter. Scanning the instruments, Abe was satisfied everything looked good in the thirty-year old plane. Easing the controls forward, he began their descent toward the approach lights of Yellowknife airport.

He'd never returned to Kenora after the war. Nothing had awaited him there. Canadian Pacific Airlines was looking for pilots with bush experience who could fly multi-engine planes. Ferrying bombers to Europe and later flying the Burma Hump into China, where he'd been shot down and rescued, had given him plenty of experience. When he'd been asked to fly for CP, he didn't hesitate. There were too many surplus pilots on the market to be fussy.

"Gear down," Abe said, more out of habit than conscious effort.

Dick Parker, his co-pilot for the flight, reached down to the floor between their seats and activated the undercarriage lever. The floorboards rumbled while both wheels dropped into the air stream with a loud thump. Dick looked up at the instrument panel as a green light came on. "Gear down, and locked," he said.

Abe had started flying DC 3's like this one when he went with Canadian Pacific, gradually moving up to heavier aircraft as they came along, and ended up flying Bristol Britannia's to Amsterdam. When the DC 8 jetliners came along in 1961, he quit.

Drifting about in the North West Territories, Abe had landed his present job flying a scheduled flight between Arctic communities, but, like the black night beyond the windshield, found the regularity of it all quickly becoming tedious.

"You going to land this plane or fly it into the ground, Abe?"

The glowing embers of a long dead fire crystalized before him. Glancing over to his co-pilot, he looked again at the landing lights.

"You've had red on the glide scope since we started down."

Abe corrected his descent without apologizing. The lights turned green. After landing, he taxied up to the terminal and shut down both engines.

Unbuckling his belt, he glanced out the side window to see Michael Redsky walking into the terminal. A wave of nostalgia swept over him. He missed his old Norseman.

After shutting down the airplane for the night, Abe picked up his battered leather briefcase that had been through the war with him, and followed his co-pilot inside the terminal. Michael, he noticed, was at one of the public pay phones. Catching Abe's eye, he held up one finger, signaling him to wait. Abe set down his case and stood some feet away while the Native man concluded his call.

"Sorry about that," Michael said, stepping out of the phone booth. "I was just checking on some arrangements for tomorrow."

"No problem. My day is done, anyway. Where're you staying?"

"The Yellowknife Inn."

"Need a ride?"

"I was going to call a cab."

"Nah, I'll give you a ride."

"Thanks."

They bundled into Abe's new GMC pickup truck and drove out of the terminal parking lot. Abe allowed Michael to sit in silence until they turned toward town. "So, what brings you up here?"

"Business."

"Kinda gathered that. This isn't a part of the world one flies into for pleasure."

"I'm looking to buy an airplane," Michael said.

"You're a pilot!"

"No. A chartered accountant."

"So you're not buying it for yourself."

"Kind of."

"You're kind of buying an airplane for yourself, even though you don't fly."

"I'm part owner in Blindfold Lake Lodge."

"Harrison's old place?"

"Yeah, we bought him out a couple years back and need another plane."

"Another plane? When I flew for him, he barely managed a trip a week. How many planes you got?"

"Three."

"And you need another one?"

Michael nodded. "You'd never recognized the place. We've been building steady for the last two years."

"So, whose plane you looking at?"

"Bill Seagram's Cessna 185."

Abe pulled up in front of the hotel. "Nice unit. Well looked after. You'll probably get it quite reasonable. I hear his widow wants to move it as soon as possible."

Michael picked up his carry-on bag. "If it goes right, we'll own it tomorrow."

"I'm off tomorrow. The plane's down at Bob Engle's base on the Back Bay. Want me to run you down there?"

"Sure," Michael said, opening his door as Abe stopped in front of the Yellowknife Inn. "How about we get together for breakfast?"

"Okay. Here?" Abe asked.

"What's the food like?"

"Good as any. The locals eat it. Eight o'clock?"

"Sure." Michael stepped out. "Thanks for the ride."

Abe waved off his comment as the door closed, but continued watching as Michael walked into the hotel, head up, shoulders back. That man's got confidence, he thought, then put the truck in gear and drove away.

SEVENTY-TWO

Next morning, Abe crossed the lobby to the Miner Mess café, acknowledging those he knew from the breakfast and gossip group while looking for Michael. Spotting him in a booth near the back, he walked past a wall of windows and slid in opposite him. Michael set the day-old *Globe and Mail* down. "Morning, Abe."

"Michael." Abe slipped off his leather flight jacket while ordering coffee from the waitress. "Eggs Benedict are good," he said, picking up a menu.

"What's the rolled oats like?" Michael asked, without looking up.

"Glue."

Michael gave a disgusted sigh, and closed the menu. Abe did likewise and threw his on top. They both ordered bacon and eggs.

"How's your Mom doing?" Abe asked.

"Fine."

The answer didn't satisfy Abe. "Still drinking?"

"Hasn't touched a drop in six years."

"That's good." Abe tried to picture Jenny. All he could come up with was a woman thirty-five years old. "She's got to be over sixty now."

"Sixty-three this fall."

"Your brother Pete, and Anna?"

"Pete still fishes a bit."

"Hope he's got a new outboard."

Michael smiled. "He used Dad's old Evinrude until four or five years ago. Bought a new twenty-five horse Johnston, and an aluminium boat to go with it. Runs like the wind."

251

"And Anna? She ever get over losing the kids in the fire?"

"I don't think she'll ever get over that. She copes the best she can with her guilt. Became one of Jehovah's Witnesses. Always tells me she'll see her babies again in the paradise."

Abe raised his eyebrows.

"She's happy," Michael said. "Still loves Pete. Does a lot for the reserve now that it's dry."

"The reservation is dry?"

"Yeah."

"What about Luther?"

"We bought him out."

"We?"

"The reserve. Friend of mine in Winnipeg set up a limited company. I run the books. Anna's brother runs the store. We employ most of his family's relatives."

"Who flies your stuff in?"

"Comes by truck. The government built an access to the logging road about ten years back."

"And Luther?"

"Lost touch, but last I heard, he and his wife are in an apartment in Saint Boniface."

"You're kidding me. Hated the Metis, then goes and lives with the French?"

Michael shrugged, then sipped his coffee, holding it in both hands. "What about you? Where you been all these years?"

"Everywhere, literally."

Michael waited.

"After the war Grant McConachie offered me work."

"This the McConachie of Canadian Pacific Airlines?"

"Yeah." Abe paused and sat back as the waitress placed their breakfasts on the table. "Started off flying a Norseman again."

"Ever fly jets?" Michael asked, forking his eggs in half.

"Nah. Flew Bristol Britannias over the pole to Amsterdam. Boring as hell. When they were replaced with DC 8's, I got out."

"So how come you're flying an old DC 3 for some small operation?"

Abe forked his hash-browns around. How do you tell someone that flying is the greatest thing in the world to be doing, while hating it? "Flying's all business now. The adventure and the romance are gone. I thought I'd find it again in a small operation." He quit fiddling with the potatoes. "Wasn't there. Couple more years, and I'm out."

Abe looked up to see Michael deep in thought, eyes focussing in the distance. Abe stabbed a piece of bacon.

SEVENTY-THREE

Cessna Aircraft Corporation started making the 185 because everyone who flew the 180 loved it but wanted more power for float operations. Thus was born the updated model that could carry five passengers. The plane William Seagram had owned before he died of a heart attack, was three years old, equipped with amphibious floats, and had only 177 hours on it. The orange Seagram Construction emblem with small red and black lettering looked out of place against the white fuselage and blue trim.

Abe had arranged for the keys and obtained permission to take it for a flight. He'd grabbed his fishing rod out of the pickup, and they were now headed for a little fly-in fishing north of Yellowknife. A fifteen minute flight brought them to Duncan Lake, and Abe landed in a bay he knew the trout would give them plenty of action.

After landing, Abe fished off the front of the left float while Michael removed his shoes and socks, rolled up his pants, and sat on the float, dipping his toes in the frigid water. "Haven't done this in years."

"Why not?" Abe asked, casting again.

"Kind of hard to do in a downtown office building."

"You don't live on the reserve anymore?"

"Sometimes. I have a bedroom at my Mom's place, but most of the time I'm in Winnipeg."

"Doing what?"

"I run an accounting firm. I set it up to help Native people, but white businesses make up the bulk of my clients."

Abe finished reeling in his lure and cast it out again. "Blindfold Lake Lodge one of them?"

"Yeah. Although we only hold forty-seven percent of the shares."

"Who holds the rest?"

"Lenny Corrigan."

Abe stopped reeling. "Lenny?"

"Leonard, Diana's boy. Thought you knew."

Diana. Dying red embers in a dark fireplace at Kate's lodge. How long ago? Twenty, twenty-two years? Why hadn't he gone back after the war? Well, she was married to Ted, that's why. It just wasn't in him to take away another man's wife. So they'd had another child, a boy at that. And now, that son owned the lodge Abe used to charter for with his Norseman. Small world, he thought.

The rod tugged in his hand. Tightening his grip, he set the hook, then began fighting to land the fish. The rod bent almost double, then straightened as a lake trout, Daredevil lure hanging from its mouth, rose from the water thirty feet away.

"He'll go six or eight pounds," Michael said, standing up.

The rod's tip bounced up and down as the fish dove for deep water and swam under the floats, spooling line off the reel. Abe sidestepped past Michael and held the rod under water to clear the rear elevator, slowly working the fish back to his side. A couple of good runs by the trout and it was played out. Abe brought him alongside the float, reached down and, hooking a finger in the gills, lifted it for Michael to see. "Feels more like nine and a half pounds."

"Too small," Michael said, grinning in mock disgust.

Abe slipped the hook out and tossed the squirming fish back in the water. "You're right. Barely enough for a seagull."

They stayed another twenty minutes, during which Abe caught two more, then gave the rod to Michael. After he hooked a couple ten pounders, they called it a day. The sun was still rising toward noon when Abe took off.

He really liked this plane. The cabin still felt like new, the engine was smooth and, after he'd trimmed it out, all but flew itself. At one moment, he caught himself thinking there was an auto-pilot engaged. "You ought to buy this plane, Michael."

"Think it's a good deal?"

"If you don't, I will."

"What would you do with it?"

Abe shrugged his shoulders. "Fly it around for the fun of it," he said, with a grin.

"I'll keep that in mind."

Michael watched lake and land slide by underneath. It reminded him of the land of his forefathers. Pristine. Unspoiled by the white man. Well that time had long faded into history. He knew that to succeed in this world he had to play by the white man's rules. What hurt most was it left so little time for his traditional way of life. Would Abe make a team player? Only one way to know. "I've heard it said my father called you *needjee*."

Abe stared out the windscreen. Jack Redsky, one of the few really good men to come into his life. A heavy feeling dragged at his heart, then, as he looked across at Jack's son, his words echoed through time. *Of all my sons, Michael is going to get a good education.* Well he did. "He certainly was my friend."

"Tell me about him."

"One of the finest men I have ever known. To him the world was not Indian or white, it was ours. I always felt he treated me as an equal. He was a hard working father who wanted the best for his wife and kids."

"I remember you holding me at the funeral."

"I shouldn't have said what I did."

256

"You held me. I trusted you. There is only one other white man in this world I completely trust. He also is *needjee*." Michael sat back and closed his eyes. He never spoke for the rest of the flight.

⁂

By four that afternoon, Michael had signed an offer to buy the plane, and Abe drove him to the airport. Parking outside the terminal, Abe noticed Michael was in no hurry to get out. Instead he sat looking out the front windshield. Abe watched him until he turned and said, "I need someone to ferry that plane to Kenora, you interested?"

Abe hadn't thought of it. Did he really want to go back to Kenora after all these years? It wasn't that the place held bad memories. Occasionally during long flights over Greenland and Scotland, the good times had played like visions in his mind. Who'd still be there after all these years? It'd be interesting to find out. "Sure. I've got a weeks holidays coming. Give me a couple of days."

"It'll take that long to close the deal." Michael opened his door. Abe got out and walked around the pickup box. Together they went inside.

"You like flying for these people?" Michael asked as they approached the ticket counter.

"It's a living. The stress is low. So is the pay."

"What's the real reason you quit CP Airlines?"

"Like I said, boredom."

Michael eyed him sideways. "And this is exciting?"

"What we did today was exciting."

"Ever think of going back to a floatplane?"

"Crosses my mind, but the hours are too long."

The woman behind the counter handed Michael his ticket. "Your plane will be boarding in a few minutes, Mr. Redsky."

"Thanks." He picked up his carry-on bag.

Abe opened the terminal door. "I'll walk you out."

Standing in the late afternoon sun, they watched workers load baggage and freight. Abe could see Dick Parker sitting in the pilot's seat today. A slight breeze blew in their faces. Abe checked the wind sock, then scanned the sky. High cirrus clouds were brushed onto pale blue. "You'll have a smooth flight."

"Think you'll have any trouble getting time off?"

"Nope. Young Parker's your pilot. He's trying to build his hours. He'll fill in."

"Good. Plan on staying a few days. I'll set aside a room for you at the lodge."

Ten minutes later, Abe watched the old Douglas airliner become a speck in the sky, then disappear all together.

SEVENTY-FOUR

Three days later, Abe eased in a notch of flap, set the prop in fine pitch, and slowly opened the throttle, running Bill Seagram's 185, now owned by Blindfold Lake Lodge, up onto the step. Another notch of flap and the Cessna lifted off Great Slave Lake, rising into a crimson dawn. Bleeding off the flaps and reducing power and pitch, he banked right, continued his climb, and leveled off two thousand feet above the earth, setting a course southeast toward Thompson, Manitoba.

Michael had phoned the night before. The lodge had purchased the plane, and the deal was signed. Abe was to fly it to Winnipeg International, stay the night at a hotel and be ready to leave at eight the next morning. That suited Abe. He planned two stops. The first was at Stony Rapids.

It was during the leg to Thompson that he finally asked himself the question he'd been avoiding. What was he going to do with the rest of his life? Flying had been his passion, but now as the years crept up, he found himself wishing he'd made more permanent relationships along the way. He'd gotten close to a few men during the war. Who didn't? They were a close-knit group. Each time he landed at some distant airstrip to be informed of the loss of a friend, it left a big hole inside that after awhile he hadn't bothered to fill.

As the miles slipped under his wings, he began to feel time had passed him by. To his left a solitary eagle circled on the thermals; it epitomized his life, gliding downhill while flying in circles. Being single, he didn't fit into the social lives of the other pilots. Why he never married remained a mystery. He was comfortable around women, had known some intimately, only to have them drift away. Diana Corrigan came to mind. He envied Ted. Where had Cindy ended up? Abe could still see the disappointment in her eyes when she learned he was selling out. Now he was flying back to all those memories. Did he really want to go there?

Thompson appeared on the horizon and Abe steered toward it. He planned on landing at Lambair's base, maybe spend some time with Tom if he was around. Turned out he wasn't. The sun was low on the horizon when he lowered the wheels in the bottom of both floats and asked for clearance to land in Winnipeg.

Eight o'clock the next morning, Abe found himself standing alone beside the left float. It was ten after before Michael and another man walked across the tarmac.

"Morning, Abe," Michael said, shouting to be heard above the thunder of a four-engine TCA Super Constellation taking off. "This is David Croft."

Extending his hand, the slight, red-haired man waited for the noise to die down, then spoke. "Good to see you, again."

Abe shook his hand. "Again?"

"You probably don't remember, but you flew Michael and I out to Long Grass the summer we passed grade eight."

"Sorry."

"Don't worry about it. It was a long time ago. Hear you're going to do some flying for us."

"Just to Kenora."

"Michael didn't make you an offer?"

"No."

David turned to the man at his side. "Well, make it now."

"Abe," Michael said, looking at the ground, "we'd like you to fly for us." Raising his eyes, he held Abe's, reading the response.

"Who's us?"

"Blindfold Lake Lodge. David's on the board of directors."

"A convenient title," David said. "I look after the legal stuff."

"For the lodge and the reserve," Michael added.

"You know I'm not interested in working dawn till dark."

"This plane," David said, patting the wing strut, "is going to fill a gap in our fleet. We have two Norseman and a Cessna 170 already. It's more of an executive aircraft."

"Winnipeg to Long Grass to the lodge," Michael said. "Trips to Kenora airport for clients. Odd one to Minnesota."

"That's why we got one with wheels in the floats." David looked at Abe. "Want the job?"

"Haven't heard anybody talk dollars."

Abe listened as his terms of employment were spelled out. They wanted him that was for sure. The pay was better and the benefits generous. He knew he'd take it, but said, "Let me think on it until Kenora."

"Sure," Michael said, stepping onto the float, sliding Abe's seat ahead, then climbing into the second row of seats.

David put one foot on the float. "Any problems with the offer let us know." He climbed in beside Michael.

Sliding the seat back, Abe got in and contacted the tower after slipping on his seatbelt. They were slotted in behind a jetliner. The Cessna lifted off smoothly then dropped ten feet when it flew into turbulent air left by the jet. Abe made a mental note to wait longer next time he found himself behind a big plane.

Next time, Abe thought. Already he had himself flying in and out of Winnipeg. On the trip down from Yellowknife he'd made the decision that if Michael offered him a job flying this plane he'd accept. The only downside was landing at airports. He wished the plane wasn't equipped with amphibious floats. He much preferred to work entirely off water. A tingle went down his spine. The lodge owned a couple Norseman. He'd make sure and snaggle a few flights in one.

During the hour it took to fly to Kenora and land in the bay, Abe tried not to listen, but he picked up bits and pieces of conversation:

custody, going to court, residential schools. It weighed heavy until David got out to ride off in a taxi.

"You probably heard," Michael said, climbing into the seat beside Abe.

The pilot nodded.

Michael sat back and sighed. "Things haven't really changed much."

"Except you now have a lawyer." Abe started the engine.

"Yes we have." Michael watched the prop spin to a blur. "But more than that, he is *needjee*."

SEVENTY-FIVE

As Anna Redsky held her grandaughter, the little girl with dark brown hair and coal black eyes curled her upper lip to form a smile. Anna kissed her on the nose. "You sweet baby." The little one turned away, then looked back at her grandmother and smiled again. Anna's heart filled with joy, then for no apparent reason, it emptied, and broken memories of Ruth played upon her mind.

Getting up, she walked over to the young Native girl lying on the couch. Placing the squirming child in her mother's arms, Anna stepped outside just as the tears flowed.

The hope of seeing her precious ones returned to her arms was the only thing that anchored Anna from drifting into chronic depression. But as she sat on the wooden steps of their old cabin, it wasn't enough and the grief she hadn't experienced in almost two years came flooding back. She wept until her heart was empty.

After the birth of High Elk, no more children had come, even though she and Pete had tried. Finally, after visiting a doctor in Winnipeg, she acknowledged it was the result of some sort of trauma about the fire. Pete never laid any blame on her. His kindness warmed her inside. Clasping both hands together, she petitioned her Heavenly Father for the strength and hope to carry on. Peace and calm returned.

Anna stood up at the sound of an airplane drifting on the wind and watched as a white and blue Cessna landed on the lake. Nobody she knew. Opening the door, she went inside.

Irene had placed Alicia on the floor and returned to her *Simpson Sears* catalogue. Anna sighed. She wished the girl was more ambitious.

There were moments when she didn't blame High Elk for abandoning her. Baby Alicia was another matter. Anna reached down and caught the little one as she crawled under the table. Wiggling in her grandmother's hands, she smiled, then protested with a wail, abruptly ceased, and smiled once more. Irene turned another page in the ladies section of the catalogue.

Holding Alicia on her hip with one arm, Anna went back to cooking and was stirring a pot of fish chowder when Pete walked in.

He sniffed over the pot. "Smells good."

Anna felt a pat on her bottom and kissed the only man she'd ever loved on the cheek. "It is only fish soup."

"This," he said, sticking his finger into the pot, then tasting it, "is not just fish soup. Its more expensive name is Walleye Chowder, and American's pay good money to eat it."

"You'll pay to eat this?"

Pete wrinkled his brow. "I look American?"

"You look handsome." Anna stood on her toes and kissed Pete. "How is your Mom?"

"Her arthritis is acting up again."

"In both hands?"

Pete nodded yes.

"Maybe I'll go over this afternoon and do a few things for her."

"Good, the place could use a little cleaning. That woman High Elk is living with isn't much help."

Dorothy Castel, High Elk's woman, as Pete had said, was useless around the house. Anna couldn't understand what her son saw in the girl. Then, looking at Irene, in her worn cotton dress, dreaming over the images in the catalogue, she had to admit, Dorothy, in her leather jacket and tight jeans, would be much more exciting to him. And, as he'd once mentioned, she hadn't saddled him with a child. Anna constantly had trouble with the new generation's view of sex and marriage. She plain did not approve of couples living together. And now that they were into this protest movement against the white society in general, Anna worried for the safety of her only son.

Pete took Alicia from Anna's arm. "How about a smile for Grandpa?" He touched the baby's nose with his finger and was rewarded with two little dimples on her cheeks. A smile soon followed.

SEVENTY-SIX

Gear retracted, Abe said out loud to himself, after checking for the second time the wheels were inside the floats. The last thing he wanted to do was flip over while landing on water with the wheels down. The reservation looked much the same as it had over twenty years ago. The new floating dock however, was a far cry from the days when he tied up his Norseman to hand-cut boards and rotten cribbing. Built in the shape of a tee, and capable of handling a half dozen planes, there was barely room for him to park.

Abe killed the engine. "Lot more boats around than last time I was here."

Michael opened his door as the plane drifted against the dock. "Everybody has one now." Hopping out, he held the strut until Abe got out and tied off the float. "We even have our own gas station." Michael pointed to a five-hundred gallon tank on legs at the head of the dock.

They walked up a path that hadn't changed in two decades. Abe noted new houses and a store. "That your new store?"

"Yeah. We built it when we were drying out the reserve, after we bought out Luther about eight years ago."

"How come? He wasn't on reserve land."

"Strictly economics. There wasn't enough business for us both. I ran some numbers and made him an offer. It wasn't what he wanted, but better than the alternative."

"So he packed up and went to Saint Boniface," Abe said.

"Well, he and his wife went to Dauphin a couple of years before that."

Near the end of a row of older houses after the store, they came to one Abe knew well. Last time he'd seen it, cardboard covering broken windows, it needed a coat of paint, and the stairs were falling apart. Now, paint and new windows made it look more like the house he'd walked out of the bush to decades ago, when his old biplane broke down. "Your mother still live here?"

Michael nodded and extended a hand, directing Abe up a set of concrete steps with a wrought-iron railing. Entering the small porch through a screen door, Abe waited as Michael opened a varnished wooden door and walked inside.

Jenny Redsky sat across the room. "Hi, Mom. Brought over an old friend."

The woman focussed on her son's companion without recognition.

Abe stepped forward. Had it been that long? Jenny had put on weight. Her face was crisscrossed with deep lines, the familiar long hair now grey with black streaks, hung limp at her shoulders. Abe wondered how much he'd aged.

Jenny's face illuminated with a smile. "Abe Williston." She tried to get up. Michael helped her. She approached Abe.

"Hello, Jenny."

"Who is this guy?" The question came from a young Indian dressed in a camouflage jacket, his red head-band standing out against jet black hair hanging over his shoulders.

Jenny touched Abe's cheek. "He is an old family friend."

"What is a white guy doing on our reservation?"

Michael's jaw hardened. "Your grandmother said he's a family friend."

"Not my family."

Turning her eyes from Abe, Jenny raised a crooked finger, pointing it at the young man. "Show some respect. This man helped your father after grandfather Jack died."

"Was killed, you mean." Walking over, he pushed his face in Abe's. "By white guys." He stood there until he knew Abe was uncomfortable.

Michael stepped between the two of them. "Sooner you come to realize that not all white men are enemies, the better, High Elk."

"Never."

"Keep up that attitude and you'll end up in Stony Mountain."

"Better than turning white." Grabbing the hand of a young Native girl standing behind him, he stormed out and slammed the door.

"I am sorry," Jenny said.

"That one of Pete's kids?" Abe asked.

"The only one alive," Michael replied.

Abe winced, remembering the fire. "I meant..."

"It's okay."

Abe wondered if coming back was such a good idea.

Jenny touched his arm. "It is nice to see you, again. Been a long time."

Abe embraced her. "Too long."

"You'll see a lot more of him, Mom," Michael said. "He's going to fly for the lodge."

"Good. You are going to stay for supper?"

Abe looked to Michael.

"Of course. We'll fly out later. I've some business at the store, but first we're going over to see Pete."

SEVENTY-SEVEN

The smell of freshly turned soil drifted in the air as Pete Redsky sat in the warm afternoon sun holding baby Alicia who slept in his arms. Anna had talked Irene into helping dig the garden. Watching them work, Pete felt his grandaughter sleep, wondering what type of world she would grow up in. A better one, he hoped.

Looking into the baby's face, Pete tried to imagine what it would have been like raising a daughter. The memory of little Ruth had long ago faded. After her death he'd searched for answers from the Kitche Manitou. No vision came. Only Mother Earth gave him comfort. Late in the autumn, after the leaves had turned, she would caress his face with the wind and blow a single leaf from a nearby tree. As it fell to the ground, Ruth would nuzzle under his chin until it touched the ground.

Even High Elk as a baby was shrouded in the distant past. Those early years had been difficult, with his own mother's drinking and Anna's depression. High Elk had been a typical boy until he attended the residential school. Although Pete found it hard to believe, Anna had many good things to say about the Sisters at Saint Mary's. She taught High Elk English, so his grades were good, but as each year passed, his attitude became more self-centered. Neither Pete nor Anna could stem the boy's prejudice against the white man.

A strong personality, something his grandfather had used for good, elevated High Elk in the eyes of many young ones dissatisfied with the poor conditions and lack of future they inherited. Leadership came easy. The power that went with it brought corruption. Dumping Irene and Alicia was clear evidence of that. Defying the drinking ban was another.

Since they had banned liquor from the reservation, there had been a lot less trouble among the older ones. It was this next generation that bothered Pete. Robbed of their culture and set adrift from their moral obligations, they ignored the elders and insisted on getting what they wanted. Pete saw a lot of their viewpoints poisoned by the white man's past.

It was a view he didn't share. Was it not Susan Two Bears' persistence and Michael's help that got them the four-room school? Now that the government was ridding itself of the residential schools, the next generation of children could get an education and also learn the traditions of the old ways. Susan was helping put together a course on Native culture. It would never be the same, but Pete felt it would once again tie his people to their past. His father would have liked that. He hoped High Elk would one day see it also.

"Hey, Pete."

Alicia stirred, then settled back to sleep as Pete looked up to see his brother Michael, and an older man, who looked familiar, walking up the path.

"Must be nice to sit around in your old age," Michael said while lowering himself into a chair beside Pete. "You remember Abe."

Pete looked again. "Abe Williston!" His voice woke Alicia, who cried as he tried to calm her.

As quickly as she started, she stopped, then puckered both cheeks and smiled at Abe who twitched his nose back at her. "Hello, Pete. It's been a long time." Abe extended his hand.

"Certainly has." Pete half reached out to shake it while still holding the baby. "You still flying bush planes?"

"Took some time off, but I'm back at it. And Redsky Fisheries?"

Pete laughed and shook his head. "There is more money in helping rich Americans catch one fish than I could make in a whole boat load."

"He guides for the lodge," Michael said while taking Alicia from Pete. "Gotta smile for Uncle Mikie?"

Little dimples formed in each chubby cheek as she grinned.

"Uncle Mikie?" Abe asked.

"It's Indian talk, Abe."

Raising his brows, Abe nodded in mock comprehension.

"You going to fly for the lodge?" Pete asked.

"Yeah."

"We bought the 185." Michael repositioned Alicia as she squirmed in his arms. "You wiggly little thing. Abe's going to fly it."

"Great," Pete said as his brother coo cooed Alicia. "It has been a long time since we flew together in your Norseman."

"Too long," Abe said, sitting on an upturned five-gallon pail. "What have you been doing all these years?"

"Existing mostly. Quit fishing about seven years ago. It wasn't paying."

"Don't let him kid you, Abe," Michael said. "He sold his license and bought a new boat."

Tires skidded on loose gravel. A rusted-out pickup, its blue paint turning to powder, braked to a halt in a cloud of dust as the passenger door swung open, and High Elk stepped out. Abe counted three people in the cab, and six more in the box. Three of them had rifles. All, including the two girls, wore hunting jackets or fatigues.

"What's with all the army clothes," Abe asked Pete.

Leaning toward Abe, he replied, "They think they're warriors."

"Who are they fighting?"

"The white man," Michael said, loud enough for High Elk to hear.

"We only want what the whites took from us." High Elk placed a boot on the bottom step.

"They did not take it," Pete said. "Our father's signed a treaty."

"Treaty Three. I spit on it. It gave us land we already owned." He gestured across the reservation. "Swamps, barren islands, and poverty. Who got the forest?" He turned to Michael. "Who, Uncle Mike?"

Michael wouldn't answer him.

"Well, we are going to get it back. Tomorrow we're going to block the logging road."

Pete jumped up. "No, you're not!"

High Elk walked up the steps to face his father. "Try and stop us."

Pete backed up. "You have been drinking."

"What do you care?"

"I care. What you do off the reserve is your business, but here," Pete pointed to the ground, "drinking is not allowed."

"You don't run this reservation," High Elk yelled.

"No, but the elders..."

"They gave away our land and forests."

Pete struck his son on the chest. "Do not speak that way of the elders."

Abe watched High Elk's glare harden as he replied to his father's aggression. "We are not going to wait for the old ones to act. All they do is talk. Nothing will happen until they die off." He jabbed a thumb at his chest. "I am not waiting that long." Turning around he strode back to the pickup and got in, then through the open window stuck out his hand and made a fist. The driver started the engine as High Elk hollered out a war cry.

Abe and his two Native friends watched the pickup speed away in a dust cloud, men in the box chanting and waving guns in the air.

"There goes trouble," Michael said.

Pete shook his head and sat down. "They'll end up doing it."

Michael handed Alicia back to Pete. "We got to go. When are you starting at the lodge?"

"In a month or so." Pete took his granddaughter. "I told Lenny to hire the young men first. They need the money more than me."

Michael kissed his niece on the nose.

Pete held Alicia up high and jiggled her from side to side. "You want to be here when she walks." Then lowering the baby girl, he hugged her to his cheek.

"Mom's making supper. You coming?"

Pete shook his head. "Anna has got fish chowder on."

"Okay, brother." Michael bumped him on the arm, "We'll catch you next time." He started down the stairs.

Abe got up to follow. Pete elbowed his arm. "Good to see you again, *needjee*."

"You too, my friend."

SEVENTY-EIGHT

During a meal of venison and canned vegetables Jenny bought at the reservation store, Michael kept the conversation light and listened to his mother talk about her garden, taking note of her request to have the store bring in some flower bulbs. Afterward, she served tea. "And what have you been doing all these years, Abe?"

"Flying."

"He flew big airplanes to Europe, Mom."

Jenny ignored her son. "I was thinking more of your personal life. You married?"

"No."

"Why not?"

"Don't know. The right woman never came along, I guess."

"I keep telling Michael not to be so fussy." Jenny placed her hand on Michael's arm. "Mary Loon is still available."

"Mom, she has two kids. Doesn't know the father of either one."

"Do not be so harsh. It was a mistake for her to go to Winnipeg, but since she has come back things are different. I see her turning into a fine young woman."

"I'm just not ready to take on that type of responsibility, yet."

"Well, do not leave it too long." She held her son's wrist with gnarled fingers. "Money is not everything."

"I know," Michael said, looking at the floor.

Letting go and sitting back, Jenny changed her tone. "You must talk to those people at the store. They ran out of milk again."

"Sure, Mom." Michael addressed Abe. "We only have a small refrigeration room."

"Then build a bigger one," Jenny said. "The Safeway store in Kenora has a whole row of them."

"Mom. It's not that easy. Those units are expensive and they take a lot of electricity to run."

"Well, I think it is a shame the children cannot get milk everyday."

"People understand the odd time we run out. Ten years ago we never had any."

"Abe used to fly it in." Jenny lifted the pot. "More tea?"

Abe waved his hand. "No, thanks. Looking back on it now, I think of all the cases of booze I loaded into the Norseman, and what little bit of space was set aside for a few bottles of milk." Abe sipped his tea. "Drying out the reserve was long overdue, even back then." He looked at Michael. "Shouldn't we be going."

"We'll stay the night."

"Oh, good," Jenny said. "Your room is all made up. Abe can sleep on the couch."

"Abe isn't sleeping on the couch, Mom. I'm sure Susan will let him use her hide-a-bed."

"Susan Two Bears?" Abe asked.

"Yeah. They moved back to the reservation when it went dry. Ignace runs a little clinic for people with drinking problems."

"On a dry reserve?"

"It is the young ones," Jenny said. "The residential schools have ruined them. They are completely out of control."

"Not all of them," Michael said. "Some of our people go to town to drink and get drunk. If they can stay out of jail, Ignace helps them out when they return." He stood up. "Anyway, Susan and Ignace will be glad to see you."

Abe rose as Michael kissed his mother on the cheek. "Don't wait up. You take your pills?"

"Yes, I do. You will talk to the people at the store?"

"I'll talk to them. Goodnight, Mom." He opened the door and Abe followed him out into the late spring evening.

SEVENTY-NINE

Ignace Two Bears met them at the door and shook Abe's hand so tight his knuckles hurt. "Abe! Abe Williston. Come in." Ignace turned and hollered into the house. "Susan! Susan! Guess who's here?"

The three men walked into the living room as Susan came from the kitchen, a tea towel in her hand. "Abe!" She ran over to him.

He caught her in a big hug. "Hello, Susan."

"Gracious, you caught me looking like a fright."

Abe didn't think so. Her hair that had a few grey strands, was shorter than he remembered, but the casual clothes she wore were definitely her. "Time has been kind to you." Susan's face retained a smoothness uncommon around the reserve.

"Thank you." She stepped back a pace. "You haven't changed a bit. Not like Ignace here." She patted his belly.

"She is like her mother," Ignace said. "Always cooking too much."

"How's your father?" Abe asked.

The light in Susan's eyes went out. "He has Alzheimer's. It's well along. Doesn't recognize anybody."

"I'm sorry to hear that."

"So," Susan said, recovering, "what brings you back to this neck of the woods after all these years?"

"I flew a plane down from Yellowknife."

"That little Cessna yours?" Ignace asked.

"No. It belongs to Blindfold Lake Lodge."

"Abe's going to fly it for us," Michael said.

"Good. If you ever need a place to stay..."

276

"How about tonight," Michael said.

"Certainly." Susan touched the top of the couch. "Got rid of the old chesterfield. This one's a hide-a-bed."

"Thanks," Abe said.

"It is good to have you back, *needjee*," Ignace said. "The young pilots at the lodge are good flyers, but they don't understand the old ways."

"Times change," Abe said.

"They do. Our young people have different views. They want many things they think we had before. Our old people want to live a simple life."

Susan interrupted her husband. "Thanks to the residential schools a whole generation have lost their Native identity. They search for their past in the future. Re-establishing the traditions by force won't succeed."

"You know about the blockade?" Michael asked.

Ignace nodded. "I tried to talk them out of it, but they only got angry."

"A whole bunch of them had been drinking by the time they got to Pete's," Michael said. "High Elk's the worse. He's belligerent when he drinks. He'll cause us a lot of trouble if they have liquor at the blockade."

"Are you still letting our people drink at the lodge?" Susan asked.

"Lenny only allows them two beers. He's made it clear that anyone who drinks too much or causes trouble is fired."

"Thank goodness that hasn't happened yet."

"Lenny's pretty fair. He's talked privately to a couple of the men. I think they realize how much having work means."

"Well, it's sure been a big help around here. Too bad the young ones can't work there."

"We've been through this before, Susan."

"I know. We sent ambitious little kids to the residential school and they came back thinking we owe them everything. Maybe it will change with the new school."

Michael sighed. "The lodge is building into a million-dollar business. If our clients are happy, they spend big. You know what would happen if High Elk and his attitude were displayed around people like that."

Susan nodded.

"We have to find something for them to do," Ignace said.

"Give it time. We need to build an economic base. Look at the income we get from wild rice."

"Menial jobs," Susan said.

Ignace interrupted his wife. "Our young people need skilled jobs, like yours."

"Then keep them in school." Michael knew regular attendance was a challenge at the reserve school. He believed in education, but deep down inside knew the path to success lay in adopting the white man's ways. Economics, yes, a little voice in his head said, but not his culture. "I don't have all the answers. I'm doing all I can."

Susan took his face in her hands. "We know you are, sweetie." She kissed his forehead. "You're doing more than your share. Maybe it'll be a bit easier now that Abe's here."

Abe didn't see how. In fact, the whole situation set him wondering if he'd made the wrong decision.

EIGHTY

Across waters once paddled by voyageurs in freighter canoes, Diana Corrigan ran flat out in Ted's seventeen-foot fibreglass runabout. Since his death of a heart attack two years ago, her life had changed, though reflecting on it with melancholy, not necessarily for the better. True, she found herself with more freedom, but also, like today, experienced times of loneliness, something she never dreamed would happen when he was alive.

The first thing she did with the insurance money was buy a fifty-horsepower Mercury outboard to replace the underpowered Johnston. Now, instead of plowing through the water, the boat rose up and skimmed across the surface of the lake. Wind blowing over the windshield whipped strands of dyed, dark-brown hair in and out of her eyes. Reaching up as the boat bounced through choppy waves, she tucked the loose hair back under her kerchief.

A trip to Kate's cabin took only forty minutes. Today, for some reason it seemed like forever. Lately, they had become less frequent since Lenny had finished school. She missed Ted. With him driving, she had sat in her own little world on the empty seat to her left. Glancing at it, she sighed. No one had come into her life to occupy the vacant space it symbolized.

They'd sold Charlie's camp to a doctor from Minnesota after Leonard came along. When Kate moved to Vancouver, she insisted they use her place. Out of necessity she had to sleep with Ted, and as time went by, Lenny drew them together, the chasm closed, and her tiny bedroom became a sewing room once more.

279

On their thirtieth anniversary, Ted gave her a card with the keys to Kate's log cabin. Kate wasn't coming back to Kenora and was happy to sell it to an old friend. While settling Ted's will, Diana found the property had been registered in her name, placing it outside of the estate.

As of late, it had become a lonely place to visit. In fact, today she didn't want to go there and turned the boat around. Approaching the bridge to Laurenson Creek, she felt let down. The big old house, too, was empty. Lenny only lived with her in it during the winter. On a whim, she swung past Marr's Marine and pulled up to the seaplane base. One of Western Ontario's dock workers tied up the boat and helped her out. She walked into the office Blindfold Lake Lodge shared with them.

"Hi, Marg"

"Hello, Mrs. Corrigan."

"Any of Lenny's planes due in?"

"Not that I know of. Why?"

"Oh, just thought I'd catch a ride to the lodge."

"Our Beaver is heading down that way."

"Got room?"

"Plane's empty."

"Okay."

Ten minutes later they were airborne. Flying over the lodge, Diana felt a surge of pride. It had been a touch of fate that brought her and Lenny together with Michael Redsky and David Croft when Ted died. She'd used all the insurance money and mortgaged the house to retain a majority position in the deal. The three men worked well together: Lenny managing, Michael overseeing the accounting, David handling the legal end. Generally she stayed out of the picture, dropping in on occasions like this to enjoy the social atmosphere. And to see her son.

An old Native guide held the Beaver's wing strut as she got out. "Hello, Lone Eagle."

"Welcome to Blindfold Lake, Mrs. Corrigan." He began turning the plane.

"How's your wife?"

"Fine."

"Really?" She waited as the Beaver began taking off, drowning out her words.

"Yes. Mr. Redsky told me when he arrived earlier."

"Good. I'm glad to hear it."

Walking along the dock, she noticed a new airplane. One of the lodge workers was removing the painted letters off its side. What remained read, Yellowknife Const.

"Hello, Mrs. Corrigan," the young white man said.

"Our new plane?"

"I guess. I was told to remove the old letters and paint our logo on it."

Diana took off her kerchief, shook out her hair, and, in her open-toed shoes, walked up a gravel path to the lodge. Her lodge. Outside of the reservation, she was the largest shareholder. Combined with Lenny's, they held controlling interest.

In the two years they had owned it, four new accommodation buildings had been added. The dining room, bar, and kitchen had been expanded, a new dock built, and this year a building to house the guides and staff was under construction.

Bookings were up, mostly millionaires from Minnesota, but more coming from New York, and a few Hollywood types from California. Money bred money and they were spending it as fast as the lodge made it. Their new Cessna was evidence of that.

Diana entered the main lodge building. Two older men, sitting at the bar, gave her a quick look and went back to their drinks. Crossing the hardwood floor, she made her way to a small door beside the kitchen, knocked once, then turned the knob and opened the door.

Recognizing the voices of her son, Lenny, and Michael Redsky, she entered to see both men in conversation. Lenny was seated behind his desk, Michael beside him, bent over looking at some papers. A third man was silhouetted against the window. He turned as she closed the door, and Diana's world began to spin. Stifling a gasp with her left hand and try as she would, she could not keep herself from leaning back against the door.

EIGHTY-ONE

Michael had risen to a sky radiating early morning rays in the east reflecting off his bedroom wall. The air had been cool and still when they had left the reservation, the Cessna's floats cutting twin vee-shaped waves across the calm water.

Coming in low to land, Abe had hardly recognized the lodge. A Norseman, a little Cessna 170, and a half dozen or so boats were tied up to a new dock. Abe had no trouble choosing where to park in all the room that was left. Two men, one Native, the other white, tied up his plane as Michael stepped ashore.

"Morning, Mr. Redsky."

"Good morning, Lone Eagle." Michael patted the old Native's shoulder. "Your wife is feeling much better. My mom said the doc told her she's got diabetes. He put her on insulin and told her to stay in bed for a couple of days."

Lone Eagle smiled and nodded his head. Abe joined Michael on the dock as he continued speaking. "Your daughter is still in Winnipeg."

The old man shook his head. "She should be at home helping her mother."

Michael wasn't going to tell him she was living on the streets and that when she did come home, she'd probably be pregnant. He led Abe further along the dock. "You get that outboard fixed, Billy?"

"No, sir," the young white lad said. "I'm waiting on parts. They're supposed to be coming on this morning's flight out of Kenora."

"Good." Michael led Abe off the dock and along a path through fresh-cut grass. Entering a screened-off veranda running the width of the lodge, Michael crossed, and held open the main door for Abe.

"This is a lot bigger than I remember."

"Should be. We added on twice." Michael started across the hardwood floor, then turned toward two men seated at the bar. "Tim McKenzie. How ya doing?"

The heavy-set man reached for Michael's hand. "Great. And you?"

"Good as ever. Don't believe I've met your companion."

"This is Neil Kent. My stockbroker from New York."

Michael shook his hand. "Your first time here?"

"Yep. Nice place."

"Thanks." Michael spoke again to Tim. "You not fishing today?"

"Just got in last night. We're going to unwind a bit." He raised his drink. "Wayne's coming in from Saint Paul later. We'll maybe do a bit of fishing this evening."

"Good. Anything you want, just ask, Andy." Michael pointed to the barman.

"Got all I want right here." Tim held up his glass, then took a drink.

"Catch you later, Tim. Neil." Michael led Abe through a door tucked in beside the kitchen.

Behind a desk cluttered with papers sat a young man with wavy brown hair, long side burns, and a small pointed nose. His short-sleeve shirt fit snug across the shoulders. Intense hazel eyes caught Abe's, then looked at Michael. "It's here?"

"Tied up at the dock," Michael said.

"I'll have someone paint our name on it. This the pilot?"

"Yeah."

The man reached out his hand. "Leonard Corrigan. Call me Lenny."

"Abe Williston."

Lenny shoved his chair back and stood up, a smile spreading across his face. "Of Williston Air Services?"

"Many years ago." Abe shook his hand.

"My father spoke well of you."

"Lot of water under that bridge."

"Well, Dad turned most of it into good stories." Lenny sat down. "You going to fly for us?"

"Michael offered me a job."

"Any problems?"

"No."

"Great. Best I can offer you right now is any empty room that's available until the new building is finished in a month or so."

"Fine," Abe said.

"You'll be in Winnipeg a lot, anyway," Michael said as an airplane roared overhead.

Lenny waited until it passed. "Well that's settled. You here for the day, Michael?"

"Yeah, I'll go back to the reserve this afternoon."

"Good. Now here's what we have booked."

Michael ran his eyes down the page. "Can we handle all that?"

"We've got the boats. I'll need another couple of guides. Pete and Alex available?"

Michael explained why Alex couldn't come. "He's been invited to show his carvings at the Toronto Art Gallery. He flies out tomorrow and won't be back for a week." Abe found himself looking out the window as they went down the list of guides. To his left he could see two men erecting rafters on top of a framed building. Beyond was one of the lodge's original cabins. From what he could see, Abe figured it was now used as a storage or repair shop for outboard motors. Behind him, he heard the office door open. Both men at the desk continued talking as he turned.

A woman, about his age, with dark-brown hair and open-toed shoes, entered and closed the door. The moment Abe caught her eye, she stopped, then fell back, supporting herself with one hand against the doorknob.

Lenny looked up. "Hi, Mom."

Abe watched the colour drain from Diana Corrigan's face.

"You feel okay?" Lenny asked.

Diana tore her eyes from Abe's to look at her son. "Yes." She hesitated, composing herself. "I'm fine. Just a little tired." Patting her hair, she wiped both hands on her slacks before crossing the room. "Hello, Abe."

"Diana."

Lenny swung in his chair. "You know each other, of course."

Diana took a couple of deep breaths. Abe stood mute.

Michael broke the silence that followed. "If you'll excuse us."

Taking his cue, Abe stepped around Diana and opened the door. She followed him into the lodge and out onto the veranda. Grabbing his arm, she yanked him to a halt. "What are you doing here?"

He swung around to face her. "Michael offered me..."

"I don't care." She closed both eyes. "Why'd you have to come back?"

Abe felt her grip on his arm tighten as the other touched his hand.

"I didn't mean that, it's just that..." Opening her eyes, she looked into Abe's. "It's been so long. You never answered my letters."

"What! I didn't get any letters. The one I did receive was so out of date I felt.., well... It just never got answered."

"So why didn't you come back after the war?"

"Had no reason to."

"I was here."

Abe didn't want to go there. "Circumstances, I guess. I started flying for Canadian Pacific and ended up all over the world. And you? I see you have a son."

Diana flushed. "Yes." Turning away, she stepped off the veranda.

Abe followed. "He's done quite well for himself here. Ted must be proud."

Diana stopped, her back to Abe. "He's dead."

Abe walked around to face her. "I'm sorry."

"He died of a heart attack two years ago fixing his outboard motor. Got mad at something and stood up to throw his wrench in the water." She faced Abe, then looked away. "After Lenny came along, he managed to get control of his temper. He loved that boy and was very patient with him." She looked out across the lake. "One slip and it killed him." She turned back to Abe. "I'm sorry. I should grieve, but I can't." Taking Abe's hands in hers, she bowed her head. "It doesn't matter, anymore."

Abe watched as she looked up and squeezed his fingers, then said, "Not now that you're here."

EIGHTY-TWO

Michael Redsky sat in his fourth-floor office looking out at the Winnipeg skyline. How far he'd come. Susan Two Bears had made him finish high school then insisted he go to college. Now he was a Certified Chartered Accountant with a growing clientele, and an assistant. More of Susan's doing. One day she walked in with him and refused to leave until the young man was on the payroll. Michael never regretted it. A receptionist followed. For someone living on the reservation, Susan still remained very well connected.

Then there was David Croft. Where would his world be without his life-long friend? David's expertise and recommendations had been an essential part of the growth in the firm, not to mention Blindfold Lake Lodge.

From the first summer David came to the reserve, he'd grown closer to the Native community and was shocked when he learned about the residential schools. Experiencing the richness of Native culture first hand, it disturbed him that the government of his country and the churches he once held sacred, had conspired to strip his friends of their language and heritage. Since then, he'd put a lot of time, and his own money, into studying the laws, and was patiently documenting sexual abuse at the church-run schools.

"We won't get the government," he had said, "but the churches are vulnerable."

Michael remembered asking why?

"Only public opinion will move the government, but the churches knew all along what was happening and did nothing about it."

288

His admiration for David grew each time he thought about this. It wasn't easy supporting Indians in a white man's world.

Looking at his watch, Michael swung his feet off the desk and stood up. When Ignace Two Bears walked in a few minutes later, he picked up his briefcase and overnight bag.

"Ready to go?"

"Sure."

"Good, because Susan's double parked." Ignace waited for Michael to lock the door. An hour later they turned off the Trans-Canada Highway. It was dark well before they reached Long Grass Reservation.

<hr>

Next morning, Michael was having breakfast with his mother when he was summoned to the reservation store's telephone.

His next call was by radio phone to Blindfold Lake Lodge where he left a message for Abe to come and get him. Hanging the receiver up, he sighed, then walked over to Pete's house. Loose gravel crunched under his city shoes. The houses along the way hadn't changed much since his youth. Derelict cars and trucks rusted away where gardens used to grow. A few new homes had been built, leaving the old places to decay, or be lived in by the poor, many dependent on a government handout to survive. Well, he couldn't help them all. Making sure his family was looked after took most of his personal resources.

Amidst all this, there were people like Susan and Ignace, who kept their place immaculate in spite of the house next to them having cardboard-covered broken windows. His mom's house had been like that until she'd quit drinking. Michael had the inside renovated and the outside painted. He wanted a decent place to stay on his trips home.

Pete and Anna still lived in the log cabin by the lake. No amount of persuasion by Pete would move Anna into a new house, so Pete had added on. With the lake so close, waves washing on the shore and birds singing in the bulrushes, Michael always enjoyed visiting. Inevitably it took him back to the memories of his youth. Today was an exception. He dreaded the news he carried.

Pete hollered for him to come in when he knocked. Anna was wiping food off Alicia's face with a spoon as he walked in. Irene was nowhere to be seen. Pete sat at the kitchen table with no shirt on. Holding up a cup, he asked, "Coffee?"

"No thanks." Michael felt his voice go flat.

"What brings you out so early?"

"Bad news."

Anna stopped feeding the baby.

Pete kicked a chair out from under the table. Michael sat down. "High Elk's in jail."

"Oh, dear." Anna took hold of Pete's arm.

"Doesn't surprise me," Pete said. "It's a wonder he stayed out of trouble this long after that business with the logging road."

"This is a lot more serious than stopping traffic and shooting guns in the air." Michael drew a breath. "He's charged with murder."

Anna gasped. "Dear Lord, no!"

Pete got up as a plane flew into the reservation. "What happened?" He moved behind Anna, placing both hands on her shoulders.

"I don't have any details. That's Abe coming in now. I can take you to Winnipeg, if you like."

Pete rubbed his wife's shoulders. "Anna?"

She shook her head.

"I'll go then."

Anna spoke softly. "I don't want to be alone."

"Irene's here."

"Sleeping. I'll go to your mother's. Give me a few minutes."

Michael waited while she gathered a few things and put the baby in an old beaded tikinagan. After putting on a shirt and coat, Pete helped her with the straps. Clouds were building in the western sky as they walked to Jenny Redsky's house.

EIGHTY-THREE

Abe set down a plate of fried ham and scrambled eggs on the lodge dining room table as he seated himself across from Diana. Stirring a little sugar into his coffee, he watched as she finished a bowl of oatmeal to which she'd added raisins and nuts. She got him to try it once, since then, he'd stuck with the bacon and eggs thing.

He'd cut two slices out of the ham before Lenny walked up to him. "Abe, you're to pick up Michael at Long Grass. ASAP."

Abe put down his fork and reached for a couple slices of toast. "Okay."

Lenny left as Abe slid the ham onto one piece of toast. "Want to come?" The scrambled eggs went on the other.

"Yes."

Abe flipped the two pieces together. "Learned this in Burma. Never leave a meal to go flying. It may be a long time before you eat again." He drained half the cup of coffee, picked up his breakfast, and headed for the plane. Diana followed. Ten minutes later they were cruising a couple thousand feet above the Lake of the Woods.

Diana watched the dull water below, whipped into white caps from the wind it appeared cold and foreboding. How long had it been since the lake was frozen and she sat beside this same man in an airplane? A lifetime. Lenny's lifetime. She had lain content beside Abe while the fire in Kate's cabin burned to embers; Hector's ring sparkling in the firelight. She'd never taken it off, and now couldn't. A link to the past she was unable to break. The embers died, and three weeks later

Abe was gone. Life returned to normal, until she discovered she was pregnant.

"Where's J D Riley these days?" Abe asked above the drone of the engine.

"Oh..." Diana blinked. "He and Genevieve still live up the hill on Second Avenue."

"See them much?"

"No. They bought a camp forty mile east of town. Seems like a long way to drive, but they do it all summer."

"And Mrs. Litynski?"

"She's in an old folk's home. Sold her place right after Yuri died. It's a shame. The new people let the garden go."

"Cindy?"

"Land's sakes, forgot about that girl. I haven't seen her since you sold your plane."

Pulling the throttle back, Abe began his descent. Ahead Diana could see Long Grass Reservation. Her heart raced. She hadn't been here since Johnnie's funeral. Whatever possessed her to come? Glancing at Abe, the answer was obvious. Well, they were only picking up Michael and flying back to the lodge. She wouldn't have to get out of the plane.

How the place had changed. They'd built a new dock, almost as big as the one at the lodge. Most of the space was taken up with big runabout boats.

Abe swung across the end. "Hop out and tie us up."

So much for not getting out, she thought.

"Nobody around." Abe killed the motor and climbed out beside her. "He's probably up at his Mom's."

Diana stood frozen to the wooden decking as Abe started off. He'd gone a few yards before realizing she wasn't with him. "You coming?"

How could she face Jenny after all these years? The woman must surely hate her.

Abe stood waiting. "Come on." He held out his hand.

Taking it, her concerns vanished, replaced by a tingle running from his fingertips to her heart. "Sorry." Squeezing his hand, she followed him up to a neat little house with concrete steps.

Pete Redsky opened the door. "Come on in, Abe." His mouth fell open. "Diana Corrigan?" He looked at Abe who'd started inside. Diana hesitated until Pete, lost for words, stepped aside and motioned her forward.

The house was much as Diana remembered it. Same old wood stove, but the furniture was new. A fresh coat of paint replaced what used to be cheap wallpaper. Across the room, seated at a chrome-trimmed table, were two women, one holding a baby. The other, whose face came alive with emotion, began standing up. The way she moved crossed a river of years to the time when Jenny Redsky was her friend. But this wasn't the Jenny she knew. Her black hair had been replaced by grey, though Diana did like the way she wore it long to the center of her back. Added weight, though rounding the brown skin on her face, couldn't subdue the aging lines leftover from too many nights in the comfort of a bottle. The woman walked up to Diana, reaching out with arthritic hands.

Diana wanted to run, but her feet refused to move. Unable to avoid eye contact, she watched as a smile illuminated Jenny's face.

"Diana Corrigan!" Jenny's threw both arms around her. "So good to see you."

"Jenny." Diana hugged her.

Michael, who'd come over to Abe, asked, "What's she doing here?"

"Came along for the ride, why?"

"I wish you hadn't brought her."

"Why?"

"Abe," Michael began, walking him away from the two women, "we've got family problems in Winnipeg. I don't want her along."

The women broke apart. "Can you stay for a while?" Jenny asked.

Diana looked at Abe.

He nodded. "I've got to fly Michael to Winnipeg. I'll pick you up on the way back."

"Good." Jenny took her friend by the elbow. "Come." She gestured to a chair. "Sit down. Oh, we have so much to talk about."

Diana made herself comfortable as Jenny made tea. Pete kissed his wife good-bye, then followed Abe and Michael out the door.

EIGHTY-FOUR

Riding in the front seat beside Abe, Michael didn't say much. Even Pete, sitting in the back behind him, had fallen into silence after a few words. Abe, who'd flown enough with managers and owners, knew to keep quiet.

They landed at the foot of Brandon Street pulling up to the seaplane base and finding David Croft, wearing a navy pinstripe suit, standing on the dock, his tie blowing in the wind. Abe surveyed the gathering storm. They'd all get wet in short order if they weren't under cover.

David grabbed the rear float line and tied it through a metal ring. Michael got out, leaving his door open. Wind whistled around inside the cabin as Pete slid the seat ahead and followed. David, ignoring the building clouds, stood and talked to the two Natives. Abe heard it all as David hollered into the wind. "It's not good."

"How bad is it?" Pete asked, brushing hair out of his eyes.

"High Elk got snarled up in a drunken brawl. They've charged him with manslaughter."

Pete looked at the ground. "Any chance we can get him off?"

David spoke directly to Michael. "We've been all through this before."

"I know. I know." Michael raised both hands in exasperation. "Petty crimes, drunkenness, prostitution, okay? This is different."

"We agreed at the start," David said, speaking against the wind, "I supply corporate legal services." He paused. "I'm not a criminal lawyer." Running his left hand through blowing red hair, he spoke directly to Michael. "We're running a business. Remember that."

295

"What if I pay you?" Pete asked.

"It'd be a complete waste of money."

"But..."

David rounded on him. "Pete! For God's sake. He knifed a white guy."

"Why?"

"How should I know? They were both drunk."

"And he is the only one guilty?" Pete asked.

"You think the justice system will be fair? He's an Indian. It's a forgone conclusion he'll go to jail. Let the government pay for his lawyer."

"If..."

David's hand shot up. "I can't help him, and I won't waste money, resources, and my time that's better spent on bringing abuse cases to court."

Abe noticed Michael and Pete's shoulders sag in the same manner. "You're right," Michael patted his friend on the shoulder. "You're absolutely right. You want to stay and see him, Pete? There's room at my apartment."

David hunched against the wind as a few spits of rain settled on the Cessna's windscreen. Abe felt his plane rocking to the motion of white caps curling on the building waves. Strands of hair blew across Pete's face as he nodded yes.

"Okay," David said. "We can do that much. But we're not holding the plane here at the peak of our season." He faced Michael. "And especially not for personal business."

David took hold of the open door. "You're out of here, Abe." By the time he closed the door, Pete and Michael had untied the plane. Abe fired up the engine and took off as the storm broke free of the heavens.

EIGHTY-FIVE

Jenny opened the lid of the stove and threw two pieces of birch wood into the dying flames. Michael paid the local boys to see that her wood pile never got low. Lately, she'd found the comfort from the wood stove a blessing as her arthritis flared up in the damp spring weather. This afternoon her knuckles felt the incoming storm.

Diana moved to stand beside her. "You will forgive me?"

Jenny turned and smiled. "You have done nothing wrong. Our worlds turned in different directions. Often I asked the Eagle to accept my prayers for you."

Diana hung her head. "I must confess, I abandoned you."

Jenny took her hand. "We were much younger then. Time has taught us many things. I am so happy you are here."

Words failed Diana. She reached out and embraced her friend of generations lost. Jenny responded and both women wept tears of joy. Diana broke away first. "Look at us." She wiped tears from her eyes. "Crying like little kids."

"So we should," Jenny replied, sniffing, and gesturing toward the chair Anna had vacated to take the baby into a bedroom. Silence hung between them until Jenny seated herself and finished pouring tea.

"You must be proud of Michael," Diana said, sipping her tea.

"Susan deserves all the credit. But yes, I'm proud of both my sons. Anna is the best thing that came into my life since Jack died. She is a true daughter."

"What about Bethy?" Diana asked.

Jenny sighed. "I am thankful Abe saved her from freezing. I believe Singing Dove's words that she is happy."

"You don't know where she is?"

Jenny shook her head.

"Well, we'll just have to find her."

"Michael and David have already tried. All we know is she was adopted by a white family."

"It shouldn't be hard to find her then."

"We don't know their name."

"There must be some record."

"David's made several inquiries but can't find any record of her adoption. He thinks it was never recorded."

"You have no idea where she is?"

"None."

"How sad."

A knock at the door was followed by Susan Two Bears entering and taking off her coat. "Diana! Heard you were here." She seated herself at the table and poured tea. "What brings you to Long Grass?"

"I flew in with Abe."

Susan stopped sipping her tea and looked at Diana over the rim. Jenny caught the look.

Diana glanced at both women. "It's nothing. He was coming this way and asked if I wanted to go for a ride." The expression on her friend's faces stated otherwise. "Really." Changing the subject, she asked, "So, Susan. What have you been doing?"

"Helping out at the new school."

"She's putting together a course on Ojibway heritage," Jenny said.

"Here?" Diana asked.

Susan nodded yes.

"So what are you working on now?"

"Pow Wows. Ignace is a great help with the men's dances, but I'm finding very few people who know how women danced." Turning to Jenny, she asked, "What about you?"

"It was such a long time ago. We drank a lot."

"Seriously."

"To be honest, I don't remember much about Pow Wows, except that those were the times Jack would drink too much. He was a good dancer, though." She closed her eyes and leaned back. "I can see him now in his chest plate and feathers moving in time with the drum, at one with our Mother."

"So what do you do now?" Diana asked.

"Nothing," Jenny replied. "There hasn't been a Pow Wow here for years."

"Why not?"

"Our Native dances have died out," Susan said. "The residential schools made sure of that."

"Doesn't anyone know how to dance?"

"Some of us older ones remember a little, but the younger ones have never learned," Jenny said.

"This course your making," Diana said to Susan, "it teaches kids how to dance?"

"In time it could, if we had a drum carrier."

"There's no one on the reserve who can beat the *Tewikan*?"

"No."

Diana shook her head. "I can't believe it."

"Our culture is almost dead," Jenny stated.

"Without a drummer, we can't dance. Our young ones need to hear the voice of the drum to become one with Mother Earth. It represents her heartbeat."

"Where can we find a drummer?" Diana asked.

"There is a Keeper of the Drum at the White Dog reserve, up north." Jenny replied.

"So why don't we get him down here?"

"Transportation," Susan said. "There are four singers in a drum group."

"Well, we can fix that. Susan, you set it up. Arrange for those people to come and I'll see they get here."

"Diana, you don't need to..,"

"Nonsense. This culture thing has gone far enough. I think we should hold a Pow Wow here before the summer is out."

There in the kitchen, now darkened by storm clouds rolling in outside, the three women laid down plans to re-establish the Pow Wow on Long Grass Reservation.

Abe arrived an hour later just as rain began falling. Dashing hand in hand with him to the airplane, Diana got soaking wet as the skies opened up. Abe took off south to skirt the thunder storm moving northeast. She looked over at him, water dripping off his hair, now tingeing grey at the temples, his hand confident on the controls as the Cessna bounced in rough air. When he glanced over with his hazel eyes, deep inside she knew the fall had started.

EIGHTY-SIX

Diana stood at the end of the dock beside the only Norseman tied there for the night. As the evening sky darkened, something welled up inside her that had long laid dormant, a feeling of spirituality. When the first star appeared, she felt the need to pray, but couldn't. What she needed was *Kineu*, the eagle to fly by and carry her request to...to whom? The Great Spirit? He hadn't helped her in years past, and, best she could see, had abandoned her Native friends. Well, so be it. Diana turned and walked off the dock alone with her thoughts.

Those thoughts centered around Lenny. Odd how he had captured her life. The two girls, living on Vancouver Island, seemed so remote. Lenny was all she had, until Abe returned.

Damn, why did he have to come back? She regretted the thought even before it finished forming in her mind, replaced by a feeling that had become all too familiar lately. Stepping off the dock, she headed straight for Abe's room.

Crossing the grass in the glow of the lodge lights, she was determined that this was the night she would tell him. How would he take it? He'd been gone all those years, missed out on a relationship every father should have. As she approached his open door, her courage began to weaken.

⟪⟫

Throughout the summer Abe was kept busy flying guests to and from the lodge. Most evenings were free, some spent in Winnipeg, many at the lodge. To fill the empty hours, he'd taken up reading, and was well into *Fate Is The Hunter*. He'd meet the author, Ernest Gann, in Chabua, starting place for the Burma hump. The book was rekindling the romance of flying.

"You still reading that book?"

Abe looked up to see Diana standing in the doorway. "Nothing much else to do. Want to come in?"

"No."

Abe watched her turn sideways and lean against the door, lifting one foot against the jamb. He knew she was crowding sixty, yet what he saw was a woman still a long way from old age. Visitors to the lodge were charmed by her grace. Workers, both white and Native respected her. Abe knew why. She spent time helping them with their problems, smoothing over difficulties, and listening to their concerns. Abe liked that, and felt comfortable in her presence. Tonight though, he sensed an aloofness about her.

Looking at him, she asked, "You want to come outside and go for a walk?"

Abe waited before replying, watching the conflict in her eyes. "Sure." Setting the book down, he stepped out and closed the door. As he moved beside her, she took hold of his hand. Abe closed his fingers over hers.

<hr />

The feeling running up Diana's arm kindled smouldering embers as Abe squeezed her hand. It had never been like this with Ted. And Hector? Hector was only a distant memory. Even his ring on her finger didn't belong to him anymore. Not since that night in Kate's cabin.

"Nice night," she said.

"Yeah."

"No bugs out."

"None," he said.

Diana lapsed into silence. How was she going to begin? Abe deserved to know he was Lenny's father, but how would he take it. Her greatest nightmare was a denial.

A frog croaked as they neared the shore. Diana wished Abe would say something. She opened her mouth, but couldn't come up with the important words. "Nice night."

"Yeah." Abe fell into a silence that Diana couldn't break.

Why wouldn't he keep the conversation going? She'd be able to find the words to fit his.

Abe bent down and picked up a flat stone, threw it across the water, and watched as it skipped three times before sinking. "You unhappy with me coming back?" he asked, as it sank.

"No!" Diana took hold of his hand again. "No." Looking down, she stroked the back of it with her other hand and said, "I needed you to come back."

Abe lifted her chin with his forefinger. "I don't want to be just a replacement for Ted."

Diana stiffened. The man she was looking at wasn't a replacement. He was the real thing. He should have been Lenny's father. He is, was. Not important. Diana knew she'd fallen in love with her son's father. "Ted's gone. I'm free to fall in love."

"With me?"

"Yes," she whispered.

Abe ran a hand over her hair. She looked at him with soft eyes which slowly closed as Abe drew her near, then kissed her.

EIGHTY-SEVEN

More and more often Abe found Diana by his side as they walked the paths or sat in the veranda with guests. He enjoyed her company, and knew the others did too. She was a very gracious host.

Late August the weather turned unseasonably hot, the temperature that day hitting ninety-eight. Waves washing on shore made the lake look cool and inviting. Diana sat beside Abe in a cotton dress. He'd been sitting with his hands clasped behind his head, left foot on his right knee. "You want to go fishing?"

"That's a good idea." She jumped up. "Give me a minute to change."

Abe grabbed a couple of fishing rods and a dozen minnows. Diana met him at the end of the dock. Abe, both hands full, stood, watching her approach. Her regular open-toed shoes, with the slightly elevated heels, complimented a pair of calf-length slacks. She'd tied her hair in a kerchief, and wore only a yellow blouse, which she'd knotted in front instead of doing up the buttons.

Abe felt he was being seduced. "Ready?"

"Always."

Abe made no move to go. When Diana saw his eyes drop to her open blouse, she grabbed his arm. "Come on. We'll take my boat."

Diana drove. Pushing the throttle wide open at the dock she swung hard right, throwing Abe off balance. Mischief danced in her eyes. Abe laughed as he recovered, and she headed out onto the lake. They dropped anchor over an unmarked reef old Lone Eagle had told her about, and threw a couple of lines over the side.

The sun crept lower toward the horizon, turning the evening pink, then red. Shades of purple gathered, and as the air cooled, Diana sat close to Abe. He put his arm around her shoulder. She relaxed against him. Across the still water came the call of a loon.

"Diana."

"Yes."

"When was Lenny born?"

Diana stiffened, then relaxed. Slowly the words she'd wanted to say came freely. "November seventeenth."

Abe could barely hear her voice in the quiet night air. He sat with his arm around her, thinking, wanting to ask the question, but afraid of the answer. The haunting cry of the loon came once more, the sound of his past returning.

He glanced at Diana. She was staring toward the fading sunset. Placing a finger under her chin, he moved her head. She looked up at him, her eyes begging him to ask.

Abe kissed her. Relaxing, she wrapped both arms around him. "You won't leave again, will you?"

"I have no reason to."

She kissed him. "Time to go."

Abe reeled in their lines while Diana dug out a jacket and started the engine. As late night shadows engulfed them, Diana headed the boat north. They ran under a star-studded sky for an hour, before Diana pulled up to a log cabin Abe recognized.

"Kate's old place."

"It's mine now."

Abe got out, holding the bow line. Diana stood at his side, waiting until Abe realized they were staying and tied the boat up. Holding hands they walked to the front door where Diana took down the key from the same hiding place she had over twenty years before.

Walking in behind her, Abe was surprised when Diana flicked a switch and electric lights came on. To his left, unchanged in all these years, stood the great stone fireplace, wood still stacked on each side.

"Build a fire. I'll get a bottle of wine." She took off her jacket.

Abe had a small blaze crackling away when she returned with two wineglasses and a bottle of Chianti. Shutting off the lights on her way by, she walked over, handing him two glasses. Holding one in each hand, he watched her fill them. Setting the bottle down, she eased in beside him on the couch.

"To us."

"To us." Their glasses clinked together.

She sipped hers, then held the glass in both hands, watching the flames dance. "Ted bought this place for me." She was silent for a long moment. "I think he knew."

"About us?"

"No. Lenny. He treated him as his own. Outside of flying off the handle at times, he was the perfect father: went canoeing, spent time with him, told him stories, mostly about the war." A smile crossed her lips. "I think Lenny knew them all by heart before he was a teenager."

Pausing, she sat staring into the fire. Abe waited for her to continue. "Never once did he even hint at the alternative. But inside, I felt he knew I'd been unfaithful."

The last twenty years of Abe's life flashed before him, a complete waste. "And Lenny?"

Diana curled her feet up on the couch. "Ted was the only father he ever knew. Now he's gone. I don't think Lenny needs another one to take his place, just yet." She sipped her wine before looking at the man beside her. "But he should know. I'd like him to know."

Abe listened to the wood snap and pop in the fireplace. He put his arm around her. "I...ah, don't know what to say. I mean, I was never here."

"You will stay?"

"Diana, I've spent a lifetime chasing dreams around the world." He pulled her closer. "I finally found what I've been looking for."

Diana laid her head on his shoulder. "After Ted died I was going to sell this place. There was no one to share it with."

"And, now?"

"I'd share it with you."

Abe kissed her on the forehead. "Will you marry me, Diana?"

She held his hazel eyes, peering to the depth of his soul. "Lenny needs to know."

Abe fell to thinking, watching the firelight dancing in his wine. Diana had emptied her glass by the time he spoke. "Yes, but not now. I'll need some time."

"We will tell him."

"Yes."

Diana lay against Abe. She was still asleep in his arms when dawn broke a new day.

Three weeks later, Diana became Mrs. Williston, and they moved into the log cabin permanently. Abe still flew for the lodge, but Diana found herself visiting Jenny more and more. Old memories came back as she discovered the devastating wreckage left behind by the residential schools. A whole generation of Native people had lost their identity and were trying to raise families in a cultural vacuum.

Through Jenny, Diana met mothers whose daughters had been destroyed by prostitution, many in jail, a few killed. Ignace and Susan revealed the plight of young Native men sent to prison to do time with hardened criminals for petty crimes, often the result of seeking refuge from a world with no hope at the bottom of a bottle. Susan's main concern was the lack of high school education on the reservation.

Commuting by boat to Kenora, or hitching rides to Winnipeg, Diana began doing research for David Croft and his challenge to have those responsible for sexual abuse brought to trial. While searching through the archives of the *Miner and News*, she came across an obituary for Father LaFrenier. At one time she wanted to see him in hell, now she just didn't care and returned the faded clipping to its file.

Although it couldn't be used in court, information about the loss of Ojibway culture began to change her view of the new generation of

Natives trying to cope with social problems forced upon them. There were nights she cried for Johnnie Redsky.

When the Cessna 170 was put up for sale that winter, she sold the big house and bought the plane for Abe. During the winter, he often flew her to the reservation when practices were being held for Native dancing. Two young men were learning the way of the drum. Twice during the winter, she and Abe stayed overnight in Winnipeg to attend performances of the city's symphony orchestra.

One afternoon in late February, they made their last overnight trip of the winter to Winnipeg. David's first case had come before the courts. It was thrown out on a technicality. David and Michael started the process all over again with the faint hope it would come to trial in three or four years. Abe and Diana flew home.

Abe flopped into his big leather chair and was soon fast asleep in front of a blazing fire. Diana brooded over her second glass of wine. The story was all too familiar, people in authority hiding behind a bureaucratic wall, waiting for time to remove the evidence. Her friends wanting justice from a system ill-equipped to deal with the wreckage it created. She should have told it years ago. How much could she remember?

Everything.

Getting up, she walked over to her desk and sat down in front of her old Underwood typewriter. Rolling in a new piece of paper, she sat staring at the blank page. They could suppress the truth, but if it was written in fiction...

Halfway down the title page, she typed:

Altar and Throne

TRUTHS AND MYTHS
ABOUT THIS STORY

There was no Long Grass Indian Reservation. It never existed, yet could be every reservation in Canada.

The greatest travesty perpetrated upon the Native people of Canada was not the sexual abuse, abhorrent as that was, but rather the destruction of their culture. This left them without a past and no prospect for the future.

The Norseman aircraft was designed and built in Canada for bush pilot service by Robert Noorduyn in 1935. There never was a Norseman CF-MAZ. I gave it that registration because those are my wife's initials. As of this writing, it is the oldest airplane in commercial service in Canada. Over twenty-five are still flying, many in Northwestern Ontario.

No story about a small town can be told without some people seeing themselves as the characters. All the main characters were created in the author's mind, yet they are made up of bits and pieces of real people, most now dead. It is to their memory I am indebted.

The Canadian Pacific Railway yard office and roundhouse have been demolished. The depot remains, a heritage to a bygone era.

The *Foxey* was a real mahogany long-deck launch that ran on the Lake of The Woods.

Two residential schools operated in Kenora. Neither was located on Rabbit Lake, nor called by that name.

The *Miner and News* is still published in Kenora.

The Aboriginal peoples of Treaty 3 are slowly rebuilding their lives and communities. It continues to be an uphill struggle filled with heartache.

QUESTIONS FOR DISCUSSION

1 What impact did the residential school policy have on the lives of Jack and Jenny Redsky?

2 How would you describe Ted Corrigan's friendship with Jack Redsky, and Diana's friendship with Jenny Redsky? In what ways did Ted's friendship and attitudes change toward Natives as compared with Diana's?

3 What conflict did Abe Williston have in flying Native children to the residential school? How did he try to compensate for this? e.g. His experiences with Pete Redsky.

4 What different attitudes toward Natives were displayed by the two policemen, Sergeant Farnell and Andy Barrett? Why was Farnell's prejudice acceptable at that time?

5 How was Michael Redsky's life successful compared to his brother Johnnie's tragic life? What role did Susan Two Bears and David Croft have in Michael's life?

6 Despite the terrible tragedies Pete and Anna Redsky experienced, how do you think they were able to cope? What do you think kept them together as a couple?

7   Do you think it was right that Jenny Redsky lost her daughter, Bethy, and that she was adopted out to a white family?

8   What caused High Elk and his contemporaries to disrespect authority?

9   Why do you think the author chose the title *Altar and Throne* for this novel?

10 What responsibility did the churches and the Canadian government have in the collapse of Native culture? In retrospect, how might this have been handled differently? How would things be different for Native peoples today if there hadn't been a residential school policy?

ABOUT THE AUTHOR

www.EdZaruk.com

Ed Zaruk grew up in Victoria, B.C., but spent his summers in Kenora, Ontario, on the Lake of the Woods. Later he worked for Ontario Central Airlines before moving back to British Columbia. He and his wife, Marian, now live in Quesnel.

Printed in the United States
127007LV00001B/130-207/P